Every Trick in the Book

Center Point
Large Print

Also by Lucy Arlington and available from
Center Point Large Print:

Buried in a Book

**This Large Print Book carries the
Seal of Approval of N.A.V.H.**

Every Trick
in the Book

Lucy Arlington

CENTER POINT LARGE PRINT
THORNDIKE, MAINE

ail

This Center Point Large Print edition is published
in the year 2013 by arrangement with
The Berkley Publishing Group,
a member of Penguin Group (USA) Inc.

The text of this Large Print edition is unabridged.
In other aspects, this book may vary
from the original edition.
Printed in the United States of America
on permanent paper.
Set in 16-point Times New Roman type.

ISBN: 978-1-61173-731-8

Library of Congress Cataloging-in-Publication Data

Arlington, Lucy.
 Every trick in the book : a Novel Idea Mystery / Lucy Arlington. —
Center Point Large Print edition.
  pages cm
  ISBN 978-1-61173-731-8 (Library binding : alk. paper)
  1. Literary agents—North Carolina—Fiction.
    2. Book industries and trade—Exhibitions—Fiction.
    3. Murder—Investigation—Fiction. 4. North Carolina—Fiction.
    5. Large type books. I. Title.
PS3601.R545E94 2013
813′.6—dc23
                                                              2013002171

To all librarians.
Thank you for inviting us to enter
the world of books time and time again.

Every Trick in the Book

Chapter 1

By the middle of October, the heat and lassitude of a Southern summer had finally loosed its hold over the quaint, artsy town of Inspiration Valley. Cool air traveled down from the foothills and encouraged the people of North Carolina to search their closets for lightweight sweaters and to spend their weekends at football games or strolling through pumpkin patches in search of the perfect gourd.

Signs of fall were everywhere. Advertisements were stapled to nearly every telephone pole, enticing the public into taking hayrides, attending apple festivals, and purchasing potted mums from the local plant store, the Secret Garden. An electric charge was present in the crisp mornings, and a bowl of warm grits or a cup of hot cider never tasted better. Folks went about their business with a spring in their step.

Although I loved autumn and welcomed the brisk breezes and the harvest moon hung from a canvas of deep indigo, I was too busy to enjoy the season. Having been promoted from a lowly intern two months ago to the position of full-fledged agent at Novel Idea Literary Agency, my schedule was full. I have cherished each and every day in this career. There's no other job in the world that would give me the chance to discover captivating new voices, unforgettable characters, must-read plotlines, or settings so original and alluring that I long to be transported to the author's fictional realm on the spot.

And those are just the query letters! I also get to sit at my desk, sipping hot caramel lattes brewed to perfection by Makayla, the talented barista who works downstairs at Espresso Yourself, and delve into a fat pile of manuscripts. Because I represent traditional mysteries and romantic suspense, much of my day is spent reading about intrigues, secrets, and schemes. You'd think that I'd quickly grow tired of those themes, but I haven't. I love a good murder mystery, no matter what its form.

This autumn, working in conjunction with the town of Inspiration Valley, Novel Idea was on the verge of hosting the area's first Book and Author Festival. The entire town was dedicated to art in all its forms, and the literary agency, located at the heart of the burg, was one of Inspiration Valley's most enthusiastic supporters. I was in charge of registration for both the participants and the guest speakers. In addition to this time-consuming assignment, I had to find our agency a new intern, because the woman I'd hired in August to take my place as intern had been forced to accompany her husband in an abrupt job transfer to Minnesota.

This meant that come Monday, my desk and email inbox would be crammed with unfulfilled tasks. Thank goodness today was Saturday and the work I had before me was of the kind I'd been looking forward to for months. Today was moving day.

Most people view this activity as a miserable one. True, it involved plenty of hard labor and emotional stress, but I was giddy with excitement when my son, Trey, pulled up in front of my mother's house in a borrowed pickup truck.

"Ready to put these guns to good use?" he asked and then flexed his biceps. As usual, he was wearing a T-shirt. Freezing rain could cover the surface of Inspiration Valley and my son would insist that he wasn't cold.

"Manual labor suits you," I told him. "If you still have energy after a day of shoveling out the goat pens or chopping wood, you could always hike down the mountain and mow my lawn."

Trey puffed out his chest, pleased that I'd noticed how strong he'd become since joining the co-op up on Red Fox Mountain. "You won't have a man around, Mom. So if there's anything you need, just say the word and I'll totally be there."

Touched by his offer, I smiled at my only child. Trey was tall with the wide shoulders of a football player and had brown eyes that were prone to twinkle with mischief. His chestnut hair was too long for my taste, but I reached up and ruffled it fondly. He squirmed away from my touch, readjusting his shaggy locks while introducing me to two young men from the Red Fox Mountain Co-op who'd be helping us transfer the furniture and boxes stacked in a Dunston storage unit into a charming cottage located minutes away from Novel Idea.

I'd had my eye on this butter yellow house with periwinkle shutters since it came up for sale. But at the time, there was a snag in my finances due to Trey totaling my car and trashing East Dunston High's football field and bleachers in the process. This prevented me from making an offer on the picket fence paradise until I sold my house in Dunston. Instead, Trey and I moved in with my mother for the summer. The moment my financial burdens eased, I rushed into the Sherlock Holmes Realty office and made an offer that was immediately accepted. I happily put down a deposit to ensure that after a mid-October closing I could lay claim to the two-bedroom house in the lovely subdivision of Walden Woods Circle.

Throughout the months of August and September, I'd fallen asleep to visions of the cottage's sunny rooms and secluded rear garden. I couldn't wait to hang family pictures on the walls and dig up the previous owner's spent annuals, to plant row after row of perennials that would burst through the ground the following spring. My head was filled with images of van Gogh's irises and sunflowers, Matisse's dahlias and daisies, and a riot of Manet's roses. I planned to transform my backyard into an impressionist painting.

As for the interior, I wanted to decorate using a combination of furniture from my old place as well as some new pieces in bright, cheerful hues. Unfortunately, I'd have to sell a few more of my clients' books to major publishing houses before I could afford to head over to High Point to pick out comfy living room chairs or a farm table for the kitchen. Up until now, I'd only sold two book series. One was a cozy mystery featuring a sushi chef and the second was a romantic suspense set in a Scottish castle. And I couldn't really take credit for the sale of the romantic suspense. That deal was already in the works when I was promoted to literary agent.

Upon our arrival at the storage unit in Dunston, I pulled out boxes of clothes and milk crates stuffed with books for the boys to load into their truck. As I worked, my thoughts focused on another client I'd inherited. I still couldn't believe that I now represented the international bestselling romance author Calliope Sinclair. If I could just convince her to make some changes to her latest manuscript, I felt certain that several publishing houses would enter into a bidding war to acquire the latest masterpiece from one of America's best-known authors.

"Stop gatherin' wool, girl!" My mother's voice startled me out of my reminiscing. "You're standin' in the middle of the path and this box isn't gettin' any lighter. What've you got in here? Cannonballs from the Civil War?"

Putting my own box on the ground, I rushed forward to take my mother's burden and set it in the bed of her turquoise pickup truck. I added the last box and then shut the tailgate, causing the magnetic sign plastered to the side of the truck to fall askew. I realigned the purple and black sign advertising the services of Amazing Althea, Psychic Advisor. "Sorry," I told her. "I was thinking about work again."

"This is work. Good work. The kind that gets you out in the open air and invites the sun's rays to paint your face. Before long, it'll be winter and we'll all be starvin' for this feelin'." My mother held out her free arms as though she could embrace the whole world. "I always feel like a kid durin' the fall. This is gonna be the best Halloween ever. I'm gonna decorate the front door and scare the masks right off the kids who toilet papered my holly bushes last year. They won't come near my place totin' rolls of Charmin ever again."

I waited until we were both inside the truck before saying, "Is that an official prediction?"

My mother swatted me with the paperwork from the storage facility. "I don't read the cards for somethin' like that. I've gotta save my spiritual energy for when someone needs me, and my appointment calendar is as stuffed as a Christmas goose."

We chatted about her clients as I maneuvered the winding roads leading to Inspiration Valley, with Trey and the guys following right behind me in his pickup truck. The town sat in a circle of low mountains like a teacup in a saucer, and I never grew tired of the view. After that last sweeping curve, the town suddenly became visible through my driver's side window—an oasis of tree-lined streets and beautifully designed houses, storefronts, and buildings. There were no concrete boxes in Inspiration Valley. Nearly every home boasted a garden, and the business district was lush with public green spaces.

Making my careful descent, I was struck anew by its charm. An army of multicolored trees surrounded the town, standing guard like timeless sentinels over the bookstore, garden center, organic grocery, restaurants, art studios, and tidy subdivisions. Today, the foliage show was magnificent. Corn yellow, pumpkin orange, and spiced cranberry leaves encouraged rich and aromatic fantasies about the first meal I'd cook in my new house.

Not for the first time, I sent up a grateful prayer

of appreciation for the circumstances that brought me here. When I was handed a pink slip last spring from my job as a Features reporter for the *Dunston Herald*, it had originally seemed a setback. There I was, a forty-five-year-old single mother with a college-bound son, having to start a new career. However, being fired had spelled not only the beginning of an exciting and unique career path, but an opportunity to make my home in this delightful town.

By the time we'd unloaded all the boxes and I'd arranged my pots, pans, dishes, and utensils in the green and ivory kitchen, I was too tired to do anything but order takeout, and the meal I had envisioned en route to the house vanished.

"What would you boys like to eat?" I asked Trey and his friends.

"Everything!" Trey answered wearily, putting his feet up on my coffee table.

I knocked them off with the sweep of one hand and held out the menu for Godfather's Pizza with the other. "Your wish is my command, gentlemen."

The three young men suddenly shucked off their fatigue and began to argue over the merits of pies made of sausage and mushroom, ham and pineapple, *quattro formaggi*, pepperoni, or spinach and feta. Before they could get too fired up, I promised to have all five delivered to my new house.

After the pizzas arrived, my mother and I set the table and put a pitcher of iced tea and a pile of extra napkins in the center and then called the boys into the kitchen.

"Thank you so much!" I told them, feeling my heart swell at the sight of my family gathered around my table.

Trey raised his glass of iced tea. "To making new memories!"

His two friends shouted a hearty "hear, hear" and then dug into their food.

Trey devoured the pizza with such gusto that I couldn't help but wonder if my son was getting enough to eat living in the self-sustained community he'd joined in June. Although I'd had my reservations at the time, I had to admit that the Red Fox Co-op had done Trey a great deal of good. He was stronger, more independent, and treated his elders with respect. He'd gained a quiet confidence and was willing to throw himself into hours of demanding physical labor. Yet at the same time, he was missing out on a college education.

In early August, Trey had received a letter from UNC Wilmington containing a welcome packet and the name and contact information of his future roommate. Several weeks later, when my son should have been attending his first class as a college freshman, he was grooming the co-op's herd of goats and preparing for a trip to Dunston to sell goat products to a selection of natural food stores and chic boutiques.

I had called the school and managed to defer Trey's admission until January, but I feared he'd refuse to attend then as well. From the beginning, I'd assumed his interest in the rustic, rather primeval way of life on Red Fox Mountain was a passing phase. It seemed that his enthusiasm had been compounded upon meeting the lovely and ethereal Iris Gyles, the co-op leader's younger sister.

Autumn in North Carolina is a gentle season, but I was worried about Trey spending a cold winter up on the mountain. The members of the co-op stayed warm with the help of woolen clothing and potbellied stoves. However, if our area received more than a dusting of snow or a freezing rain, the dirt road leading to the mountain-top community would be impassable. I hated the idea of my son being cut off from electricity, medical care, and me. I was ready for him to resume the life of an average American teenager, and was terrified that he would never do so.

Pushing these irksome concerns aside, I focused on one last task before a dessert of raspberry sorbet. I had picked up a fabulous mirror at Dunston's largest consignment shop and was given an enormous discount by the owner. When I was still an intern, I'd passed along her query letter on decorating with vintage objects to

Franklin Stafford, the agent representing non-fiction books. He had found her idea compelling and later signed her as a client. As a result, the oval mirror, set in a wood frame embellished with carved flowers and small birds, didn't cost me much more than tonight's pizza order.

Trey had drilled a hole and secured a wall anchor right inside the cottage's front door, and I was just about to lift the mirror onto the hook when my mother entered the hallway.

"Everything's comin' together," she said with a smile.

I balanced the heavy mirror on the top of my foot and nodded. "Yes, it is. And not just the house. Everything. I love my job, I'm dating a great guy, and Trey and I haven't gotten along this well since he was a little boy."

My mother raised her brows. "So you and the good-lookin' man in blue are finally knockin' boots?"

Blushing, I turned away from her bemused gaze. "If you must know, we haven't progressed beyond the kiss good night stage."

"Why the hell not? You're a grown woman. More than grown." She grunted. "Shoot, Lila. Don't you know that havin' gray hair means that you get to sleep with a man without anybody's permission?"

I frowned at her. I spent a pretty penny keeping my shoulder-length hair a gray-free, roasted chestnut hue. "I'm not looking for permission. Work just keeps getting in the way. Sean's been assigned a string of night shifts, and with the festival coming up at the end of next week I—"

"How about a little afternoon delight?" my mother suggested with perfect aplomb. "When your daddy was alive—"

Thankfully, Trey called out for my mother before she could elucidate on the ecstasies of her marital bed. I'd heard them before, usually after she'd consumed a few fingers too many of her lifelong beau, Mister Jim Beam, but I really didn't want to hear her conjugal anecdotes before dessert.

Returning my attention to the mirror, I hefted it against the wall and slowly eased it onto the brass hook. The moment I drew back, the wire attached to the frame snapped. My fingers shot out to catch hold of the mirror, but I couldn't move quickly enough. The vintage work of art tilted sideways and hit the hardwood floor. The sound of glass shattering echoed down the narrow corridor.

I screamed in dismay and both Trey and Althea came running.

"Did you cut yourself?" Trey asked, worry clouding his handsome face.

"I'm fine, honey, but I doubt I can say the same about this." I bent over the mirror. It had fallen facedown, concealing the extent of the damage. Gently, I flipped it onto its side, listening to the sickening crunch of broken glass coming loose from the frame and crashing onto the ground.

I sighed in relief. The delicate birds and flowers were unscathed. There was a small scratch on the right-hand side that could be easily repaired with a dab of stain, and the glass could be replaced by the local art supply store. I'd seen their custom frame jobs and knew they'd have my mirror fixed in no time.

Trey disappeared to fetch a broom and a dust-pan, but my mother stayed rooted in place, her features pinched in concern.

"Mama," I said softly, touched that she was so upset over the thought of my being injured. "I'm okay. See?" I presented both of my pink, healthy palms as proof.

She shook her head and did not meet my eyes. She couldn't seem to tear her gaze from the jagged shards of glass. "Oh, darlin'. It's not fine. Not at all."

To my surprise, she knelt down on the floor, picked up a piece of glass shaped like a lightning bolt, and began muttering under her breath.

"Mama?" I began to feel a stirring of alarm.

She waved Trey away when he appeared with the broom, insisting that she needed to collect the pieces and take them far away from the house.

"Whatever for?" I asked her, utterly perplexed. "All that nonsense about broken mirrors and seven years of bad luck is just that. Nonsense."

She took a deep breath and answered in a tremulous voice. "You should believe. I'm takin' these to protect you, Lila. Trouble's comin'. It's comin' hard and fast as a runaway train."

My uneasiness grew. Memories of my brush with violence during my first month in the Valley could still fill me with dread, although the sharp edges of the fear had dulled somewhat. "That was this summer. It's all over now."

She pointed at the debris on the floor, and I was disturbed to note that her finger shook as she said, "You're wrong, Lila. This is only the beginning."

Chapter 2

Monday morning started off crisp and bright. Despite the sun, my hands were cold as I rode my yellow Vespa the short distance to work, and I decided that I would need to pick up riding gloves for the cooler weather. Parking the scooter, I walked to the office with determination. My day would be full, starting with the interviewing of two hopefuls for the intern position. The job had been advertised in the *Dunston Herald* last week but had generated only two responses. I'd decided to interview the applicants back-to-back so I could compare the merits of each and hopefully hire one of them by the end of the day. There was so much to do to prepare for the Book and Author Festival that the agency desperately needed an extra pair of hands.

I smiled as I remembered how Bentley had hired me based on a quick phone interview. She, too, had been desperate to recruit an intern at the time. Until I joined the agency, Novel Idea had had a difficult time holding on to their interns because of the demanding workload and the necessity that they be booklovers, which was often not the case. I was determined to find someone who was a motivated bibliophile.

When I entered the agency's reception area, I was surprised to see one of Trey's co-op friends sitting on the leather couch. Doug looked very different from the last time I'd seen him, however. His dark hair was short and tidy, and he wore a pair of pressed khaki pants and a white collared shirt. If it wasn't for his distinct bushy eyebrows and pale blue eyes, I might not have recognized him as the same young man who hefted bales of hemp, dressed in patched jeans, and tied his long hair in a ponytail with a thin piece of leather.

As I approached, he stood and held out his hand. "Good morning, Ms. Wilkins. I'm a bit early for my interview, but I wanted to make sure I didn't keep you waiting."

Interview? In my mind, I ran through the names on my appointment calendar. Doug Cooper at nine, Vicky Crump at nine thirty. I hadn't realized that Doug Cooper was Doug from Red Fox Mountain and tried to cover up my surprise by shaking his hand enthusiastically. "Well, it's good that you're punctual. Give me a few minutes. I'll call you in when I'm ready."

In my office, I hung up my jacket and pulled out the interview file. Doug's résumé didn't mention the co-op as an employer, but he did give Jasper Gyles, the co-op leader, as a reference. Doug had one year of college under his belt, had done odd jobs at fast-food stores in Dunston, and listed his most recent employment as farming. Uncertain how he would fit into the agency, much less have an eye for sifting through queries, I wondered why he hoped to work here and why he was leaving the co-op. Seeing him cleaned up, however, gave me hope that one day soon Trey might also choose to withdraw from Red Fox.

Doug appeared bright-eyed and eager as he sat across the desk from me. I leaned back in my chair and studied him. "Why did you apply for this job, Doug?"

He ran his fingers through his hair, as if he was not quite used to the shortness of it. "I decided it was time to make a change," he replied. "I'm done with the hippie thing, and the direction that the co-op is taking just doesn't mesh with me anymore. I want to go back to college, but since I was kicked out a few years ago I kind of have to prove myself to be accepted back. So I thought, since you're Trey's mom, you might give me a chance."

Dismayed at his expectation that our tenuous connection would land him a job, I hoped that he at least was an avid reader. "What kind of books do you like to read?" I asked.

"Well, not much, really. Do I have to read books to work here? I thought the job would be like an assistant or something, a gofer, get your coffee and stuff."

I strived to make my tone kind. "Why would

you think that? Did you read the job description in the advertisement?"

He shrugged.

"This is a literary agency, Doug, and it's our job to sell books to publishers, so yes, you have to read books to work here. You need to know what makes a book good, what will sell and what won't. We represent writers, and the intern is most often the first person to decide whether a query ever reaches an agent's desk."

"Oh." He slouched in his chair. "I guess I'm not really a good fit for this job, then. I just thought . . ." Sighing, he stood up. "I'm sorry, Ms. Wilkins. I shouldn't have wasted your time."

"You'll find something more suitable, I'm sure. And I'll keep your résumé on hand in case we need extra help at the Book and Author Festival at the end of the week, okay?" As I showed him out the door, I touched his arm. "You certainly clean up well. You look very professional."

He beamed at that and descended the stairs with a light tread. I was disappointed, however. Now all my hopes for hiring an intern rested on Vicky Crump.

Her résumé looked promising. Ten years as a court clerk and a librarian for twelve before that. At precisely nine twenty-five, I heard her footsteps on the stairs and went to the reception area to greet her.

A petite woman entered the agency. Barely five feet tall, she wore a navy pleated skirt with the hem just above her knees, a white blouse, and a navy cardigan. Her silky white hair was parted at the side and held back with a bobby pin.

When she saw me, her eyes lit up behind her blue-rimmed glasses. "Hello. I'm Vicky Crump," she announced with a strong, confident voice that made me want to stand a little taller. "I'm here for a job interview."

"Hi, Vicky. I'm Lila Wilkins." I waved my arm in the direction of my office. "Please come in."

She lowered herself into the visitor's chair and placed her purse on her lap, waiting expectantly. She sat with ramrod straightness and met my gaze directly. Feeling as though I was back in a grade school classroom, I hastily perused her résumé to refresh my memory, but before I could say anything, she spoke.

"You'll probably ask me why I haven't worked for the last four years."

I nodded. "As a matter of fact, that was going to be my first question."

"I retired four years ago, same time as my husband, and we thought we'd have years of travel ahead of us. But my husband died last year and my days have become . . . quiet." She seemed to find the word distasteful. "While I can bide my time with gardening and bridge club—Franklin, who I believe is one of the agents here, plays bridge there, too—it just isn't fulfilling enough. There's still a lot of life left in me." She smiled, revealing a row of perfectly shaped white teeth. "I've lived in Inspiration Valley for the better part of my adult life, and I've been watching this agency since it was established. I've also read most of the authors represented by Novel Idea, and I think I can be of some use to you."

"Really? You're that familiar with our clients?" If this were true, then she certainly had the background for the position.

"Oh yes!" Her enthusiasm sounded like a bark. "One of my favorites is Calliope Sinclair. Her romances are just divine. And I love Meteor Granger's spy thrillers. I can't put them down and have lost many a night's sleep devouring his books."

"Well, your reading interests are certainly an advantage." I reached for the file containing sample query letters. "You are aware that this job is for an intern position?"

She pushed her glasses up. "Yes, I am. But I'm wondering if you'd entertain a proposal. I know this seems forward of me . . ."

Uncertain what to expect, I put the query file down and nodded. "What kind of proposal?"

She folded her hands and placed them on the desk, and I suddenly wondered who was in charge of this interview. "I'm sixty-nine years young and have no aspirations to be a literary agent. But I *love* books. And I love the idea of being a part of bringing them to life. I've seen the newspaper ads looking for an intern pop up again and again, and I believe you haven't found the right person for the job. And when I called here, there was only a general voicemail. No one answers the phones? No one greets guests?"

"Well . . ." I said, feeling like I was failing some kind of test. "That's the intern's job and that's why we placed an ad—"

Vicky plowed on. "I think what this place needs is consistency in the clerical tasks. You need a receptionist and someone to manage all the paperwork. I'd still do the intern's job of vetting the queries and mailing out rejection letters and such, but I could do so much more than that." She cleared her throat. "For a slightly higher salary, of course."

I gawked at the tiny older woman who possessed all the authority and charisma of Napoleon. "I think your idea has merit, but I can't really make that decision. Let me run it by Ms. Burlington-Duke and we'll see what develops." I opened the folder and passed her a sheet of paper. "I received this on Friday. Our guidelines stipulate that one should only submit a query letter and no manuscript unless requested to do so. How would you respond to this?"

She leaned forward and read aloud:

Dear Agent,

Attached is my 150,000-word manuscript for my mystery novel called *Murder in Montana*. I know you didn't request this manuscript, but it's so well written and so exciting that I'm sure you'll be grateful that I sent it to you first. I look forward to hearing from you by the end of the week.

Vicky adjusted her glasses and sat back. "I would reply by saying, 'I recommend you reread our agency guidelines and send us a properly crafted query letter.'" She grinned as if I'd asked her a ridiculously easy question.

I chuckled. "Perfect response, Vicky." Turning to the bookshelves, I pulled out three large tomes and placed them on the desk. "These are reference books containing guidelines as to what makes a good query. I hope you will read them because I think you'd be perfect for the intern position. Will you accept the job whether it becomes a permanent office manager position or not?"

Her eyes sparkled and she nodded. "Yes, I shall!" She reached for the first volume. "Don't worry, Ms. Wilkins, not a single line of subpar material will get past me."

"And if a pushy aspiring author shows up here and demands to see one of our agents without an appointment?" I asked teasingly. "What will you do then?"

Vicky rose from her chair, tugged on the hem of her cardigan, and answered without a trace of humor. "They will have their knuckles rapped."

I don't know how Vicky did it, but two days after she had a single phone conversation with my boss, Bentley Burlington-Duke, the reception area at the top of the stairs was rearranged to accommodate a new desk, a file cabinet, and a leather swivel chair with adjustable back and seat cushions. Seconds after the furniture delivery-men left on Wednesday morning, a man from Dunston's largest office supply store arrived and installed a complicated telephone system with a headset attachment, a PC with an enormous screen, and a fax machine at Vicky's new station.

Delighted by the prospect of turning over the query letter screening to Vicky, I headed down to Espresso Yourself to tell my friend Makayla about the new reception area in Novel Idea.

"She may be small of stature, but she's capable of wiping out an entire drug cartel with a stern look," I told Makayla before taking a sip of my caramel latte.

Makayla laughed, a sound that reminded me of wind chimes, and her jade green eyes glimmered. "I'd better not screw up her order, then." She slid the latest Tana French novel across the counter to me. "You can read this before I put it out in my lending library. I finished it three days ago and scenes are still echoing in my mind. Lord, but that woman can write!"

"That's high praise coming from you," I said, glancing at the pair of bookshelves in the corner of the coffee shop where Makayla and her customers traded gently used novels.

The beautiful barista had a shaved head, and her silken, chocolate-colored skin made her appear ageless. She could have been gracing the catwalks of Paris or Milan, but she loved her little coffee shop and glowed with contentment from the moment she brewed the first pot until she locked the doors at the end of the day. A bibliophile and art lover, Makayla supported local artists by inviting them to display their wares in her shop. I had my eye on a water-color of an old woman perched on the edge of the town's Fountain of the Nine Muses, her bare feet submerged in the water and her wrinkled face glowing with childish delight, and I planned to buy it as soon as I made another deal.

Makayla caught me staring at the painting. "I know how much you want to bring that home, girl. You can get it on layaway. The artist is a friend of mine."

I shook my head. "No, thanks. Seeing it every day inspires me to work harder. I've got to convince Calliope to cut the out-of-body experience from the end of her latest novel or it won't sell. The entire chapter is just wrong, but she doesn't want to hear that. She wants me to tell her the book is perfect and send it out to the publishing houses."

Makayla handed a cappuccino to an attractive man in a seersucker suit, thanked him, and then turned back to me. "Sounds like she's itching to delve into the supernatural, but isn't this book historical romance?"

"Yes, it's Elizabethan. And it's wonderful until the main character suddenly dies and begins to narrate the last chapter in first person as she's looking down at her own corpse. Calliope insists she'll return to her body in the beginning of the next book and that her heroine can only realize that she's in love with her sworn enemy by temporarily dying, but I disagree. There's got to be another way for her character to have an epiphany without an out-of-body experience."

Makayla was about to offer her opinion when the customer she'd just served returned to the counter. "Do you have any nutmeg?"

She nodded. "Sure, hon. There's a shaker on that little stand where the milk jug and sugar packets are."

"I couldn't find it," he answered. "Just cinnamon."

"I'm sorry," she told him with genuine regret.

"I think I'm fresh out. Can I get you anything else?"

He grinned mischievously. "How about your phone number?"

Makayla pretended to swat him with a dish towel. "Shame on you, George McAllister! Go buy a dozen roses for your sweet wife."

The man saluted her. "Already did. The love of my life made me a rib roast for supper, so the least I could do was bring her flowers."

Makayla and I exchanged smiles.

"So has Sean shown up at your door with a bouquet lately?" she asked once George had left.

"He hasn't stepped foot in my new house yet," I complained. "It's not his fault. More night shifts. And I'm so wiped by the end of the day that I'd be terrible company. One glass of wine and I'm snoring on the sofa."

Coming out from behind the counter, Makayla began wiping off the tiny circular tables nestled in the narrow eatery. "Are you ready for the festival?"

I shrugged. "On paper, sure, but I'm worried about having booked four hours' worth of pitch appointments. I've never listened to a pitch in my life. I'm going to be more nervous than the writers."

"I seriously doubt that, my friend. Most of those poor souls will be shaking so hard you'll think they had one of my triple espressos." She came over to my table and mimed pulling on a base-ball mitt and adopting a pitcher's stance. "Do you want me to toss a pitch at you? I've got a wicked fastball."

It was hard to take my friend seriously as she raised her left leg, pivoted her body, and pretended to throw a speedball at my coffee cup.

"You're too confident," I scolded her. "You're supposed to be more jittery. You're a writer who'd do anything to impress me and you know that I'm going to be listening to dozens of people before and after you. Your idea has to be dazzling and well presented or you'll have blown your chance. See? Give me jittery."

"Okay." Makayla sat down opposite me and laced her hands together. She glanced anxiously around the café and then drew in a deep breath. "My book is a paranormal romance set in a coffee shop. Mena Lewis is a shy, hardworking barista by day and a dangerous, untamed shape-shifter by night. She keeps to herself because she doesn't want to hurt anyone. One day, she's attacked in the forest surrounding her town by a strange, nightmarish creature and is rescued by a handsome but secretive park ranger. He heals her and, during a full moon, witnesses her change into a snarling cougar. He seems amazingly unfazed by her transformation, and Mena wonders if she might have finally made a human connection. But as she gives her heart to him,

Mena doesn't know if the hot ranger is a hero or a shifter even more dangerous than herself. The end!"

I sat back, impressed. "You came up with that out of the blue?"

Makayla shrugged. "I could tell you dozens of ideas. They're swimming around in my head like a school of fish, but that's all they'll ever be. Ideas. I can't turn them into a book. I just don't have it in me."

"Too bad," I said.

"Listen, Lila. You're going to be hearing from folks who've poured a piece of themselves into page after loving page." She gestured at her little library in the corner. "I don't know how anyone does it. To have that kind of devotion, to sit there day after day and lasso the things churning around in your mind into organized thoughts. Can you imagine how those people feel when they finish that last sentence? And so many of them won't ever see their books for sale in a store."

"That's what makes these pitch sessions so tough," I said. "I know that these writers have devoted a huge part of themselves to their projects and yet I'll have to turn down dozens of them."

"You'll find the right words when the time comes. I just know you will." Suddenly, she grabbed my arm and beamed. "I forgot to thank you for making sure I was picked to handle the beverage service for the festival. My piggy bank is about to get a whole lot fatter."

I squeezed her shoulder. "I simply put your name in the suggestion box, so to speak. Anyway, I can't survive this weekend without you and your lattes."

"There'll be good food, too. Big Ed is going to set up a Catcher in the Rye kiosk, and the Sixpence Bakery booth will be there to handle all the sugar cravings." Makayla lowered her voice to a whisper. "I snuck over to the bakery before I opened to get myself one of Nell's cherry cheese Danishes. Lord have mercy, but that is no ordinary pastry. It's a tiny glimpse of heaven, I swear."

"I'll pick some up tomorrow to celebrate Vicky's first day on the job. But for now, I've got to tackle the six proposals stacked on my desk. See you later."

Wishing me luck, Makayla returned to her position behind the counter and began taking orders from the group of college-aged students who'd entered Espresso Yourself in a wave of laughter, raised voices, and tinny music emitting from the earbuds of more than one iPod. They were all dressed in collegiate sweatshirts, jeans, and boat shoes.

I'd noticed an unusual number of college students hanging around Inspiration Valley over the last few months. It hadn't seemed odd for so many of the older teens to be present in the summer, because many of them held food service jobs and worked as camp counselors, but today was a weekday at the end of October. Why weren't these kids in class?

Berating myself for having become suspicious of anything out of the ordinary, I decided that the students were probably on a midsemester break or had just finished a series of grueling midterm exams and had come to our idyllic town to shop in the hip boutiques, eat delicious food, or hike the beautiful mountain trails.

Back in my office, I picked up the first proposal in the tidy stack on the center of my desk and began to read. Within a few sentences, I was transported to an old house in New England. In a cobwebbed attic, a young woman knelt in front of an antique steamer trunk and was on the verge of setting free an evil that had lain dormant since the witch trials of Salem. Unfortunately, the suspense that grabbed me in the opening scene gave way to forty pages of dull backstory.

I reread the author's original query letter and wasn't convinced that the idea was marketable. The writing certainly wasn't.

This didn't mean that I would respond to the author with a firm rejection. Instead, I emailed her a short note saying that while I loved the beginning of her book, she would need to completely rewrite the remainder before submitting it to me again.

This done, I reached for the next proposal. It was so riddled with spelling and grammatical errors that it took me forever to read the first chapter. When the font size shrank and the spacing went from double to single, beginning with chapter two, I gave up.

"This was your big chance and you couldn't be bothered to send me your best work." I reprimanded the author as though he were sitting in my office. "With computers able to spell and grammar check, there is no excuse for such a sloppy submission."

The email I sent out to this author was short and direct. I wouldn't be offering him a second chance. I explained that his project was not for me, recommended that he revise his work before querying another agency, and wished him luck finding representation.

Shaking my head in puzzlement over the behavior of some aspiring writers, I pulled the third proposal in front of me and began to read:

The pine floorboards of the four-room house were stained with blood.

The stain was mahogany brown and had been there for decades. People had tried to cover it with straw, rag

rugs, and at one point an avocado-colored shag carpet, but it remained—a persistent oval stain. It would forever mark the room with its gruesome presence.

Men had died in this house, in this room. Hundreds of them. Soldiers clad in frayed gray uniforms had lost their lives here, drop by crimson drop. Others had lost legs or arms or feet. Limbs chewed up by cannonball fire, appendages shredded by musket shot, flesh turned black by infection.

I could almost hear the men screaming. The smell of their fear hung in the house-turned-museum like smoke. It hovered over the daguerreotypes and weapons locked in glass cases, clung to the archaic surgical equipment and tattered flags.

Why did I keep coming to this place?

Did I feel empathy for the soldiers? Because they had sacrificed in vain? I had sacrificed, too, and there had been no victory for me, either. We were connected by loss, these men and me. We had wasted our future because others ordered us to do so.

My eyes kept returning to the stain on the worn pine floor.

Did I long to witness death? To see the blood running from another's veins drop by crimson drop? Is this where my anger will lead me one day?

Only you will see that I am capable of taking what is mine.

Only you will know when I will choose the next victim.

I let the paper fall from my hands, unwilling to read more. This story was not for me. It was too dark and I had a hunch that the narrative would eventually become too graphic for my tastes. I also wasn't sure what I'd been reading. It wasn't a proper proposal. There wasn't a single line explaining what the book was about, nor was there a letter accompanying the document. The author had sent an entire chapter without pre-amble and without following any of the guidelines listed so clearly on the agency's website. The only note in the personal voice of the author was one line at the beginning that read:

I plan to pitch this project at the book festival.

The whole thing was bizarre.

Despite my lack of interest in the work, this

author, Kirk Mason, illustrated a measure of talent. I decided to hand the packet over to Jude Hudson. He represented thrillers and was always on the lookout for a fresh voice. This voice was unique enough to give me chills.

Unfortunately, when I flipped through my file to see if I could locate the original query letter from Kirk Mason, all I found was the large brown envelope the chapter had arrived in, stamped and addressed to the agency, but not to a specific agent. No letter. Curious, I turned to my laptop and searched through my list of sent messages, looking for the email in which I'd requested more material from Mr. Mason. My email didn't contain a single correspondence from someone by the name of Kirk Mason.

Setting the packet aside, I read through the rest of the proposals and liked the last one well enough to request the entire manuscript. It was a cozy mystery set in an isolated mountain town and featured a women's sewing circle. All five of the book's heroines were married to members of the local police force. When their husbands failed to solve crimes in a timely fashion, the women secretly took over, only to give credit to the men in the end. I loved the humor and pluck of these women and couldn't wait to read more about their exploits.

After tidying up my desk and sending a few confirmation emails to festival guest speakers and volunteers, I picked up the writing sample by Kirk Mason and headed down the hall to Jude's office. Perhaps the author had meant to query Jude all along and somehow part of his first chapter had ended up on my desk. Things had been rather disorganized as of late. Without an intern, we were all trying to divvy up the incoming queries, and they hadn't always ended up where they belonged.

Jude had his feet propped on top of his desk and was studying an image on his computer screen with such concentration that he didn't hear me enter. Even though I'd been working with him for months, I couldn't help but pause on his threshold and stare. He had the appearance of a classic film star—a rugged jaw, warm brown eyes framed by long lashes, and waves of dark hair. His lean, muscular body looked good in the tailored suits and cashmere sweaters he favored, and his full lips begged to be kissed.

I'd kissed him over the summer, and though we'd generated enough heat to cause a five-alarm fire, it had been a mistake. Jude loved women. He loved to flirt with women, chase women, and woo women, but I wanted a man who only had eyes for me. If my heart interpreted the signals correctly, that man was police officer Sean Griffiths.

Jude turned his head and smiled. My pulse raced a little faster, but I called forth the memory of my last dinner date with Sean, and my coworker's allure instantly dimmed.

"Hi," he said, leaning back in his chair. "I was just admiring the festival page on our website. Good job."

I shrugged at his praise. "That's the handiwork of our web designer. I can't take the credit." I lowered myself into his guest chair. "It does look sharp, though, doesn't it?"

"Don't be so modest. It was your concept, your design. Mandy just did the technical stuff to get it on the Internet."

"Thanks." I grinned. "We've processed over two hundred registrations through the website and more by mail. I think the convention is going to be a great success. Based on the emails I've received, both the young adult fantasy panel and the one featuring members of area law enforcement are going to be standing room only."

Jude's eyes twinkled. "Isn't your boyfriend participating in that session? You'll have to make sure not to schedule any of your pitch interviews then."

"Very funny." I had, in fact, cleared my calendar for that hour, because I really wanted to see Sean in action. The other participants would include the DA's assistant, a coroner, and a private investigator. The session promised to provide a plethora of information for mystery writers.

Jude leaned forward and clicked his computer

mouse. "I'm excited about the festival, too." He turned his monitor toward me. "I just wish the Marlette Robbins Center for the Arts could have been ready in time. It would be a much better venue than the old town hall. Look at the layout of the building. This entire wing"—he indicated to the right of the screen and then again to the left—"and this one are both closed to the public. They branch out from the central area where we're holding our sessions, and I'm hoping that the wooden barriers we erected will deter attendees from poking around in those spaces. They're littered with construction debris. A total lawsuit waiting to happen."

"We'll just have to strategically place our message boards and information signs to keep people away from those areas."

He nodded. "Good thinking. But we have to make sure people can't get into those sections of the building. They have minimal lighting and they're not safe. We must consider our liability."

I gazed at the computer screen. The parts of the town hall we were using for the festival were labeled and coded in various colors according to their usage. The restricted wings appeared as ominous blocks of black. "It'll be fine, Jude. And the Marlette Robbins Center will be ready for next year's festival." Inspiration Valley had been bequeathed the funds to build the Arts Center in honor of the late Marlette Robbins, a former homeless man and posthumously published author.

I handed over the packet from Kirk Mason. "I wanted you to look at this. It's definitely not for me and is more your kind of thing. It was unsolicited, but it might be marketable."

As he scanned the first page his eyes darkened. "This is a bit twisted, but you're right. It *is* up my alley. I might be able to sell it. What do you know about this Kirk Mason?" He flipped through the pages in befuddlement, clearly searching for an actual synopsis.

"Nothing." I shook my head. "I couldn't locate a proposal or a query about this novel, or any emails or correspondence of any kind from a Kirk Mason."

"That's strange."

"I know. If you wanted to consider the manuscript, how are we supposed to contact the author if we don't know how?"

Jude shrugged and placed the proposal in his in-tray. "Well, Kirk Mason says he'll be at the festival."

I sat back and tried to imagine what a writer of such dark material would look like. I envisioned a tall, slim man with a hooked nose, dark, deep-set eyes, and pencil-thin lips. He'd be dressed all in black and have a dagger tattooed on his neck. At the pitch session, I'd have to sit across from him, listening to his scabrous voice as he described his novel in chilling, graphic detail, his cold, piercing stare making me want to look anywhere but at him. Involuntarily, I shuddered. "Then I hope this author is scheduled for one of your pitch sessions and not mine!"

Chapter 3

The Inspiration Valley Book and Author Festival got under way Friday morning beneath a bank of low clouds, dark and heavy with rain. The attendees didn't seem to notice, and the buzz of excitement that traveled among them reverberated through the lobby of the old town hall. In fact, the organized bustling of the crowd combined with the hum of many voices reminded me of an energetic beehive.

I was stationed at one of the check-in tables, issuing badges and schedules to panel speakers and other special guests. Vicky was seated at another table with Flora Meriweather, the agent representing children's and young adult books at Novel Idea, and I couldn't help but grin over their contrary appearance.

Flora, a plump, jovial middle-aged woman who favored bright colors and cheerful patterns, was wearing a floral blouse and a mango-colored skirt. Her lipstick was the same tropical hue, and she'd secured her hair beneath a lime green headband. Her Peter Pan charm bracelet jingled merrily each time she handed one of the writers a welcome packet. It took Flora twice as long as

Vicky to complete the check-in task, as she engaged each of the attendees in conversation, making fast friends with every person in her line.

Vicky, on the other hand, kept her face as blank as a world-class poker player. She ticked off names on a spreadsheet she'd created during her first hour of work at the agency, answered questions in a clear-cut monotone that could have rivaled the loudspeaker announcements heard at an airport, and sent people on their way. And even though her attire resembled that of a Catholic school nun, from her shapeless black sweater down to her square-toed orthopedic footwear, I was delighted to have her onboard.

The woman had transformed our office within hours of her arrival yesterday. She'd appeared at the top of the stairs at two minutes to nine, thanked Jude for the flowers on her desk, thanked me for welcoming her into the fold with an offering of Danishes and coffee, placed her purse under her desk, and then tapped on a little gold watch. "It's nine o'clock. Time for work. There's much to be done."

Whenever I passed by her desk, I found her seated with perfect posture. And while she rarely moved her body, her hands were like whirling dervishes over the keyboard. Vicky could certainly multitask. I'd never seen an office manager who could calmly answer the phone with one hand, type with another, and not lose focus on either job. It was as if she had two minds.

By the end of Vicky's first day on the job, the agents' inboxes had been graced by a fresh pile of well-written query letters, dozens of minute details relating to the festival had been addressed, and our break room had been cleaned and sterilized until it resembled a hospital ward.

Now, sitting here in the lobby of town hall, I would have loved to be able to emulate Vicky's self-confidence. The reputation of our agency would be affected by the success of this festival. Novel Idea would either gain more clients and esteem from this weekend, or people would question whether a premier literary agency could really flourish this far from New York City, the heart of the publishing world.

My boss, Bentley Burlington-Duke, tobacco heiress and philanthropist, had left the bustle of Manhattan and returned to her home state to open the foremost agency in the South. So far, she'd made good on that goal, and we all hoped this festival would finally prove to our doubters that we could operate from Tahiti and still be successful. As long as we had the Internet and a group of ambitious agents, we'd continue to rival any of the agencies from the Big Apple.

Just as this thought was passing through my mind, one of the guest speakers arrived at my table and stared at me in awe. I returned the slack-jawed stare, for this woman could have been my twin. Like me, she appeared to be in her midforties. Tall with feminine curves, coffee brown eyes, and hair the color of roasted hazelnuts, the only noticeable difference was that her skin was more peach-toned than mine. Remarkably, we'd both paired a paprika-colored blouse with slacks. Mine were black and hers were tan, and I'd chosen flats while she'd opted for heeled boots in highly polished leather, but still, the overall resemblance was extraordinary.

"They say everyone has a double," I said and held out my hand to her. She clasped mine and shook her head in wonder.

"I'm Melissa Plume." Her voice was lower in timbre than mine. "Senior editor for Doubleday Books." She handed me a business card, which I slipped in my purse without looking at it.

Handing her a packet, I smiled and told her my name. "And we have books in common, too. I don't suppose pepperoni is your favorite pizza topping."

Returning my smile, she said, "Anchovies. Still, we could fool my husband, if not my mother. How'd you like to fly up to New York and pretend to be me whenever I need to tell an author that their series has been canceled?"

I waved away the offer. "No, thank you. I have to deliver plenty of rejections as it is. That's why this festival is going to be so much fun for me. At this stage, the place is teeming with possibility. The writers are determined, eager, hopeful. They're like marathon runners poised at the starting line, their adrenaline pumping, their hearts filled with expectation." I stopped, knowing that I was getting carried away. "I wish it could always feel like this."

"The serious writers won't give up, no matter how many rejections they get," Melissa said, gazing at the crowd. "They take classes, join critique groups, and edit their books again and again until someone like you believes they are ready. It might take them ten years to get published, and their first book might tank. But the real writers, the ones whose veins run with ink, who talk to characters in the shower, who'd make the perfect material witness because of their powers of observation, those people never give up. They can't. Writing is an addiction. If they stop, they dry up and wither away."

"I hope that speech is part of your lecture."

She laughed. "Oh, I've got a whole notebook of such inspirational gems. See you in there."

Once all of the morning's panelists and guest speakers had checked in, I waded through the clusters of aspiring writers milling around the Espresso Yourself and Sixpence Bakery kiosks. Makayla, who was steaming milk in a stainless steel pitcher, called me over and handed me a caramel latte without skipping a beat. I told her we'd catch up later and forced myself not to be tempted by the sight and smell of chocolate croissants, pecan twists, cinnamon buns, triple berry muffins, and apple strudel that Nell was selling with the alacrity of a newspaper boy with a dramatic headline.

Walking around the room with my latte, I double-checked the signage and was reassured that the rooms designated for the panels were easy to find. Vicky had me pose with a few of the attendees as she snapped some photos.

"I want to post a bunch on the agency's website," she explained. "Good PR."

I decided to sit in on "Crafting Your Nonfiction Proposal," which was being mediated by my coworker Franklin Stafford.

The room was packed. I had to settle for a seat in the last row, and my heart swelled with pride when Franklin switched his microphone on and introduced five of his clients. Under his guidance, the published authors shared stories of how they'd become published. Their narratives were heartfelt and humorous, and it was clear that all of the writers had faced challenges on the road to publication. The allotted hour elapsed before anyone was prepared to leave.

After attending Melissa Plume's insightful lecture on the future of the publishing industry, I rounded out my morning by serving as a mediator on my own panel: "Cozy, Soft-Boiled, or Romantic Suspense: Identify Your Mystery Genre."

I'd invited four authors to sit at the table in front of the room and discuss which elements helped classify their novels as a particular genre. The most engaging speaker turned out to be Calliope Sinclair. Flamboyant as ever, the author of dozens of bestselling romance novels was a local hero. She was the small-town North Carolina girl who'd made it big, and her love of the craft shone through every piece of advice and anecdote. Dressed in a voluminous royal purple muumuu, turquoise leggings, and an emerald green scarf, Calliope was as showy as a peacock, but she responded to questions from the audience with a passionate sincerity that stole the show. The other authors didn't seem to mind. Being far more reserved than Calliope, they were certainly happy to let her represent them all.

At the end of the panel, I sidled up to Calliope and asked if I could treat her to lunch.

"We really need to talk about your current project." I was determined to convince her that she'd have to revamp the final chapter of her book if I stood any chance of selling it.

Calliope consulted a diamond-encrusted watch. "All right, but I'd rather not wait in line for one of Big Ed's sandwiches. I have a facial this afternoon and don't want to be late." She put her hands to her cheeks. "My skin always gets *so* dry in the fall."

Knowing I would likely regret asking, since Calliope had expensive taste and I tried to keep my business expenses within budget, I said, "Where would you like to go?"

"Let's walk over to How Green Was My Valley. They're featuring Indian dishes on their hot food bar and I simply *adore* lamb rogan josh over a mound of basmati rice."

It was a relief to leave the din inside town hall and step out into the brisk air. We made our way to the organic grocery store, passing storefronts decorated with fluttering ghosts, black cats with electric yellow eyes, jack-o'-lanterns of all shapes and sizes, and glow-in-the-dark skeletons. Usually, Calliope didn't like to walk anywhere, especially under the threat of rain, but she was in an especially good mood. She pointed at an Elvira costume displayed in the window of a trendy boutique with delight.

"I haven't bought an outfit for tomorrow night's Halloween dinner dance. What do you think? Should I try it on?"

I struggled for the right reply. Calliope couldn't fit one leg in the black latex dress, let alone two. "Why don't we eat first? I don't want you to miss your facial."

Diverted, Calliope increased her pace. In the grocery store we were welcomed by the scent of warm apple cider. A clerk handed us samples and we sipped the cinnamon-spiced brew as we perused the hot food bar. Later, after we'd both made a dent in our lunches, I swallowed a mouthful of fiery chicken curry and put down my fork.

"You were amazing during the panel." I'd learned to begin conversations with Calliope with a compliment. "You kindled the writers' dreams, yet tempered them just enough with a dose of reality."

Calliope's eyes glimmered. "It was such fun! I remember exactly what it felt like to be one of them." She put a hand over her heart, her jeweled rings twinkling. "I remember that burning sensation in here. Night and day. I knew that I'd either publish . . . or perish!"

We laughed over her theatricality. "And do you still think you have room to grow? To learn new things, even though you're already an international bestselling author?"

She smiled. "I never get tired of hearing people say that. But the answer to your question is yes, I am absolutely open to stepping out on a limb. That's why I dearly want you to sell my latest project. And that's why you're helping me find a new publisher who will allow me to break out of my genre. History, romance, intrigue! It's a winner." When I failed to agree, Calliope eyed me warily. "Don't you think so?"

Summoning my courage, I said, "Right up until

the last chapter. It's a gem, Calliope, and you know that's not just lip service. I'm a true fan. And have been since long before I was lucky enough to become your agent." I paused. My next statement required delicacy. "You mentioned some of this project's best qualities. The lovers from different social classes, the historic London setting, and the murder of a chambermaid blend beautifully. But the out-of-body experience in the final chapter doesn't. It appears out of left field. It would be like Santa Claus delivering the State of the Union address."

Calliope shuffled a forkful of rice around on her plate, her mouth stretched into a deep frown.

"We've discussed this before and I'm aware of your feelings on the subject," I pushed on. "I believe that last chapter will prevent this book from selling, and I know how much you want this series to be a success. Calliope, if I didn't truly care about your work, I wouldn't be saying any of this." I reached across the table and touched her hand. "Will you rewrite the ending?"

After a long moment of silence, Calliope squeezed my hand. "I trust you, Lila. I don't know why, since you're a relatively green agent, but I do. I'll revisit the finale."

I could have hugged her, but instead I applauded her flexibility and told her I'd be anxiously awaiting the revised version.

Calliope wanted to mull over her project on the

way back to her car, so we parted inside the grocery store.

Heading back to the festival, I was so buoyed by self-satisfaction that I barely noticed the rain. By the time I showed up for my first pitch appointment, however, my suit jacket was peppered with wet drops.

Just outside the former courtroom where Jude and I planned to host our pitch sessions, I bumped into Vicky. She looked me up and down, made a noise that clearly expressed she found me wanting, and then rummaged in her handbag for tissues and a compact. I hastily wiped away the raccoon eyes created by my running mascara and applied some fresh lipstick from my own purse.

The buzz from within the room tied my stomach into knots. "I'm nervous," I confessed to Vicky.

"Follow your instincts. You have good judgment. After all, you hired me, didn't you?"

I could have sworn I saw her lips twitch with amusement, but there was no time for further study. I took my place at one of two small tables set up at the front of the room.

Jude caught my eye and winked. Standing, he cleared his throat. "Welcome, writers." His words silenced the chatter in the room. "I'm Jude Hudson, agent for thrillers and suspense novels, and this is Lila Wilkins. She represents romantic and traditional mysteries. We know you are all energized and maybe even a teeny bit anxious, but try to stay calm and present us with your best pitch. I promise we'll be kind." Judging by the worshipful stares he was receiving from the majority of the women in the audience, he could have been talking about the nuances of tax law and they would have listened attentively.

After Jude relayed instructions on how we would proceed, each of us called the first name on our appointment schedules, and the pitch sessions were under way.

A slim woman in her midtwenties approached my table, papers vibrating in her hands as rapidly as hummingbird wings.

"It's okay. I know exactly how you feel," I said gently. "Just breathe."

The young woman gave me a grateful smile, took a seat, and told me her name. She then took my advice, inhaled deeply, and presented her pitch.

"I've written a young adult trilogy similar to *The Hunger Games*. You've heard of the books by Suzanne Collins?"

I nodded, disappointed that she'd begun her pitch by concentrating on another author's work instead of pointing out the merits of her own.

"In my series, starting with *The Ring*, gladiator matches are fought between supernatural creatures. For example, goblins fight dwarves, fairies battle trolls, et cetera. The winner of the games gets extra magic for their race. It's really fast-paced and I've done a ton of research on mythical creatures. Anybody who likes J. R. R. Tolkien will love *The Ring*."

The young woman's idea wasn't half bad. In fact, it was quite creative, but her pitch was overly brief and too focused on name-dropping. Hers might have been the first pitch I'd ever heard, but I didn't need to be a veteran agent to recognize that I'd been given no sense of voice from this writer. She hadn't even mentioned the existence of a main character. Tactfully, I thanked the woman, gave her advice on the information she needed to include during future pitch appointments and queries, and wished her the best of luck.

With the first pitch session out of the way, my initial anxiety abated. I leaned back and took a deep breath. This was certainly more direct than dealing with written queries, and it was important for me to be sensitive to the person sitting across the table, but I felt a certain satisfaction in giving an immediate verbal response. I could only hope that all the writers I'd meet today would be as receptive to my advice as the first.

I looked around the room at the tense and nervous aspiring authors. Along the wall, people were sitting and standing. Most were clutching papers, and although a few were chatting to one another, the majority waited in silence. Jude was listening intently to a woman wearing a maroon cape.

I caught the eye of a man who made me suck in a quick breath. His appearance reminded me of my imagined Kirk Mason. Tall and thin, the man wore jet-black pants and a blazer over a black turtleneck. His beard had been trimmed into a pencil-thin goatee, and his raven hair was short and spiky. A silver ring pierced both of his thick, dark eyebrows. It was eerie how closely he matched the image my mind had created for him. It was entirely possible that he was Mason. After all, the aspiring author had registered for the festival.

The man in black stood with one shoulder leaning against the wall near Jude's table. His cold ebony eyes bored into mine. I quickly glanced away and called the next name on my list.

Ten pitches later, I felt as if I'd been participating in a bizarre form of speed dating. The stories presented to me had all jumbled together in my mind, and the writers' faces had become a blur. I'd been regaled with clichéd tales of romance and murder and had yet to hear a pitch worthy of consideration. Heaving a big sigh, I scanned the remaining hopefuls in the room while calling my next person, one Ashley Buckland.

The sinister man in black narrowed his eyes,

causing his eyebrow rings to glitter, and pushed away from the wall. Good Lord, he was coming to pitch his novel to *me*. I struggled to compose myself and straightened my papers. But then he veered away from me at the last moment, leaving a cloying, musky scent in his wake, and sat down in a vacant chair not far from Jude's table. Jude, having just had a rotund, bald man push himself out of the seat across from him, turned and winked at me.

"Hello, I'm Ashley Buckland."

A pleasant voice drew my attention back to my own table, and I looked up to see a gentleman of average height with short brown hair and wire-rimmed glasses standing by me. "Please, sit," I said, gesturing to the seat at the other side of the table.

He cleared his throat and chuckled. "I guess you don't usually get a man pitching a cozy, do you?"

I didn't feel inclined to tell him that today was the first time I'd had anyone pitch anything to me, so I said, "I think a man can have a unique voice and perspective in a genre primarily written by females. Please, tell me your story."

He glanced at the sheet of paper in his hands and placed it on the table. "I've written a humorous cozy about a group of househusbands who call themselves Men at Home. My main character, Will, is a relatively new stay-at-home dad, so he is invited to join these guys who, like him, have left the nine-to-five world to raise their kids while their wives are in the corporate rat race. They get together once a week at a play-group for their kids to swap recipes and advice. When Will's former boss gets murdered, Will becomes the chief suspect. The Men at Home band together to try and discover the real murderer, in between loading up the Crock-Pot, carting babies around in strollers, and folding laundry."

"That's definitely a unique approach," I said. "And I could see it having a certain appeal to both the typical cozy reader and to men who don't normally pick up the genre. Do you envision yourself writing more than one title?"

"Oh yes," he said, nodding vigorously. As he described his ideas for the second, third, and even fourth book, I realized this could be a winner. Of course, I cautioned myself, it would depend on the quality of the writing.

When he finished, I handed him my card. "Email me your first three chapters along with your query, and put 'Requested material for Lila Wilkins' in the subject line. That way our assistant knows to forward it directly to me." I smiled at him. "I hope to hear from you soon."

Reenergized after that pitch, I felt that maybe something good would come out of this very long afternoon after all. I glanced around the room and called the next name on my list, T. J.

West, the last appointment before a much-needed break. As the name left my tongue, I wondered if T. J. was a male or female.

Jude was deep in discussion with a young woman whose vibrant red hair was tied back in a ponytail. The creepy guy in black still sat near Jude's table, staring intently at me. By the door, a woman stood chatting with a man with brown hair and glasses. When I called out for T. J., that man turned in my direction, but my eyes instinctively darted back to the man in black. At that moment he rose and walked to my table while at the same time, the man with the glasses was also approaching me. I knew I should have been focusing on him, because in all likelihood he was T. J. West, but I kept my attention on the sinister-looking man, who stopped at my table and placed a large raven feather in front of me without saying a word. Then he turned and left the room.

I picked up the feather, wondering what on earth it could mean. The barbs radiating from the vein were silky smooth and glossy in their blackness, and even the downy afterfeathers at the base of the shaft were black. I had no idea why that disquieting man would give this to me, as I had never seen him before today, and made a note to ask Jude if he knew anything about him.

T. J. West turned out to be a pseudonym, and the writer was unwilling to give me his actual name. His pitch was for a cozy based in a small lakeside town and featured a widow who ran a bed and breakfast. His depiction of the town and description of the protagonist were strong, but I have to admit that the writer didn't have my full attention because I could not keep my eyes off the black feather. What did the creepy guy mean by leaving that plume on my table?

I returned my focus to the man's voice. After all, he should be given as much consideration as the others who preceded him.

"So the clue that my widow is convinced will help her solve the murder," he was saying, "is something that the murderer left in the victim's arms. A child's much-loved teddy bear."

I sat up. "A teddy bear? I don't think cozy fans would like that. Children are untouchable in a cozy, unless they serve as cute or humorous minor characters."

"But it's the key to the murderer's motivation. She kills the woman because—"

At that moment a cold, wet drop fell on my forehead. Two more fell onto my appointment schedule, blurring some of the names. T. J. West directed his eyes upward and a fat droplet splashed onto the lens of his glasses. "The ceiling is leaking!" he exclaimed.

I looked up. Sure enough, drops of rain were collecting at a crack directly over our table. Another plopped on me, this time on my nose. I shoved the table out from under the leak and handed one of my cards to the man. "If you take out the teddy bear, you can email me the first three chapters, with 'Requested material' in the subject line."

He took the card. "But—"

"I like your setting and your protagonist. However, before you send me your proposal, check our agency guidelines on what constitutes a cozy and make sure your book fits the criteria, okay?" I held the door open for him. "I'm sorry to cut this short, but I have to find a bucket."

I ran to the lobby where Vicky was sitting at her table sipping from a cup.

"Vicky, the ceiling is leaking in the courtroom!" I exclaimed. "Do you know where I can find a bucket?"

"No need to panic, Lila." She put her cup down. "One of the presentation rooms has a dripping ceiling, too. Zach found a bucket for it in the janitor's closet down that hall."

She pointed to a corridor behind one of the large easels displaying the panel schedules. We had placed it there to prevent attendees from entering that part of the building.

"But that area is cordoned off because of the renovations," I protested.

"The entry is simply obstructed by barriers and our signs. You can get in easily." She glanced down at my shoes. "I'm glad to see you're not wearing a pair of unstable high heels. Just watch out for the construction debris."

"Okay. Where's the janitor's closet?"

"Fifth door on the right. And I'll get Jude to mop up the water on the floor in your room. We can't have any lawsuits on the first day of our festival."

Ducking behind the easel and then under the wooden barrier, I found myself in a dimly lit passageway that disappeared into darkness. The floor was littered with chunks of plaster, pieces of wood, and dirt, and I couldn't see past the first three doors. To get to the janitor's closet I'd have to venture into the dark.

The rainy weather made the air in the corridor dank, and I felt a chill. " 'Deep into that darkness peering, long I stood there wondering, fearing,' " I whispered, quoting Edgar Allan Poe's "The Raven." Rubbing my arms, I gingerly picked my way around the debris.

My eyes became accustomed to the gloom, but I still couldn't see very clearly. The rubble on the floor was a shadowy obstacle course. My steps echoed in the hollow-sounding, somber space, and I felt edgy, even though there was absolutely no reason for me to be skittish. I was just getting a bucket, for heaven's sake.

I passed the fourth door and was almost at the fifth when I stumbled on a crumbly brick. I reached out my arms and my hands caught the wall to keep me from falling. Vicky had been right about the shoes, and in that moment I was glad I'd worn flats. Wiping my hands on my pants, I continued.

A noise sounded down the corridor, almost like an echo of my stumble. I stopped and held my breath, listening. Hearing nothing, except for the beating of my heart and the rain assaulting the roof, I waited a minute more and then moved forward.

The fifth door opened easily, revealing a small cubicle. At one end, a tiny square window shot a shaft of dull light onto a set of metal shelves and a troop of mops in the corner. I felt along the walls to the side of the doorway for a light switch and was jubilant when my fingers touched one. However, flicking it produced no result. In the gray light shining in from outside, I could see two buckets under the bottom shelf to the left of the window. I darted over and grabbed both of them. The door slammed behind me with a loud thump.

I cried out in surprise. Annoyed with myself for being so jittery, I left the room, pulling the door closed firmly behind me, and started to make my way around the maze of debris.

Ahead in the corridor, footsteps approached in my direction.

"Jude, is that you?" I called out.

No one responded, but the footsteps came closer.

"Who's there?" I demanded, tightening my grip on the bucket handles.

In the gloom, a man appeared, casting an eerie light ahead of him with an open cell phone. It was difficult to make out his features, but his tall, thin body filled the narrow corridor with more shadow. His dark clothes allowed him to melt into the blackness.

"This wing is closed," I announced. "Festival attendees aren't allowed in here."

As he moved his head, there was a glint at his brow. I suddenly realized that I stood in front of the creepy man in black, the one with the eyebrow rings who had unnerved me in the courtroom during the pitch appointments. He was the one who'd left the feather on my table.

"Who are you? What do you want from me?" I inquired in my best authoritative voice.

"You." The single syllable rumbled from his throat like a growl. It echoed in the emptiness, replete with undeniable menace. "Finally. I've found you."

He advanced, his hands reaching out for me.

Chapter 4

For a moment, I stood in that dark corridor like I had been hewed from the same stone as the floor. My mind couldn't seem to come to terms with the fact that a strange man was reaching for me with a pair of long, spidery hands. It didn't make any sense. Why me? I'd never seen his craggy, pierced face before in my life.

These fleeting thoughts were quickly replaced by a more primal urge—my instincts took charge and my body reacted like any cornered animal. My muscles were now in control, the message issued to my nerve center commanding me to fight.

Just as the creep's bony fingers were about to close on my forearm, I swung the metal bucket in an upward arc. It connected with his chin, the impact forcing his head to snap back. His head bobbed on his neck like one of those plastic drinking birds dipping its beak in and out of a glass of water.

"HELP!" I shouted before my attacker could recover. I stumbled down the hall toward the public area. As the light grew brighter, I could hear the tread of heavy footsteps behind me. He was coming after me again.

Then I realized that those footfalls sounded like they were ahead of me. But how could they be behind *and* in front? Was someone now blocking my path to freedom? I pulled up short and gasped. Another man was entering the shadows.

"Lila?" a familiar voice called.

Thank heavens! My coworker Zach Cohen had come to my rescue.

"Zach!" My panicked shout reverberated off the walls. "Someone's chasing me! Help!"

To his credit, Zach didn't waste another breath. He charged past me into the gloom, carrying a bucket just like mine in one hand. "YOU!" I heard him bellow as my potential attacker's steps changed direction. "STOP! *NOW!*"

Part of me wanted to follow Zach. He was a strong young man in his midthirties, and though he was nearly impossible to intimidate and I was confident he could take care of himself, I was still worried. After all, there was something sinister about the man in black. Menace oozed out of him like foul cologne. I could easily picture him slipping into a nook to wait for Zach to pass by. What if he picked up a loose brick or another makeshift weapon from the construction debris? Zach would have no chance. No chance at all.

That terrifying thought propelled me into the

lobby. I grabbed Vicky, told her to call the police, and then looked around for backup. Just then, Zach reappeared. His face was flushed and he was breathing heavily, but he was unscathed.

"He . . . got . . . away!" Zach put his hands on his knees and bent over, sucking in air. "Out the fire door."

My eyes traveled beyond the town hall's double doors to the sidewalk below. Since the festival was now officially over for the day, people were streaming outside, spilling over the sidewalk and into the street. There was no sense searching for the man in black. Despite his height, it would be impossible to spot him in the crowd. Because of the weather, dozens were clad in dark-colored coats.

Moving closer to the exit, I gazed out at the gunmetal gray thunderclouds and crossed my arms over my chest, rubbing the goose bumps away from the skin of my arms. Beneath my suit jacket and blouse, I felt chilled.

"Are you okay? Did he hurt you?" Zach put his hands on my shoulders and examined my body with his gaze. Normally, I would have pushed him away and let loose a snide remark or two, but instead, I hugged him and gave him a grateful kiss on the cheek.

"I'm fine. Thank you for rushing to my aid."

Zach preened, glancing this way and that to see how many women had witnessed his act of heroism. Unfortunately, the only audience he had was Vicky, and she appeared entirely unimpressed.

"I won't have much to tell the police," I said to her.

She shrugged. "No need to worry. I didn't place the call because there was nothing for me to report. I make it a rule not to jump to conclusions, and once again, it's proven to be a good rule. It looks like the imminent threat has passed."

I scowled at Vicky. "That horrible man could be back tomorrow! We need to identify him and be prepared in case he comes back. Where's Jude? The psychopath had a pitch appointment with him, so we must have a record of his name and contact information."

This was the type of action Vicky was eager to pursue. She pushed away her chair and stood with the straight-backed discipline of a marine heading to the front lines. "I'll see to this immediately."

Zach watched her march away. "What a pistol! The Zachmeister likes her."

My coworker had a particular way of referring to himself in the third person. Looping his arm through mine, he led me outside. "Come on, we'll head over to the restaurant for the agency dinner. I found a maintenance guy to deal with the leaks and Vicky can handle the detective work. You and I will order some booze. After today, I could use a tall, frosty mug of Octoberfest ale."

A drink sounded good to me, too. I was more of a red wine kind of gal, but after my run-in with the stalker in the shadows, I had half a mind to down a shot of whiskey. Or two.

However, by the time Zach and I joined the rest of the agents from Novel Idea at Voltaire's, Inspiration Valley's new French restaurant, the frightening experience had lost its edge. It was difficult to concentrate on anything unpleasant inside Voltaire's. The interior was resplendent with crystal chandeliers, red velvet and gilt chairs, and gold brocade tablecloths. The mirrored walls cast splintered refractions of light onto a ceiling painted with winged cherubim and ethereal celestial goddesses.

I sank into one of the soft chairs and smiled with relief as a waiter placed a napkin on my lap. "Good evening, madam. May I pour you a glass of champagne?"

Bentley gestured at my empty glass. "We're celebrating the completion of a very successful first day. I am immensely proud of my agents." She hesitated. "Where are Jude and Vicky? We can hardly have a toast without them."

"They are searching for the identity of Lila's crazed writer stalker!" Zach announced and then proceeded to tell Bentley, Flora, and Franklin how he'd scared off a veritable giant in the deserted town hall wing.

After listening to his inflated version of the

event, Bentley eyed me curiously. "Perhaps you should mention this incident to your policeman friend, Sam? Or is it Scott?"

Bentley rarely remembered the names of people she had no use for, so I patiently replied, "Sean," before she could list every name beginning with the letter "S." "I'll definitely tell him. And since Officer Griffiths is a guest speaker tomorrow, I'll certainly feel safer should that . . . man . . . return."

Jude and Vicky arrived at that moment, shrugging out of rain-drenched jackets and easing into the red velvet chairs with the same sigh of relief I'd uttered.

"Well?" Zach demanded excitedly. "What's the psycho's name?"

"We're pretty sure it's Kirk Mason," Jude answered. "He was booked for my last pitch session of the day, but in the confusion of the leaking ceiling, everyone cleared the room and I didn't actually meet with him."

Vicky fiddled with her silverware until the forks, knives, and spoons were perfectly aligned. After taking a prim sip from her water goblet, she said, "We're tardy because I wanted to review Mr. Mason's registration form. He paid by check —a cashier's check, I assume, considering the address he provided is incomplete. The street is missing. He only filled in the state and a zip code."

"Then Kirk Mason could be a pseudonym?"

Flora's eyes widened. "Oh, this sounds like a Nancy Drew novel!"

The other agents gave Flora an indulgent smile.

"No offense, Flora," I said, "but I'd prefer to have Sam Spade by my side should Mr. Mason come back to the festival tomorrow."

"But why did he go after *you*, Lila?" Franklin wanted to know. "He was supposed to pitch to Jude, so you couldn't have caused him offense." He turned to Jude. "Do you know anything about Mason's pitch?"

Jude consulted his legal pad. "Only from a proposal he sent to the office. His thriller-suspense intrigued me, and I had really hoped to speak to him." He shook his head. "It certainly held a lot more promise than the last pitch I heard. The story was your run-of-the-mill serial killer stuff, full of graphic detail with no character development." He frowned in distaste. "The killer's signature was that he pierced a body part on all of his victims with a safety pin. The author was more than happy to describe all the gory details, but I wasn't hooked."

"As fascinating as this discussion may be," Bentley said in a tone that belied how she truly felt about the topic, "I would like to review the highlights of the day." She gave a regal wave of her hand, indicating that she was ready to make a toast. After praising the agents and Vicky for their hard work, Bentley ordered a sampling of the most decadent food on Voltaire's leather-bound menu and the waiter scurried off to the kitchen. Another waitress materialized with loaves of warm baguettes and a sun-dried tomato cheese spread and presented Bentley with the wine list.

Later, after sampling indulgent appetizers like brandy and peppercorn steak tartare, butter-basted sea scallops, and artichoke hearts with shitake mushrooms in a white wine garlic sauce, we went around the table and shared some of the most memorable moments from our pitch sessions.

"I've got one for the history books," Franklin declared. "Hold on, I need another gulp of vino to bolster my courage." He took two long swallows and then cleared his throat. "Well, then. I actually had a gentleman propose that I represent his how-to book on the alternative uses of, ah, prophylactics."

"Someone pitched a book on what to do with a condom?" Zach asked and began roaring with laughter before Franklin had the opportunity to answer. "How many pages could that take?"

Jude grinned. "Perhaps there are meant to be dozens of colorful illustrations."

"No, no, you misunderstand the young man's intent," Franklin interjected, his cheeks flushing the same hue as the velvet on his chair. "His book centers on nonsexual uses. For example, a few hundred can be stitched together and dyed to make a fashion-forward dress. They can be turned into balloon animals at children's birthday parties, swimming gloves, replacement rubber bands, Christmas tree—"

Bentley stopped him with a stern look.

When the laughter had died down, Flora told us that her most memorable appointment had been with a twelve-year-old girl. "This young lady showed me a picture book filled with skull-splitting trolls and killer vampires and fairies ripping one another's wings off. Her mother told me all she ever does is closet herself in her room penning these extremely violent fantasy stories." She shook her head. "I believe it's all the child does. She was as pale as my napkin. Reminded me of that strange little girl from the Addams Family."

"Was this a case of age discrimination?" Jude teased.

Flora put a hand over her heart. "Certainly not, but the girl's books are far too frightening for the intended age group. I suggested she focus her attention on middle grade fiction."

"Hey, the average sixth grader could have run circles around my worst pitch of the day," Zach said. He'd eaten everything on his plate with gusto and was now reaching for a second hunk of bread. "I met with this retired high school football scout who wanted me to represent his tell-all on the dark side of recruiting. The subject was *awesome*, but the guy could barely string two words together. When I told him he'd have to give me a few examples, he had the gall to say that he wasn't going to speak a word until I coughed up *ten grand* in advance!"

Bentley let loose a nearly inaudible snort, and her eyes gleamed with amusement. "That's all? And were you supposed to write him a check then and there?"

"Totally!" Zach bellowed in theatrical indignation. "I tried to explain that I wasn't buying anyone's book, but this meathead could not be made to understand how the publishing world works no matter how simple my vocabulary was. Man! He was thicker than a two-by-four. Stormed out when I wouldn't pay up, too!"

Before I could discuss my pitches, a quartet of waiters cleared away our hors d'oeuvre dishes and set warm dinner plates before us. Empty wineglasses were refilled, and succulent entrée platters were arranged in the center of the table. The waiter hovering behind my right shoulder informed us that we were being served veal medallions in a creamy cognac sauce, filet mignon with a dusting of peppercorns, sautéed chicken breasts in marsala wine, and a pan-seared rockfish. Side dishes included spaghetti squash, white-striped beets with goat cheese, and tamarind-marinated eggplant.

For several minutes, no one spoke a word. Our taste buds were in ecstasy. No words could describe the layers of flavor, the tenderness of the meat, or the freshness of the herbs and spices. We were reduced to groans, our eyes half closed in pleasure. Between the wine and the rich food, I had nearly forgotten about the man in black and could barely recall experiencing even a moment of fear in this glittering haven of tantalizing aromas and superb cuisine. In the company of my coworkers, I felt relaxed and happy.

I'm ashamed to admit how much I ate, but it was worth it. Only Vicky and Bentley refrained from cleaning their plates, and both women passed on dessert, settling for decaf coffee instead.

As the waiters served us shallow cups of ginger and vanilla bean crème brûlée, I wondered how I'd ever zip my skirt tomorrow morning.

"Tell us about your pitches, Lila," Flora prompted, splintering the crust of her crème brûlée with the edge of her spoon.

"I guess the most unusual thing about my session was that I had not one, but two men pitch cozy mysteries to me. The first was about a group of stay-at-home dads turned amateur sleuths, and the second was a village-style cozy featuring a widow who runs a B and B."

"Are you sure they were real dudes?" Zach winked at me. Clearly, the younger agent had consumed too much wine.

Vicky stared at him in confusion. "As opposed to what?"

Before Zach could elaborate, Franklin broke into an elaborate coughing fit and then asked me to pass the creamer. After pouring a splash into his coffee, he asked, "Were their pitches any good?"

I nodded. "Yes, actually. I told both of them to send me their first three chapters. Unfortunately, I was a bit distracted during the last pitch because the man who came after me in the hall dropped this feather on my desk." I reached into my purse and drew forth the black feather. "He didn't say a word. Just dropped it and kept walking."

Flora shuddered in distaste. "Be careful tomorrow, Lila. This man might be so desperate to get published that he may have taken on the behavior of his character."

"I hope not!" Jude declared as Bentley handed the waiter her credit card. "In his proposal, Kirk Mason's killer murdered someone with a meat cleaver."

And just like that, I was ready to get home, lock the door, and call a policeman. *My* policeman.

It was no longer raining when we left the restaurant, and the moon cast a luminous glow in the velvety blackness of the sky. The night was pleasant but I paid it little heed. I was just eager to get off the street, as my mood was colored by a lingering disquiet from our final conversation. Water sprayed onto my shoes and pant legs as I rode my scooter through puddles left by the rain, so that by the time I got home I was damp and cold. It was a relief to walk into my warm and comfy house.

I immediately removed my wet clothes and put on pajamas, even though it was barely eight o'clock. Sean would not be coming by, as he was on duty tonight, so I had no fear of him seeing me in plaid flannel pants and a T-shirt that said, *Chocolate is the fifth food group*. Curling up on the couch with my phone, I threw a chenille blanket over my legs and punched in Sean's number. As it rang, I hoped my call wasn't interrupting an arrest or other important police business.

"Hey, you," he answered with enthusiasm. "How'd it go today?"

It was such a balm to hear his deep, masculine voice. "That's a loaded question," I replied. "The first day of the festival was a huge success, but it had its pitfalls, too." I proceeded to tell Sean my experiences with the disturbing Kirk Mason, starting with the way he kept watching me from across the room, describing the feather he dropped on the table, and then relating how I belted him with the bucket before running away. "I was terrified and don't know what might have happened if Zach hadn't shown up when he did."

"It sounds as if you were quite a match for him—the way you decked him with that pail," Sean said with a hint of admiration in his voice.

"But seriously, Lila, this guy could be dangerous. You'd better be careful and take some precautions."

"Like what?"

"Like perhaps keeping a cop close by?" he said in a playful voice.

He'd barely finished his sentence when the doorbell rang. The sound was so unexpected that it made me jump, and my heart pounded a few extra beats per second.

"Sean, stay on the phone while I answer the door," I said as I made my way to the front hall. "I have no idea who it might be."

"I'm right here."

Peering through the peephole, my wariness turned to delight when I saw Sean standing on my front porch, in uniform, holding his cell phone to his ear. He was not wearing his policeman's hat, however. Instead he'd donned a Greek helmet with red plumes sprouting from its crown. His free hand was raised in a salute.

I whipped open the door. "I didn't expect to see you tonight! Aren't you on duty?" My joy at seeing him overshadowed any reaction to the fanciful addition to his attire.

Stepping inside, he removed the helmet and said with a grin, "I do get donut breaks, you know."

"I'm so glad you're here." He truly was a welcome sight. Standing there in his policeman's uniform, his handsomeness was intensified. He seemed taller, leaner, and more muscular; his eyes were bluer, and his face was more ruggedly captivating.

I reached up and kissed him, then took the helmet from his hands. Examining the craftsmanship, I said, "This is great, Sean. You're going to look just like Paris." I placed it on the hall table.

"Just a few years older than the original," he said with a smile. "I rented a breastplate and arm guards, too. I'll need to look my best, as I'll be escorting the beautiful Helen of Troy to the costume party tomorrow night." He pulled me close and kissed me again. "Move over, Orlando Bloom and Diane Kruger."

I laughed and took his hand. "Come into the living room. Can I get you a coffee or something?" I peered at him impishly. "I have no donuts, I'm afraid."

"No, I don't want anything, thanks. I just came over to show you my helmet. But I need you to tell me more about this creep at the festival. We have to find him and ensure that he won't be a threat to you anymore." He sat down on the couch and glanced around. "This room feels homey," he said. "Your personality is all over it."

"Thanks. I forgot you hadn't seen the place yet. Want a tour?"

"Not now. Let's save that for another time." He patted the couch next to him. "Come sit down."

I lowered myself beside him and rested my head on his shoulder. "Thanks for coming, Sean. You are just what I needed."

"No problem." He placed his hand on my thigh. "Nice jammies, by the way," he teased as he stroked the flannel pants leg. "Too bad I'm not appropriately dressed for a pajama party."

"Maybe next time." I placed my hand over his, entwining our fingers.

Bringing them up to his lips, he kissed them and then freed his hand. "Okay, let's get down to business. You say this guy's name is Mason?" He pulled a notepad and pen out of his shirt pocket.

"Kirk Mason. But we're not sure that's his real name, because the address he wrote on his registration form was incomplete. Vicky thinks he paid by cashier's check, so that's untraceable, too."

"And you've never seen him before? You have no idea why he was targeting you?"

I shook my head. "All I know is that he was going to pitch a gory serial killer novel to Jude and for some reason he has something against me."

"Can you describe him?" Sean had his pen ready.

I leaned back. The last thing I felt like doing was conjuring up the image of that man again, even if it was merely in my mind. But I closed my eyes and verbally sketched every detail I could remember.

"Good recall, Lila." He sighed as he folded closed his notepad. "I hate to leave so soon, but I do have to get back to work. I told my partner I'd only be ten minutes."

"Wait. I want to give you that feather he left on my table." I grabbed the plastic bag in which I'd placed the black raven feather. "Isn't it just too weird?" I asked, handing it to Sean.

"It is inexplicable acts like this that cause me the most worry," he said in a troubled voice, "because they illustrate the perpetrator's unpredictability. I'm glad I'll be at the old town hall tomorrow."

I walked with him to the door. Opening it to the darkness, I saw Sean's police cruiser.

"There's my ride," he quipped. "I'll leave the helmet here until tomorrow, okay?"

I nodded and we stepped out on the front porch. The night air was crisp, and the moon shone high in the dark sky. We faced each other, clasping hands. "See you tomorrow," I murmured.

"Be careful, Lila. Lock that door tight." He caressed my cheek and lowered his lips to mine.

I wrapped my arms around his neck, and there, under the glowing orb in the sky, we kissed. His arms encircled me, enveloping me in warmth and affection. Our kiss intensified, and when our lips finally parted, I held his eyes with mine. " 'Soul meets soul on lovers' lips,' " I murmured, quoting Shelley. Sean's smile crinkled the corners of his eyes, and he brushed his lips against mine once more before letting go.

Chapter 5

The next morning was so beautiful that it was easy to forget about my encounter with Kirk Mason. The late October sun set the ocher and paprika petals of the chrysanthemums in my garden afire and illuminated the lavender asters until they glowed.

I had bought an old Radio Flyer wagon at my neighbor's yard sale, lined it with hay, and set it on my front porch. I then stuffed it with miniature gourds of all shapes and sizes. The yellow, green, and creamy white vegetables looked terrific mixed in with a dozen small pumpkins.

Now that my son was independent and living away from home, I wasn't too interested in decorating for Halloween. However, there were plenty of children in our little subdivision who'd be ringing my doorbell in hopes of acquiring a few pieces of candy, so I hung a wreath of black cats and witches on the front door just to show that I welcomed trick-or-treaters. In fact, I'd had to hold off buying bags of candy for fear I would eat them all before the big night.

This year, Halloween fell on a Sunday. Because it was a school night, the neighborhood committee had voted to send the kids around just after sunset. They could collect their goodies, burn off some of the sugar they'd eaten, and be home at a reasonable time. The elementary kids had to be at the bus stop at seven o'clock each morning, so I knew their Halloween evening would be a low-key affair. I, for one, was glad. After a three-day book festival, it would take every ounce of remaining energy to drag myself off the sofa. It would be all too easy to ignore the doorbell and gorge on snack-sized Milky Way bars, but I knew I wouldn't let the children down.

I was getting ahead of myself, however. There were still two more festival days to get through, and I was ready to face Day Two. Even though my sleep had initially been riddled with anxiety thanks to Kirk Mason, I'd woken well before my alarm sounded feeling surprisingly well rested. Lingering over my breakfast in a kitchen cheerful enough to dispel the gloomiest of memories, I'd filled in the *Dunston Herald* crossword before putting on my favorite autumn work outfit. My camel-colored skirt, espresso brown cashmere sweater, and polished leather boots made me feel chic and youthful. Hopping on my scooter, I quickly indulged in one of my favorite fantasies in which I starred as a wise and glamorous celebrity, known and admired by everyone in the literary and publishing circle. It was easy to pretend that all the automobile drivers were staring at me. The majority of them probably were casting curious glances in my direction. After all, I was the only woman in her midforties zipping around Inspiration Valley on a canary yellow Vespa.

I loved being able to fit in tiny parking spaces all over town, but today, I didn't try to get close to the old town hall. My heart was featherlight and the world was bathed in vibrant color and I wanted to walk a few blocks. Between the pumpkin banners hanging from each lamppost, the holiday-themed shop decorations, and garden urns filled with the perky faces of orange and purple pansies, Inspiration Valley was an autumn utopia. Leaves scuttled across my boots in a blur of red, brown, and gold until I left them behind and jogged up the front steps and into the lobby of the spacious stone building.

Vicky was already in her position at one of the check-in tables, a thermos of hot tea and a banana stationed by her right hand.

"Good morning," I said brightly, my voice bouncing around the cavernous lobby. "I'm going to grab a cappuccino from Makayla. Can I get you anything?"

"No, thank you." She indicated her thermos. "I only drink noncaffeinated herbal teas."

I nodded, though I couldn't imagine achieving a state of mental acuity without a significant jolt of caffeine first thing in the morning. "Danish?

Bagel? Something to accompany your banana?"

Vicky's mouth turned down in disapproval. "Too many processed carbohydrates. I prefer to begin my day with fruit and whole grains." She gave her plum-colored cardigan a prim tug and eyed me closely. "Are you all right after yesterday's excitement?"

Not the noun I'd have chosen, but I wasn't about to correct our formidable office manager. "I am. One of today's guest speakers, Sean Griffiths, is a police officer. He's agreed to remain in the building until the conference is over this afternoon. I've already given him a thorough physical description of Kirk Mason, and since Mason is rather hard to miss, Sean—I mean, Officer Griffiths—is certain to spot him if he dares to make an appearance."

"That's good." Vicky produced her camera from her purse. "Should Mr. Mason be foolish enough to enter by the front door, I'll be prepared to take his photograph and email it directly to the police station."

Vicky brandished the camera like it was a can of Mace, and I had to suppress a giggle. Still, if I were forced to pick a winner in a duel between Vicky and Kirk Mason, I'd choose my coworker. She seemed like the type to have a knife built into one of her square-toed shoes just like an Ian Fleming character.

The scent of fresh baked goods lured me into

the makeshift café area of the town hall, and I was delighted to overhear Nell declare that she'd sold out of nearly all of her stock yesterday. Makayla had had an equally profitable day.

"I've got to hang with writers more often!" the beautiful barista called out. "They drink more coffee than any other population group. I'm going to tell Lila to host one of these book festivals every month."

"Forget it!" I told Makayla as I strode up to her booth. "I'm going to need a week's vacation after this."

Makayla's lovely face grew tight with concern. "I heard about your run-in with Mister Crazy last night. Are you doing okay?"

I smiled. "I'll be just fine the moment I take a sip of your new vanilla cappuccino."

"Then I'd better make it a double." Makayla began steaming milk. Over the hiss of the espresso machine, she asked, "And when is your handsome policeman going to show up and dazzle the crowd?"

"Sean's got a morning panel. He's been joking around all week about putting some of the audience members in handcuffs. I couldn't really tell if he was serious or not." I watched as Makayla sprinkled cinnamon over the cloud of white foam on top of my cappuccino.

She handed me the drink and cocked her head to the side. "So have you two played around with those cuffs?" Her jade green eyes were alight with mischief. "Does Sean accuse you of shoplifting maybe? Or is it something more scandalous?"

I balled up a napkin and tossed it at her. "Stop it! You know perfectly well that Sean and I haven't slept together yet."

"There's always tonight after the costume party. With you and Sean dressed up as Paris and Helen of Troy, you could do some serious role-playing." Makayla gave me a saucy wink. "Helen's got to show Paris her gratitude for being whisked away by a handsome lover. And after knocking back a few of the witches' brew cocktails they're serving tonight, Helen might just end up handcuffed to a bedpost."

Warmth rushed to my cheeks and I knew that they had turned a deep shade of pink. It's not as though I hadn't thought about making love to Sean. I had. Plenty of times. I knew my libido was more than ready, but my mind wasn't quite there. We just hadn't spent enough time together to take things to the next level. I hoped Makayla wasn't right about the witches' brew cocktails. Getting drunk and making out with my boyfriend in public would hardly be professional behavior.

However, the idea of doing exactly that struck me the moment I saw Sean walk into the lobby. His authoritative presence seemed to fill the vacuous hall. Even Vicky wasn't immune to his poise and rugged good looks. Sipping my cappuccino, I wondered if Vicky would be put under the spell of Sean's tropical sea blue eyes. I was tempted to pull him aside and lose myself in those shades of cerulean and cobalt, but I greeted him formally and led him to the courtroom, where his panel was being held.

"You'll be in the audience?" Sean asked. "After all, I want to look down from my lofty perch and see the face that launched a thousand ships."

I laughed. "Hold on to your Paris persona until tonight. This morning, you're all cop."

His smile faded. "I'm afraid that's a skin I never quite shed. And after yesterday, my eyes are going to be on everyone. If that Mason creep shows up today, he'll be dealing with more than a woman armed with buckets." Sean gestured at the table where a private investigator, a crime scene tech, and a corrections officer waited to introduce themselves to the crowd. "I know all those guys. It would only take a word from me and Mr. Mason would be pinned to the floor, cuffed, and Mirandized before he could say 'boo.'"

I squeezed his arm. "I love it when you turn protective. Now get up there and educate these writers on how to create a realistic law enforcement character."

I needn't have worried. Sean and the other professionals were captivating. As he'd hinted to me earlier in the week, he did handcuff several volunteers from the audience. He then allowed other attendees to unlock their fellow writers. Some volunteers practiced reading pretend criminals their rights. Sean allowed people to try on his loaded utility belt, minus his sidearm, so they could see why most cops walked with a noticeable swagger.

It was a good thing that I'd given this panel a ninety-minute allotment, because once Sean and the other men had conducted a variety of demonstrations and answered dozens of insightful questions, it was time to empty the room for the next panel. However, it was obvious that the writers were reluctant to leave. At least ten participants still had unanswered questions, so Sean and the rest of the guest speakers promised to continue their Q&A session at the tables near the Sixpence Bakery kiosk.

Swallowed by the tide of chattering writers, I drifted out to the food area and noticed Melissa Plume waiting in line at Nell's kiosk. She looked up from the enticing array of pastries and our eyes met. With a little wave, she beckoned me over.

"We're not matching today," I said.

Glancing down at her black turtleneck dress, patent leather pumps, and leopard print scarf, she shook her head. "I should have called you to coordinate. I love your outfit. I bet I'd have a great time raiding your closet." She excused herself while she paid Nell for an apple and raisin turnover and then asked if I'd like anything to eat.

"No, thanks. I'm posing as Helen of Troy this evening and I don't think I can channel the world's most beautiful woman after consuming both a vanilla cappuccino and a chocolate hazelnut croissant."

Melissa immediately ordered the croissant and passed it to me. "Have you ever seen renderings of Helen on a Greek amphora? She's as curvy as the road leading into this town. My kind of girl."

We settled at a two-top table and discussed how the festival was going so far. Melissa loved the town's B and B and assured me she'd return every year if given the chance. "This place is heavenly. I expected some one-horse town with a pancake house and a barbeque joint, but the food is sophisticated and delicious, the shops are filled with hip, artsy items, and the scenery is breathtaking. I haven't seen this much color since the city's Pride Parade."

I laughed and tucked into my croissant. "I detect a hint of a Southern accent—are you from the South?"

"As a matter of fact, yes. I'm from Dunston. I used to work there before I met my husband and moved to New York. I was trying to get my book published, actually, and that's how we met."

Impressed, I asked, "What was your book about?"

"Oh, it was an exposé sort of thing that never got published. It focused on my work with kids in the foster system. My husband was a lowly editor then, to whom I naïvely sent the manuscript. Something about my proposal got to him, and while he was in Raleigh on personal business, he took the time to swing over to Dunston to tell me his publishing house didn't want the book. Over lunch, it became clear that he was mighty interested in me." A dimple appeared in her left cheek as she smiled at the memory. "And the rest is history." She sat back in her chair and glanced around. "I just can't believe I spent so many years living within a train ride of this little paradise and never knew it. But back then, the only people who talked about this place were flaky, free-spirit types who were searching for their past-life identities or the secret voice of Mother Earth. Not exactly reliable spokespeople, if you know what I mean."

As we enjoyed our treats, we watched the attendees milling about, their faces flushed with animation. A woman in a multihued poncho with fuchsia lipstick and a loud voice reminded me of Calliope. Wiping chocolate from my fingers with a paper napkin, I asked Melissa if she would mind my pitching Calliope's new series in the middle of our coffee break.

"This is the first time I've relaxed in years," my look-alike gushed in reply. "You could ask me to donate a kidney and I'd say yes, so pitch away!"

I was so familiar with Calliope's work that the story line unfurled like a flower opening its petals to the sun. Melissa took bites of her turnover as I spoke and then held up a finger to stop me.

"I'm not the acquiring editor for historical suspense, but I am absolutely positive that my friend Kate would adore this series. Let me call her right now."

It was hard to say no to such an opportunity, and I was certainly passionate about my client's project, but it was a Saturday. Would Melissa's fellow editor be annoyed to receive a work-related call over the weekend, and if so, would it hurt Calliope's chances? I voiced my concern to Melissa even as she was dialing Kate's number.

"Trust me. Our husbands are out playing golf together and she's stuck at home with the twins. She'd love to talk shop."

After a brief exchange with her coworker, Melissa passed the cell phone to me and gave me a thumbs-up sign. I introduced myself and repeated my pitch. Kate didn't hesitate.

"I love Calliope's books and I definitely like this idea," she told me. "But why is she looking outside her own publishing house?"

"Her current editor wasn't interested in histori-cal suspense. She wanted Calliope to come up with a new contemporary romance series, but that's not what my client wanted to write."

Kate whistled. "Lucky for me, then. Can you email me the proposal?"

My pulse quickened and I tried not to shout into the phone. "Absolutely. I can get it to you today."

"Brilliant! I'll have something to look forward to after I put my kids down for their afternoon nap. I'll start reading as soon as the email lands in my inbox."

After promising to drive over to my office right away, I handed Melissa her phone. She chatted with Kate for another minute and then hung up.

"Thank you, that was really nice of you," I said. "Now I wish I'd bought *you* a pastry and not the other way around." I got to my feet and shook her hand. "But I'll make it up to you at tonight's costume party. I heard they're serving some killer cocktails."

Melissa shook her head, a solemn look appearing in her eyes. "I make it a point to stay sober around aspiring writers. I've had . . . uncomfortable exchanges with a few of them. Especially if I've recently rejected one of their projects. Once, someone even accosted me while I was in the park with my son. He was really creepy. At one point he actually stroked the fur of Silas's teddy bear." She shuddered and then held out her fist. "Don't get me wrong, I'm a tough New Yorker, but one can never be too careful these days. Sometimes passion can taint a person's judgment. Artistic people can want a thing so badly that they forget we all live by a code of conduct. Not to speak in clichés, but some of these writers can cross the line."

My mind flashed to the shadowy figure in the dark corridor and I gazed nervously around the food area, and then shifted my attention to the lobby. Thankfully, there was no sign of a tall man with pierced brows. I looked at Melissa and nodded. "You're right. And when people are wearing disguises like they will be tonight, inhibitions might not be held in check."

Melissa rolled her eyes. "A room full of inebriated introverts dressed as literary characters? This is going to be *some* party."

The old town hall was transformed that evening. The hours we'd put into decorating had paid off, and with the lights dimmed and candles lit, the effect was one of eerie elegance. As Sean and I, or I should say, Paris and Helen, stepped through the black and orange–ballooned archway, a whistle escaped from his lips.

"This looks fantastic," he said as his arm slid to my back, gently guiding me into the hall.

Glowing ghosts and skeletons hung from the ceiling, and streamers of bats and black cats swooped above our heads. Orange folding chairs and black-covered tables surrounded the dance floor. At the center of each table sat a pumpkin candle nestled in colored autumn leaves, a flame dancing on its wick.

I absorbed the atmosphere and smiled. "Look," I said, pointing at the bar. "There's Captain Ahab, speaking to Dracula and Edgar Allan Poe."

"And there's another Edgar Allan Poe talking to a third Edgar Allan Poe." Sean chuckled, directing my attention to the food table.

I swiveled my head around the room. It seemed that the majority of attendees had chosen to emulate the founder of the modern mystery genre by wearing black suits, high-collared shirts, wavy black wigs, and a little black moustache.

"It looks like a Poe convention," I said in wonder, trying to recognize people behind their disguises.

"This is brilliant, isn't it?"

I turned toward Flora's voice, only to find myself looking at a roly-poly Harry Potter. Her round, dark-rimmed glasses and Quidditch cape left no question as to the identity of her character, although her gardening clogs were in slight contradiction with the rest of her outfit. "Flora, you look great."

"Well, thank you," she giggled. "So do you, Helen of Troy. That's a beautiful dress." She fingered the flowing folds of my chiton. "And I must say, Officer Griffiths, you make a handsome Paris."

At that moment, Hagrid joined us and handed Flora a martini glass filled with an orange liquid. "Some witches' brew for you, my dear." He turned to us and held out his hand. "I'm Flora's husband, Brian. Hagrid for tonight." He was a good head taller than his wife. With his matted wig and beard and dusty oversize coat, it was easy to view him as a giant.

Just as we introduced ourselves, Zorro leaped over to our small gathering. "This shindig's a smash!" Zach declared, tipping his gaucho hat and winking behind his black mask. "Have you seen all the Poes?"

I surveyed Zach's jet-black pants and shirt and remarked, "There must have been a sale on black suits."

Sean touched my shoulder. "Would you like a drink?"

I nodded. "Thanks. Something fruity and nonalcoholic," I said resolutely. "I must maintain my professionalism tonight."

As I waited for him to return, I mingled about, joining a conversation with Miss Marple, Rhett Butler, Scarlett O'Hara, and, of course, an Edgar Allan Poe. I had no idea who these people were in their costumes as they discussed the future of e-publishing. Actually, Rhett and Miss Marple did most of the talking while Scarlett concentrated on her drink and Poe seemed more interested in studying the faces of the other revelers. Rhett was emphatic that digital books would be the death of print books, but Miss Marple maintained that not everyone wanted to read from a screen and there would always be people who valued the look and feel of a beautifully bound book or an artistic cover. "And don't forget that a wall of book-lined shelves adds to the décor of any room," she declared with passion.

Poe, who had been silent throughout the conversation, suddenly blurted out, "What a load of crap! Books aren't written to serve as decoration! The very idea is an insult to authors. Have you no clue of what we writers put into our work? How much of ourselves is present in each and every word?" Anger tinged every word, and when I looked down at his clenched fists, I saw that he held a black feather in his right hand.

I stood stock-still and tried to swallow with a mouth that had suddenly gone dry. That voice! *This* Poe was Kirk Mason! Blood roared in my ears. Should I confront him or get Sean? It was obvious that Mason didn't recognize me in my Helen of Troy costume and my wig of long blond corkscrew curls. Not wanting to spook him, I smiled at the group and backed away, as if I was simply doing the party shuffle and planned to socialize with another group.

As soon as I was some distance away, I turned

and rushed toward the bar, almost running right into Sean. "Whoa!" he said as he tried to avoid spilling two tumblers of orange liquid garnished with black straws and slices of lime. "I didn't realize you were that thirsty."

"I saw Kirk Mason. Over there!" I pointed in the direction of the group I had just left, but they had already dispersed. Rhett and Scarlett were now laughing with Robin Hood and Maid Marian, and Miss Marple was conversing with a vampiress whose white face was a stark contrast to her black high-collared cape. Poe was nowhere to be seen.

I should correct myself. Poes were all over the room, but I couldn't recognize the one I believed to be Mason. "He was just here." I described how I'd instantly recognized his voice.

"We'll find our man," Sean assured me, handing me a drink. "Look closely at all the Poes, and see if you can distinguish him from the others."

I sipped the chilled mango-flavored beverage in my hand and scanned the characters in the room. It was hopeless. Except for a rather diminutive Poe and an overtly rotund one, they all looked alike. "I don't know . . ." I muttered as I approached Miss Marple.

"Excuse me," I said as I held out my hand. "Sorry to interrupt. I was standing with you a few minutes ago. I'm Lila Wilkins, from Novel Idea."

She nodded. "I remember. We were talking about e-books. I'm Shawna York, a soon-to-be-published author." She grinned. "And this is my editor, Melissa Plume."

"Melissa?" I stared at my look-alike incredulously. Red-tipped fangs stuck out of her mouth, starkly crimson against her colorless skin. "I would never have recognized you. What a fantastic costume."

"Thanks. I thought I'd take some artistic license and dress up as a forty-year-old Bella from *Twilight*. By the time she reaches my age she's bound to be a vampire." She grinned wryly. "You make a pretty good Helen, too."

I smiled in acknowledgment. "Congratulations on your book, Shawna. I'd love to hear more about it later, but at the moment I'm wondering if you know the real name of the Edgar Allan Poe you were talking to a few minutes ago."

"That obnoxious man?" She shook her head. "I have no idea."

Sean joined us. "Did you see where he went by any chance?"

Both women looked up and stared at the Greek warrior in confusion.

"This is Officer Sean Griffiths of the Dunston Police Department," I quickly explained. "He's my Paris tonight."

Shawna smiled at him. "Nice to meet you, Paris. I'm sorry, but I didn't notice what happened to that abrasive man. I left that group just after you did, Lila."

"You'll have some trouble finding him in this sea of Poes," Melissa mused, glancing around.

I rolled my eyes. "You've got that right."

The speakers crackled and Bentley's voice filled the room. "May I have your attention, please?"

All eyes turned to the front. An elegant Queen Guinevere stood at the microphone, her green velvet gown and floral head wreath belying the professional garb she usually wore at the office.

"Welcome to the first annual Inspiration Valley Book and Author Festival. I'm Bentley Burlington- Duke, owner and founder of Novel Idea Literary Agency, the main sponsor of this event. I must say, I am overwhelmed with the success of the festival. Attendance is beyond our expectations, and I hope you are all enjoying yourselves as well as acquiring useful information and contacts."

People began clapping, and Bentley waited for the clamor to quiet down before continuing. "The festival offers something for everyone, and tonight's masquerade party is a wonderful bridge between the workshops and sessions for authors that were held yesterday and today, and tomorrow's classes on book repair, preservation, and illustration. In the vendors' hall I've had the pleasure of speaking to authors and editors, librarians and bibliophiles, and, most important of all, readers."

A thunder of applause interrupted her once again. She held up her hand. "I won't keep you from your revelry too much longer, but I'd like to thank my agents and all of our helpers who transformed this town hall into a Halloween ballroom. They did a marvelous job. In a few minutes, the tapas stations will be open, and afterward, our local band, the Valley Warblers, will entertain you. Enjoy yourselves tonight."

Throughout Bentley's speech, I kept glancing around, feeling as if I were in a magical library in which characters in the books had stepped out from the pages. The enchantment was marred, however, by my uneasy awareness that Kirk Mason was one of the black-shrouded individuals in this very room and I couldn't recognize him.

Dinner was a delicious romp through different taste experiences. The tapas stations set up by the Nine Muses Restaurant presented a fantastic feast. I filled my plate with shrimp satay and a dollop of peanut sauce, a quinoa salad with tomatoes and a hint of cilantro, sliced sirloin with capers and onions, little fresh spring rolls with fresh vegetables, and grouper in a tantalizing curry sauce. I relaxed my no-alcohol resolve to complement the meal with a dry, crisp Riesling, and for dessert I simply could not resist a chocolate orange pot de crème.

After dinner, Sean and I went from table to table under the pretense of chatting with the guests, but we had no luck finding Kirk Mason. Even as we spun on the dance floor, we both kept a look-out for the sinister man, noting every Edgar Allan Poe who passed by. Still, Mason eluded us.

As the evening drew to a close, the last dance was announced. The Valley Warblers, who were surprisingly good at jazzy numbers, crooned out Nat King Cole's "The Party's Over." Sean took me in his arms, and I molded into his embrace. For a brief time the synchronized swaying of our bodies allowed me to forget about Kirk Mason, Edgar Allan Poe, and everything else. There was just my Greek warrior.

The dance ended all too soon. Almost instantaneously, it seemed, we were saying good-bye to the partygoers, blowing out candles, and taking down decorations. The hall had to be ready for tomorrow's workshops, and although the maintenance staff would do the cleanup, the decorations were the responsibility of the agency.

I gathered the pumpkin candles into a box. Sean started taking down the bat and cat streamers. Still humming "The Party's Over," I began daydreaming about what might transpire later when Sean took me home.

However, I was startled out of my reverie by Vicky, who was dressed like Virginia Woolf. At her side was Franklin, looking remarkably like an older Sherlock Holmes.

"Lila, did you move those barriers to the restricted section?" Vicky stuck her hands in the pockets of her long sweater and eyed me accusingly.

"The hallway where Kirk Mason came after me? No way." I put down the box I was holding. "Why?"

Alerted by our conversation, Sean came over. "What's up?"

"The barriers have been pushed aside. I know for a fact they were in place when I draped those cobwebs over the doorway earlier."

"And I swear they were still in position during dinner," added Franklin.

"But not anymore," insisted Vicky. "Come along, I'll show you."

Sean followed Franklin and Vicky, and I stayed close behind him. My earlier uneasiness returned, and the image of Kirk Mason came to the forefront of my mind.

"See? It's as if someone hurriedly pushed them out of the way." Vicky pointed to the opening that led into that dark hall. "Even the cobweb is torn."

The two wooden barriers had been roughly shoved clear of the doorway, one rammed up against the other. And the large synthetic cobweb that hung across the entry had been ripped in half, unveiling the portal into the black passageway that had been the site of my encounter with Mason.

Sean went closer and examined the cobweb. "From the direction of the tear, it looks as if someone split it by running out of the hall rather than going in." He looked up. "Does anyone have a flashlight?"

"I have a torch," Franklin said in an English accent. He pulled a thin black Maglite out of his pocket. "I know Holmes wouldn't have had one, but I believe in always being prepared."

Sean took it from him. "Thanks. I'll go check it out." Flicking on the light, he shone it into the darkness and ventured across the threshold.

I could not stay behind wondering what Sean might find. I inched behind him and followed, heartened to discover that Franklin and Vicky were coming as well.

We crept after Sean, following the dim illumination of the flashlight beam shining in front of him. Our footsteps echoed quietly in the dank corridor and we carefully stepped around the rubble, making our way through the passageway, peering around Sean to see what he was seeing on the floor up ahead. A curved white shape glowed in the darkness.

We all saw the conspicuous item at the same time and stopped.

"What is that?" whispered Vicky.

"Let's find out." Sean moved toward the shape,

shining the flashlight directly on the surface of the mysterious object, which seemed to have increased in mass as we neared.

It was a familiar shape, yet it didn't make sense for such a thing to be here, residing in the middle of the shadows, surrounded by silence.

"Oh no." Sean lurched forward, crouching onto his ankles and drawing in a quick breath. The air about us changed, becoming heavy with questions. And with fear. "Call an ambulance!" he shouted. The volume of his command was intensified in the lonely corridor.

Vicky and Franklin raced back to the entrance while I squatted next to Sean. "Who is it?" As the question left my lips, I recognized the high-collared cape, the white makeup, and the red-tipped fangs. "Melissa!" Her eyes were closed and she wasn't moving.

Sean held her wrist, feeling for a pulse. "You know her?"

"Yes. She's an editor from New York. I had coffee with her this morning." I dropped down but Sean held me back.

"Don't come too close," he said, handing me the flashlight. "Shine the light for me."

Trying to hold my hand steady, I directed the beam on Melissa as Sean placed two fingers on her neck.

"No," he whispered angrily, and at that moment I saw a dark inkblot shape the color of deep burgundy wine on the floor beneath Melissa's head. My eyes met Sean's as the implication sank in.

"Point the light over there." Sean gestured at a brick lying not far from Melissa. It was stained the same dark red as the floor.

"Someone killed her," I croaked, my eyes welling with tears. "Someone ended her life using that brick." Weakened by despair, I lowered the flashlight. "I bet it was that Kirk Mason."

Sean said nothing. He exhaled slowly, shaking his head in disgust, and I knew he was also feeling grief and anger over Melissa's murder.

I suddenly went cold as another thought came to mind. "What if Mason thought Melissa was actually me? What if I was supposed to be his target?"

Staring at Melissa's waxy visage, I believed that I'd never feel warm and safe again.

Chapter 6

Noises invaded the tomblike stillness of the corridor. I both welcomed and resented them. I knew that the voices bouncing off the walls meant reinforcements were on the way. Members of the police force were hastening toward us. I could practically hear the clink of their gear, the swish of their uniforms as they moved, and the tread of heavy footwear on the lobby's marble floor. They'd enter the gloom fearlessly, filling the silence with the sound of their tasks. The darkness would be banished by portable lights, and while that was a relief, those same lights would put Melissa on display, highlighting her wounds and the lack of life in her body. She would no longer be a smart, savvy, inspirational editor from New York. Her roles as wife and friend and mother would lose their significance.

Instead, her identity would forever be changed to "the victim." Her name, her lovely face, and the way her eyes danced when she laughed would not be considered relevant. People would examine her injuries, take pictures of her corpse from all angles, and write reports on the cause of death. File folders would be filled with evidence statements and crime scene data. They would smell of printer toner and cigarette smoke, holding not the slightest trace of her sweet pea scented perfume.

I looked at Sean and saw that his mouth was pinched into a thin, grim line. It was as if he was also reluctant to yield this woman to the ministrations of his colleagues. The warmth that had fled from me upon discovering Melissa's body returned as I stared at this strong, sensitive man. Dressing in gladiator attire, he should have appeared incongruent in the dim space as he knelt beside my fallen look-alike, but at the moment, he appeared as fierce and powerful as Hercules.

"You'd better go join your coworkers," he told me, but I shook my head in defiance.

"I'm not going anywhere. It wouldn't be right. She doesn't have anyone else. I don't want to . . ." I trailed off.

Sean took my hand and squeezed it gently. "You don't want to leave her. I know. But this is a crime scene now, Lila. And I've got to assist in any way that I can. Finding out what happened to this woman is my responsibility."

"And mine!" I was surprised by my vehemence. "I had coffee with her today. She went out of her way to help me with one of my client's projects." I pointed toward the main room where the party had been held, my ire rising. "Melissa was just down that hall, eating the same food we did. She was talking shop and encouraging writers and laughing. Look at her now! Why? Why is she here?"

My tirade finished, Sean helped me to my feet and wrapped his arms around me. "Something drew her to this place. And if the killer was able to succeed in convincing an intelligent woman to enter a dark and deserted corridor alone, then he had leverage over her. That makes me think he wasn't after you."

I curled my hands into fists. "It doesn't matter which of us he wanted. If Kirk Mason—"

"We can't jump to any conclusions, Lila. We don't know who did this." Sean's tone was firm. His arms slid away from mine, and I could feel a chasm growing between us as his professional side took over. He was about to continue when he suddenly eased the flashlight from my hand and pointed the beam at Melissa's right hand. It was curled around a crumpled piece of paper. I only saw it for a moment, but I could tell that the paper was made of thick stock, like a notecard. The edge of a photograph protruded from between the card's folds. Every fiber in my being longed to reach out and pry the card loose from the woman's fingers. I wanted to know what had led her back here, what had lured her to her death. The answer was inside that note or on the photograph; I was certain of it.

Sean sensed the tension in my muscles and

pivoted me away from Melissa. "Come on, hon. I can't touch it, either. No gloves."

He escorted me toward the lobby, holding an index finger out to his coworkers from the station as they passed by. I knew that the signal meant he would immediately return to the crime scene, leaving me to wrestle with my shock and fear without his comforting presence.

And that's exactly what happened. Franklin and Vicky had rounded up the rest of the agents and they were waiting in the lobby, huddled close to one another as if they were all seeking shelter from a rainstorm. Sean spoke hastily to Vicky, but Jude interrupted their conspiratorial exchange.

"I'll take her home. She'll be safe with me," Jude told Sean and whoever else was within earshot. "And I'll stay as long as you need me," he added in a low whisper only I could hear.

Sean nodded his thanks, made eye contact with me for a brief second, and then disappeared down the dark corridor. At that moment, I began to question whether I really wanted to be in a relationship with a cop. We'd hardly seen each other over the last few months, and now, when I wanted Sean with me most, he wasn't available. I knew I was being selfish and childish, but seeing Melissa had stripped me of my usual aplomb. I didn't want to be alone tonight. Glancing at Jude, I nodded in gratitude. He draped his coat over my shoulders and put a protective arm around my waist.

The faces of my coworkers mirrored my own. The news of Melissa's death had frozen their expressions into blank stares. They each gave me a sympathetic nod as I said good-bye, and I knew they were too stunned to do more than that.

"I hope you have something stronger than wine at home," Jude said as we turned to leave. "You need a shot of the hard stuff."

I managed a rueful smile. "I always keep a supply of Jim Beam on hand. My mother won't drink anything else. After I moved in, she made me put a bottle on my shopping list before I could finish unpacking my first box."

Jude raised his brows. "Amazing Althea. Maybe she knew that you'd be in need of a splash of whiskey tonight."

"Maybe. Her intuition is better than most people's, but she never warned me of any danger lurking at the book festival," I said, refusing to mention the warning she'd delivered after I'd broken my mirror on moving day. Once again, anger welled within me. I had no one to take it out on so I directed it at my mother, and I murmured darkly, "I guess there are limits to her psychic powers."

I drew the coat lapels tighter over my chest, feeling one of the tresses from my wig brush against my skin. I pulled the collection of curls from my head in disgust. All traces of the gaiety I'd felt earlier in the evening were gone, evaporated like the wisps of smoke from the spent candles in the jack-o'-lanterns. The other agents had piled all the hollowed pumpkins from the party tables into a large garbage can, and the topmost pumpkin stared at me over the can's edge, its slanted eyes and crooked grin morphing into a wicked leer.

"Get me out of here," I pleaded, and Jude didn't need to be told twice.

He led me out into the night and drove me home under a black and starless sky.

After two fingers of whiskey, the shock had loosed its hold on me and I was left feeling drained and taciturn. I apologized to Jude for being such bad company and told him that I'd prefer to be alone with my thoughts. He left reluctantly and only after I promised to call him if I felt the slightest bit scared.

My body was weary, so I lit a fire and stretched out on the couch, watching the flames flicker as I replayed my conversations with Melissa Plume. I recalled her mentioning that she'd had several uncomfortable exchanges with aspiring writers and that a few of those authors had behaved inappropriately after she'd rejected their work.

"They crossed the line. Those are the exact words she used," I said to the crackling kindling in the fireplace, my eyes glazing as I got lost in the memory. Had she rejected Kirk Mason's work? Did he kill her because of the rejection?

The heat of the fire made the room feel close and cozy. Setting the whiskey tumbler aside, I pulled my purse over to the couch and dug around inside for Melissa's business card.

I hadn't looked at the card when she'd first given it to me, and I don't know what compelled me to do so now, but the moment it was bathed by the soft, dancing light of fire I drew in a sharp breath.

Wasting no time, I dialed Sean's cell phone.

"Lila?" His voice was filled with concern and I instantly regretted how I'd entertained thoughts of breaking up with him earlier.

"Sean, I think Kirk Mason is the killer."

A pause. "Have you remembered something specific?"

"Just a conversation Melissa and I had about writers. For some reason, it made me want to look at her business card. I've got it right here in my hand." I tilted the card so that the shadows from the flames stretched over its creamy surface like twitching fingers. "She had a black feather embossed on her card, probably because her last name is . . . was . . . Plume."

Sean caught on right away. "And Mason dropped a raven's feather on your table during the pitch appointment session."

"Yes. But I don't think he was in the room when I introduced myself. If he hadn't heard my name, he might have mistaken me for Melissa Plume. He gave that feather to a woman he believed to be Melissa Plume to convey some kind of warning or message." I worked through my theory out loud. "He thought I was Melissa, so maybe, when I didn't react to the feather, his rage grew even stronger. The feather could have been his way of saying, 'I know you.' Maybe it was supposed to terrify Melissa. It spooked me, and I have no history with this man."

I could practically hear the gears in Sean's mind turning. When he didn't respond for several seconds, I asked, "What was in her hand?"

After another long beat of silence, Sean sighed. "We're going to keep some of the case details close to our chests, Lila, so don't share what I'm about to tell you with anyone." He waited for me to swear not to discuss the contents of the note or the photo with another soul and then continued. "The picture was of a Winnie the Pooh. A stuffed bear. The note said, *If you want to know how I got this, meet me in the restricted hallway. Walk until you see an exit sign. Come alone or something might happen to the owner of this bear.*"

"Why would she—?" I began but then stopped short. "Melissa's son!"

"Yes," Sean answered solemnly. "Silas. He's four."

This information hit me like a blow to the stomach. The vague recollection of a query involving a toy bear tugged at the corner of my mind but was wiped away by the image of a little boy clutching a Winnie the Pooh plush toy. The room suddenly felt too warm, the air swelling in my lungs. I saw a little boy snuggling up to the bear at night, hugging it when he was scared and taking it along to preschool, the yellow fuzzy head poking out of the top of a zippered book bag. It was easier for me to focus on the bear. To think about the boy, who would now have to grow up without his mother, was far too painful.

"Does he know?" I asked in a choked whisper. "About his mom?"

"Not yet. I spoke with Ms. Plume's husband at length. He has a different surname—Delaney. Logan Delaney. His sister is taking care of Silas. Mr. Delaney is coming down on the next flight."

I visualized the shell-shocked husband walking through an airport terminal with the blank and expressionless eyes of a zombie. I had to blink back more tears. "That poor man. What did he say about the Winnie the Pooh bear in the photo?"

"That Silas carries the thing with him every-where. He still has it, as a matter of fact, so the one in the photograph was a decoy."

Rage surged through my blood. "The murderer tricked Melissa?"

"Silas's bear has a blue bandanna tied around

his neck, and the killer must have known that. The bear in the photo looks fairly new, but I doubt Melissa studied it too hard, and it's also wearing a blue bandanna." Sean sounded sorrowful. "Her protective instincts probably overruled all other emotions. She saw that picture and ran."

I nodded, even though Sean couldn't see me. "I'd have done the same thing. I would have been totally blinded by fear for my son." I glanced across the living room at a framed drawing Trey had made for me on Valentine's Day over twelve years ago. Yes, I would most certainly have reacted exactly as Melissa had. "Did Mr. Delaney mention Melissa having trouble with overly aggressive writers before?"

"Nothing beyond a few nasty phone calls or emails. He'd never heard the name Kirk Mason, but that doesn't surprise me since Mr. Mason doesn't officially exist."

My mouth had gone dry again. "I feel responsible for this, Sean. We invited a killer to Inspiration Valley. My agency accepted this man's registration information at face value. He breezed into our event under a false name and with malice in his heart."

"It's a book festival, Lila. No one expected you or anyone else from Novel Idea to run the attendees' IDs through a federal database," Sean argued. "This happened because an individual gave in to a darkness inside himself. End of story.

You couldn't have stopped this. If the killer was Kirk Mason, then I was in the same room with the guy and *I* didn't stop him." He sighed heavily. "Now we need to look ahead. I have to find Mason, and you know how crucial these first few hours are. I can't talk to you anymore, Lila, until I have some answers. However, there's something I may ask you to do."

"Anything," I quickly replied.

"If I can't track down a photo of this guy, I'd like you to come to the station and meet with our sketch artist."

"Of course. I doubt I'll ever forget what he looks like."

Sean said good-bye, and after wishing him luck, I hung up and sank deeper into the couch cushions. There had to be something I could do to help bring Melissa's murderer to justice. Once again, I recalled her description of writers whose blind passion for their work had caused them to cross a line. Perhaps Kirk Mason had done just that with other agents or editors. If he'd queried several agencies or publishing houses using the same pen name, perhaps they had a more complete record of him. Perhaps they even knew his true identity. I resolved to reach out to my fellows in the publishing world as soon as possible. Unfortunately, most of them wouldn't read or respond to my email until Monday.

By then, the Dunston Police might have Kirk

Mason in custody. I wanted to believe that, because the alternative was too frightening. The idea of Kirk sneaking around the festival tomorrow filled me with dread. True, he could no longer disguise himself as Edgar Allan Poe, but it was possible that he didn't care and was willing to risk his freedom for the sake of his work. Perhaps he believed that by becoming famous as a cold-blooded killer he would finally land a book deal.

Curling my hands into fists, I grabbed the steel letter opener from my little desk in the corner of the room and held the blade up to the firelight. I watched for a moment as the yellow and orange flames licked the metal until it seemed to glow in my hands. I then stuffed the letter opener in my purse.

If Kirk Mason planned to hurt another person at a book festival set in *my* town and sponsored by *my* agency, he was going to have to get by me first.

Even though Sunday's workshops had nothing to do with the agency, we felt it was important for Novel Idea to maintain a presence at the festival. With that in mind, some of us had registered for classes. I'd signed up for a demonstration on paper and book making, Franklin was attending one on book repair, and Flora, a seminar on illustration. Jude and Zach, who had no interest in the workshops, would be taking turns at the agency booth, and Vicky would continue manning the registration and information desk. I offered to relieve her for the afternoon, knowing that things would be winding down and it would be a quiet job where I might have the chance to read through some manuscripts.

Approaching the town hall that morning, I felt for the letter opener in my bag, reassured in knowing I had something with which to defend myself. If only Melissa had had something with her when she'd been lured into that deserted corridor.

The Dunston Police had anticipated that the news of Melissa's death would draw a significant media presence, and it had. Early this morning, television vans had grabbed all the parking spots closest to the old town hall's entrance and intrepid reporters were filming backdrop scenes while I was still at home drinking coffee and putting on makeup. In response to Bentley's considerable influence, a trio of policemen arrived before the festival opened for the day and cordoned off a wide area leading from the sidewalk to the front doors.

"No members of the media inside," they told the disgruntled journalists. "This is a private event and it's too late for you folks to register."

A reporter called out, "What ever happened to freedom of the press?"

One of the veteran cops smirked and answered, "You can be as free as you wanna be as long as you stay on the other side of this rope. If any of the book people feel like talking to you, they're all yours, but if you stick one toe on the wrong side of this rope, the only footage you'll get is of me putting you in the back of my car. Got it?"

It appeared that none of the media felt like arguing with the man, who bore a close resemblance to Paul Bunyan. Flora, who climbed the steps seconds behind me, commented, "I truly believe that officer could carry an ox in each arm without breaking a sweat."

I responded by quoting a line from Shakespeare's *Measure for Measure*. " 'O! it is excellent to have a giant's strength, but it is tyrannous to use it like a giant.' "

"Tyranny can be quite useful at times," Flora quipped in reply, glancing back at the colossal policeman with admiration.

When I walked through the door, the din of voices besieged me. People milled about the main hall; more, it seemed, than had been there for both of the previous conference days. As I made my way to the registration desk, I glanced about, wondering if Kirk Mason was among the attendees. Would he be so bold as to show up here today?

"What's going on?" I asked. "Are all these people signed up for the classes?"

Vicky shook her head. "Not by a mile. Somehow word got out that there was a murder at the festival, and now we've got curiosity seekers mixed in with legitimate attendees . . ." She sighed. "Once the first sessions start, I'll weed out the people that shouldn't be here."

"Just be careful," I cautioned. "There might be a killer in the crowd."

At the Espresso Yourself kiosk, the lineup for coffee stretched long. I was just debating whether I'd get to the front of the line in time to make my workshop when Makayla waved me over.

"I'm making your latte right now," she said, despite the disgruntled looks being directed her way. "When this hubbub dies down, we need to talk. Are you holding up okay?"

I nodded. "Thanks," I said, taking the cup she handed me. The warmth in my hands gave me unexpected comfort. "I'll come back after my class."

Despite feeling unsettled because of Melissa Plume, I was looking forward to this workshop. A newcomer to Inspiration Valley, Sandra Pickwick, was teaching it. She'd recently opened a stationery store in town called Pickwick Papers, which sold, among other things, beautiful handmade cards, notepads of handcrafted paper, and unique journals and scrapbooks. On its opening day I had visited the shop and purchased a set of notecards decorated with delicate violets. I had asked Sandra how the violets had been incorporated into the paper and added that I'd like to try making cards using blossoms from my garden, so Sandra suggested I sign up for this class.

Just by the entrance was a table containing merchandise from the shop. I spent a minute admiring the beautiful wares before finding a seat near the door, on which I placed my jacket.

At the front of the room, tables were set up with pieces of equipment and materials. One table had two large bins on it, another, two blenders, and a third, a large paper press consisting of two flatbeds that could be forced together with a large screwing mechanism. Sandra Pickwick, wearing black slacks and a blue flowered blouse, stood at the lectern studying her notes.

I approached her and reintroduced myself.

"I remember you," she said. "You were very intrigued by our floral collection."

"That's why I'm here. I'm curious to see how that beautiful paper is made."

She leaned in close. "Is it true?" she whispered. "That someone was murdered here yesterday?"

"There was . . ." I stopped myself, unsure of what to say. I knew that I shouldn't reveal anything about Melissa, since the police had yet to release an official statement. "The incident is under investigation. That's all I know," I lied, glancing at my watch. "I'd better get to my seat."

As I sipped my coffee, I scanned the room for

Kirk Mason and listened to Sandra introduce herself to her audience. Among the twenty people in the room, I knew Mason wouldn't be there, but I'd keep looking for him until he was apprehended. Everywhere I went, he'd be a shadow lurking on the fringes of my vision.

Shifting my thoughts, I directed my focus to Sandra.

"You all probably know that the first paper was made by the ancient Egyptians; the word 'paper' deriving from the name of the papyrus plant. The Egyptians pressed sliced, wet sections of papyrus stems together and then dried them. Paper that we are familiar with today is made of pulped cellulose fibers like wood, cotton, or flax." She pointed to two large containers on the table beside her. "Today, we're going to press paper out of cotton and hemp. The result will be thicker and more fibrous paper than what you usually use, but we can adjust that by the amount of processing we apply, and we'll add some decorative elements into it, like flower petals and seeds. The hemp and the cotton have been soaking overnight, and the hemp has also been cooked with some soda ash, so they are ready to be turned into paper. When they're pressed, we'll do a quick dry with some blow-dryers, but they won't be completely dry until tomorrow."

She continued to describe the step-by-step process of producing paper, which included mashing the pulp in a blender, adding dye if desired, and pressing the pulp between towels in the large paper press.

"Now we're all going to get our hands into it and make some paper. Half of you come to the hemp, the rest to the cotton."

I now understood why registration was limited for this workshop. We each had to wait our turn at the press, adding our unique character to the paper using dye or flower petals. I chose to make hemp paper, since Trey worked with the material for other purposes at the co-op and I thought it would be fun to write him a note on it. I crumbled some dried cornflower petals into mine and pressed in a few thin stems as well.

The ninety minutes allotted for the workshop went by quickly. Proudly carrying my homemade paper, I sought out Makayla at the Espresso Yourself kiosk. Business had slowed down when I arrived, and there were only two customers in line.

"Look what I made," I said to her after she handed a chai latte to the person in front of me. I held out my sheet of paper, the blue cornflower petals providing a striking contrast to the textured, slightly beige speckled paper. I felt a little like a schoolgirl showing off her project, but I was proud of what I had produced.

"That's beautiful," Makayla said, stroking the soft, fibrous sheet. "Are you going to pen some sweet nothings to a certain hunky policeman using that special paper?" She wriggled her eyebrows.

My peripheral vision caught a movement of black, and I immediately turned, thinking the shadow might be Kirk Mason. A woman wearing a black sweater walked past us toward the exit. I exhaled in relief and then saw that I'd gripped my homemade paper so tightly that a deep crease had formed in the right-hand corner.

"Girl, you're as jittery as a fly in a pond full of frogs," Makayla said, touching my shoulder. "Not that I blame you, considering what happened yesterday. I'm going to make you a nice peppermint tea. I'm cutting off your caffeine supply."

The refreshing mint of the tea did calm me, even while I told Makayla about the events of the previous day. As I went on to explain why I was sure that Kirk Mason was the murderer, she frowned.

"I wouldn't put all my eggs in one basket," she countered gently. "Like I already told the police, baristas are keen observers. Yesterday, for example, I saw Melissa Plume arguing with another woman right at this very table." She tapped her finger on the tabletop. "And how could I *not* remember Melissa? When that woman ordered a caramel latte and I turned and looked at her, you could have knocked me over with a feather. She was your twin, Lila! Melissa introduced herself and we got to talking. She seemed like a great gal." Her face lost its typical illumination for a moment. "What a terrible shame."

"It's amazing how alike we were," I noted sadly, but if Makayla was aware of another suspect, I needed to be fully briefed. "How did the argument start?"

"Melissa was sitting here reading through some notes when this other woman plunked herself down in the chair opposite her. After a few minutes, things got tense between them and the other woman kept pointing her finger angrily at Melissa. I was busy with other customers so I didn't hear what they were saying, but they were causing quite a ruckus. Then the other woman got up, knocking her chair over, and shouted, 'You'll regret this!' And then she ran off. Made quite a spectacle of herself."

"What did Melissa do?"

"She apologized to everyone, picked up the chair, and then left, too."

I was having a difficult time envisioning a woman luring Melissa to her death using a picture of Silas's teddy bear, but I couldn't mention this to Makayla since I'd promised Sean I wouldn't tell anyone about the photograph. Instead, I argued, "But would a woman have the strength to strike Melissa down?"

"This woman was pretty combative. And those finger points were meant to be a threat. I don't have to be an FBI profiler to read that kind of body language," Makayla insisted. "Besides, that wasn't the only time I saw this crazy lady. She confronted Melissa again last night and her claws were showing even more then."

"When? At the costume party?"

Makayla nodded. "I was just arriving and heard raised voices in the parking lot. I saw an Edgar Allan Poe push a vampire against a car, so I ran over to see if everything was all right. The vampire was—"

"Melissa!" I interjected, sitting forward. "But Kirk Mason was dressed up as Edgar Allan Poe last night. How do you know it wasn't him?"

"I know a man when I see one, Lila," Makayla said with a snort. "This Poe had green eyes, auburn hair, and a whole face full of freckles. It was as if someone upturned the pepper shaker and started sprinkling. Only one person at this festival had that face. And no matter how tight that gal's suit coat was, she couldn't hide those double Ds! Not many Poes running around with that bra size, no, ma'am."

I sat back in my chair and sighed. "What happened after you approached them?"

"I asked if everything was okay and the green-eyed woman glared at me and said, 'We're fine.' When I looked at Melissa, she told me not to worry. But I hung around long enough to hear the woman roar, 'You'll be sorry. I'll make sure of it!' before she stalked off like a lioness on the prowl. Melissa and I walked into the party together, and she told me that the woman was an irate writer with the personality of a spoiled pop princess."

"Do you think she was capable of murdering Melissa?"

"It didn't occur to me then that she might be dangerous." Makayla shook her head. "But after I heard what happened to Melissa, I thought about her words some more and decided that she might have gone off the deep end. So I told the police everything that I saw."

I pondered Makayla's narrative. Had the green-eyed woman lured Melissa to her death? Could her hostility have turned into a murderous rage while they were in that dark, lonely corridor? My certainty that it had been Kirk Mason began to waver. "What did the police say?" I wondered.

"Not much." She frowned in disappointment. "If only I'd heard her name, the police would stand half a chance of finding her. But Melissa never said it."

"I wonder what they were quarreling about."

"Maybe Melissa rejected her book and the woman took leave of her senses. Of course, killing someone over a book is pretty damned over-the-top, but you know writers better than most. Nuttier than a bag of circus peanuts at times, aren't they?"

" 'There's the scarlet thread of murder running through the colorless skein of life,' " I said, quoting Sir Arthur Conan Doyle. We both stared blankly at the shifting crowd, unable to comprehend the workings of a murderer's mind.

I had been correct in assuming that my shift at the information desk would be a quiet one. The festival was winding down and people didn't approach me except to say good-bye. I had brought along some manuscripts to read, but I was too distracted to concentrate. I kept going over all the reasons I thought the murderer was Kirk Mason and saw him in every thin man with black hair who walked by, but Mason did not make an appearance. I was also watching out for a green-eyed, freckle-faced woman with short auburn hair, but didn't catch sight of her, either.

The tireless police officer was still at his post. I was convinced that he hadn't moved from his position once today. I'd yet to see him eat or drink anything, and he'd only changed his formidable posture to exchange a few words with Sean before resuming his military stance again.

However, with the lobby nearly empty and the members of the media aggressively intercepting festivalgoers heading for their cars or Inspiration Valley's train station, I assumed Officer Bunyan would relax.

Despite the fact that I was reassured by the police presence, I couldn't shake the guilt I felt over my part in Melissa's violent demise and kept thinking about the poor little boy with the teddy bear who would grow up without his mother. Melissa's husband would have arrived by now, and Sean would have interviewed him. Had Mr. Delaney given any insights that could help lead the police to an arrest?

Reaching for my cell phone I punched in Sean's number.

"Hey," he said, answering after one ring. "I was just about to head over there. Are things winding down?"

I surveyed the hall. People were packing up, hugging one another, and waving good-bye. "Yes. We close up shop in a half hour. Sean, Makayla told me about the woman Melissa was arguing with. Have you been able to track her down?"

"I figured she'd tell you about that. No, we haven't found the mystery woman yet. But Makayla's account does add another suspect to our list. The killer may not have been Kirk Mason after all, though we won't know until we locate him."

"Did you meet with Melissa's husband? How is their little boy doing?"

"He's young and doesn't really understand, but while his father was on the phone with him he kept asking for his mother." Sean was quiet for a second. "The husband is grief-stricken, but on the flight over he remembered something. There's an editor at Melissa's publishing house who has some animosity toward her. This guy, a Mr. Ruben Felden, claims she lured an author from him— one who subsequently ended up on the bestseller list for nearly a year. Apparently, this author specifically requested Melissa as her editor, even though Ruben was originally approached by her agent. He maintains that Melissa influenced the agent to bring the author over to her. And you won't believe this, but Mr. Felden's hobby is creating art with ornithological motifs. To be more specific, he makes murals and sculptures using feathers."

"The raven feather!" My brain was churning. "Do you think Felden could be Kirk Mason?"

"He wasn't at the office today; in fact he's been absent for a few days. New York's finest are trying to locate him. And this guy may or may not be Kirk Mason, Lila. The general description of this man could fit, but we don't have details yet."

Suddenly I knew how I could help. "Sean, I can assist you with that. If I go to the office—"

He sighed. "Please keep the investigating to the police, Lila. Remember what happened the last time you got involved."

I didn't want to travel back to those memories. This time my participation would be different.

After all, I was the one who had access to information on publishing houses and their editors. At the office I could research this man who was angry with Melissa.

When I first became a literary agent, I hadn't anticipated that my love of books would end up bringing me in close contact with a murderer, but I wasn't going to back down now. It didn't matter whether the killer was an aspiring writer or an established editor. What mattered was that this warped individual had murdered a good woman during my agency's festival. Now, I was going to use all my resources to bring that person to justice, and I wasn't going to stop because the event was over or because Sean had asked me to. This crime was personal and I was involved. End of story.

Chapter 7

When Sean showed up at the old town hall, his face was pinched and grim and I sensed he was about to deliver a piece of bad news. Unfortunately, my instincts proved correct.

"I'm sorry, Lila," he said softly, touching the tip of my chin tenderly. "I can't come for supper tonight. We've got a dozen interviews to conduct regarding the argument Makayla witnessed between Melissa and a female writer, and then I've got a conference call with a fellow officer in New York."

My heart sank. I'd really needed Sean's company tonight. It wasn't just the murder that had me feeling down—though Lord knows that was enough to cast a pall of gloom over the entire weekend. There was something unaccountably disheartening about the festival coming to an end. All around me, attendees were shouldering the ocher-colored canvas bags provided by Novel Idea, saying good-bye to friends and acquaintances, and heading out into the crisp October afternoon. The final classes were almost finished and the food service kiosks were closing down. The vendors who'd sold scores of bookmarks, writing journals, funky mouse pads, and inspirational posters were placing their remaining wares into boxes.

"A rain check, then," I'd told Sean, mustering a smile. After all, bringing Melissa's killer to justice was far more important than my having a case of the blues.

He'd hardly made it out of earshot before I began dialing my mother's number.

She picked up after the first ring. "So you're cooking for me tonight? And Trey, too?"

"Is there a tarot card layout that predicts supper invitations?" I asked acerbically.

Althea tried her best to soothe me. "You've had a hard weekend, shug," she said gently. "It'll be good for you to spend some time with your family. I bet Trey would get a kick out of givin' treats to the little kiddos tonight—it'll make him feel like a tried-and-true grown-up." She sighed nostalgically and I instantly regretted taking out my negativity on her. "I recall the time he dressed up as a wizard. He couldn't have been more than six or seven and he used that pack of sparklers for his magic wands. Remember what a ruckus that caused?"

I laughed. "How could I not? He nearly set fire to the neighbor's rose trellis and *then* he went after their cat! He swore to me that he only wanted to change it into a dog!" For a moment, I was lost in the past, transported to another

Halloween night in which my young son dumped his bag of treats onto the floor and begged me to pick my favorite candy from his spoils.

"Those are yours, Trey," I'd protested with a smile. "You walked a mile to get all of those treats."

He'd given me a hug, pressing his shining head of chestnut hair against my belly. "But I want to share with you, Mom. You share things with the person you love the most, right?"

Tears pricked my eyes, and though I was reluctant to let go of the memories, I turned my attention back to my mother. "Thanks for bringing me back to that moment," I told her warmly. "And nothing would make me happier than to see you and Trey seated at my table tonight. I'll give him a call."

"No need," my mother assured me. "I already let him know we were expected and that you were servin' chicken in some kind of sauce. See you soon!"

Marveling over my mother's insight, considering I had planned on making chicken piccata with a side of snow peas and a small mound of wild rice for Sean, I watched the departing festivalgoers stream through the lobby. The last two classes had let out and everyone was exiting. Several camera crews were waiting on the sidewalk to capture sound bites on the murder of Melissa Plume. Even though the ambitious reporters were hoping for new information to squeeze into the six o'clock reports, I doubted the attendees had anything to offer other than gossip. Tall tales and ridiculous theories had been circulating around the old building since the doors opened this morning.

As Vicky and I packed up the last of the agency's literature, I realized that today's police presence had definitely made me feel safer. I hadn't seen any sign of Kirk Mason, but I was still plenty nervous about the possibility that he hadn't left town. Thank goodness Trey and Althea were coming over. Halloween had never been a spooky holiday for me before, but the knowledge that a murderer was loose transformed the approaching night. These last hours of October loomed ahead like a thundercloud. I was likely to be jumping at the slightest sound and peering out the windows at my dark yard in search of a shadow moving in the blackness.

With the festival officially over, I was thankful to have a meal to prepare. Shopping and cooking a nice supper for my mother and son would occupy my mind until I returned to work Monday morning and could start researching Melissa's coeditor as well as the unstable author who'd threatened my look-alike.

I spent an unusually long time selecting ingredients at How Green Was My Valley and purchased all kinds of rich and comforting food that wasn't on my grocery list. In addition to snow peas and a box of long-grain wild rice, I selected a wedge of creamy Brie, a block of Havarti, two apricots, a bunch of red seedless grapes, a French baguette, a bag of chocolate-covered raisins, and a bottle of pinot grigio. I knew the lemon, vanilla, and almond flavors of the wine would be the perfect accompaniment to chicken piccata. At the register, the cashier handed me a lollipop decorated with a white icing ghost.

"It's mango flavored," she told me. "All organic and completely delicious."

She didn't need to twist my arm. I loaded my groceries into the basket behind my scooter's seat, pulled the wrapper from the candy treat, and popped it into my mouth. I paused there for a moment, my weight resting on my leather seat, the scooter's engine still quiet, and felt the bliss of fruit-flavored sugar coating my tongue.

The scene around me was breathtaking. Perched on my scooter I gazed upward and watched the sun sink behind the perimeter of trees surrounding Inspiration Valley. It sent its last gasps of light shooting into the foliage, igniting a fire of scarlet, russet, and marigold hues across the base of the hills. There was a distinct line of shadow where the light could no longer reach, and above this demarcation the forests had been plunged into darkness. I was literally witnessing night laying claim to the land.

The air became much cooler and I shivered, suddenly longing for the small fireplace in my living room and my warm and cozy kitchen. I bit my lollipop into small pieces and turned on the scooter, pointing it toward home. As I drove, I couldn't help glancing in my side mirror, fascinated and slightly chilled by the surrender of the day.

By the time I pulled into my driveway, there wasn't a sliver of light left in the sky, but Althea's turquoise truck was parked along the curb at the end of my flagstone walk. My mother and Trey had made themselves comfortable in the pair of rockers on my front porch.

"Why didn't you go on in?" I gestured at the pottery chicken perched by the doorframe. "You know where I hide the spare key."

Althea shrugged and made no move to get out of her chair. "I knew you were on the way. Besides, there's nothin' like a Halloween sunset. You can just feel the kiddies bouncin' up and down with anticipation, beggin' their mamas and daddies to hurry, hurry, hurry!" She reached over and poked Trey in the ribs with her index finger. "You sure you don't want to grab a pillowcase and run around with the tykes? I know what a sweet tooth you've got."

Trey smiled at her indulgently. "I'll just eat the good stuff out of Mom's trick-or-treat bucket. I'd actually be doing the kids in this neighborhood a service. Maybe she could hand out dental floss or toothbrushes instead."

I pretended to be horrified. "Do you seriously want my house to be covered in eggs and toilet paper?"

With the grace of an athlete in his prime, Trey unfolded his long frame from the chair and crossed the porch to where I stood. He wrapped his arms around me and gave me a tight squeeze. "I heard about what happened at the festival. Are you okay?"

I returned the embrace; relishing his scent of wood smoke and the goat's milk soap he helped produce at the co-op. "I'll be all right, honey. But let's not talk about it tonight. I only want to hear about you. That always makes me feel better."

He stepped back to pick up the grocery bags. He peered into them and grinned when he saw the delicious ingredients I had purchased to prepare dinner. "Wow, Mom. This looks way better than candy."

"So which chicken did you go with?" Althea wanted to know. "Piccata, Parmesan, or marsala?"

"Not marsala," I said, opening the front door. "You still don't like mushrooms, do you, Trey?"

His mouth turned down in disgust. "I think they're gross," he replied and walked inside.

I gave him time to settle at the kitchen table with a cutting board boasting an array of plump grapes, sliced Havarti, and salty wheat crackers before I asked what was wrong. After she poured me a glass of pinot grigio and sat down with her tumbler of Jim Beam, Althea nodded at Trey encouragingly.

"Come on, get it off your chest. Whatever's troublin' you has been sittin' on your shoulders like a big, fat cat." When Trey said nothing, she continued. "I know you men like to keep things to yourselves, but women have a way of seein' a problem from a different angle." She leaned forward on her elbows. "Go on, son. Spill."

Trey released a heavy sigh. "Something's changed at the co-op. In the beginning, I felt like I really fit in there, you know? They got who I was. And I had stuff to offer them, too, like the new product designs. Everything's been going so great. I have friends, a job, and . . ." He left the rest unsaid, but I knew he was thinking of Iris Gyles. Trey had had a crush on her from the moment they'd met, but I didn't know if she felt the same way. Could she have turned down his romantic advances? Was he nursing a broken heart or had something more serious happened?

"Please tell me it's nothing violent," I murmured softly, and he quickly shook his head.

"Jasper spent all summer telling me how the co-op didn't operate in hopes of making a profit —that the people of Red Fox were looking, you know, for something deeper." He blushed, slightly embarrassed over having to find words to aptly describe the socialist-type lifestyle he'd adopted. "But he's been charging kids my age to hang out with us. They're not working or anything. They just meditate with him for a few hours and then go. And they seem totally cool about paying him what he asks."

I dipped the last of the chicken cutlets in an egg wash before coating it with breadcrumbs and poured some oil into a skillet. As the flame of the cooktop burner sprung into blue life, I said, "Do you think Jasper is taking advantage of these kids?"

Trey shrugged. "I dunno. But I heard him talking about buying all these expensive space heaters and laptops and stuff. And people have never had to pay to walk the trails or to just find a quiet place to chill out before. We don't own the land."

"Yet Jasper's actin' like he's king of the mountain?" Althea guessed.

"Yeah. He's just . . . different than when I first moved up there."

Even though I was focused on browning the chicken, I could sense Trey's reluctance to badmouth the co-op's leader. Still, he sat rigidly in his chair and the grip on the cheese knife was too firm. My son was truly troubled.

I waited for the chicken to cook, transferred it to a plate covered with paper towels, and then placed my hand on my son's shoulder. "Can you talk to him? Tell him that it doesn't feel right to collect money from people who just want to get away from it all for a bit?"

Trey opened his mouth to speak, but before he could say anything, his eyes became guarded and he averted his glance. "It's cool. I'm sure Iris will handle it."

Althea and I exchanged worried glances, but I knew we wouldn't get another word out of Trey. Instead of trying to elicit more information, I blended chicken stock, white wine, lemon, garlic, fresh basil, and capers. At the sound of the doorbell, Trey leapt up from the table to answer the door, his face transformed by a boyish grin of anticipation. While the piccata sauce was thickening, I had time to catch a glimpse of a pint-size Miss America, a devil missing his two front teeth, a wounded soldier, and a fairy with a glittering purple dress. Trey gave the children generous handfuls of candy and wished them a happy Halloween.

"Go easy on the treats," I chided, waving my wooden spoon at him. "Or I won't have any left to eat while I watch *Ghostbusters* later tonight."

Trey grabbed several boxes of Milk Duds and brought them into the kitchen. "Then these are mine. Can't handle cheesy flicks without them."

"You're going to watch the movie with me?" I was thrilled. When Trey was younger, we'd always spend Halloween night sampling from his trick-or-treat bag while *Ghostbusters* played on the small television set in our living room.

Althea gestured toward the front yard. "He's already got a change of clothes in the truck. Neither of us thought you should be alone tonight. Strange things can go on when spirits are roamin' around."

"It's not the spirits I'm worried about," Trey insisted, studying me gravely. "The book festival killer is still out there and I don't want you to be on your own, Mom."

I gave him a grateful smile, once again noticing how brawny he'd grown after months of manual labor, fresh air, and healthy food. "I'll definitely feel much safer with you in the house, Trey."

He smiled, pleased that I thought him a worthy protector.

"Maybe you can get that hunky cop to spend tomorrow night with you. It's about time that man unlaced his boots and stayed for a spell. A *long* spell," Althea said with a leer and then refilled her tumbler with another inch of whiskey.

Ignoring her, I poured the thickened sauce over the chicken and garnished the cutlets with sprigs of fresh parsley. After putting several spoonfuls of wild rice on each plate, I lifted the lid from the pot of snow peas. Steam billowed forth, flushing my face with heat. The rush of warmth made me think of Sean.

Trey and Althea were right. I didn't want to be

alone. Not tonight. Not tomorrow night, either. I was ready for Sean to become a real-life Paris to my Helen, for him to lay down his shield, kick off his sandals, and take me in his arms. I was just getting to the part in my fantasy in which Sean's fingers were deftly removing my long, white Grecian dress when Trey asked me to pass the pepper shaker. At the same moment, the doorbell rang and I offered to handle the next batch of trick-or-treaters.

As I walked to the door, I made another silent vow to help find Melissa's killer. As soon as he was caught, I could have Sean to myself, and when that time came, I was going to show him just how passionate a middle-aged single mother could be.

When I entered the office on Monday, the first day of the new month, its uneasy atmosphere was like a tangible entity. The enthusiasm over the success of the festival was blighted by Melissa's murder, and my coworkers were unusually listless.

Instead of hunkering down to work at our desks, we hung about the coffee room, hugging our mugs as we dissected the events of the weekend. Zach paced back and forth while Flora and Vicky dipped their tea bags in and out of their cups in tandem. As conversation lulled, Jude pushed back his chair with a loud scrape and stood.

"I need to get to work. I'm sending out an offer of representation this morning." Without further elaboration he strode out of the room.

Vicky dangled her tea bag over her cup before dropping it into the trash. "I, too, must tick some items off my list," she said. "There are numerous wrap-up tasks from the weekend cluttering my desk, including sorting through the scores of photos I took and entering the number of people who preregistered for next year's festival in my database."

Following Jude and Vicky's lead, the rest of us headed for the door. There was a stack of proposals waiting for me, and the manuscripts I'd intended to work on at the festival still needed to be read. Before tackling those, however, I intended to research Ruben Felden, the editor at Melissa's publishing house, and try to discover the identity of the mysterious green-eyed woman.

There were not many steps from the coffee room to our respective offices, yet before any of us could get through the doors, Bentley appeared in the hall, wearing an elegantly tailored teal suit. I marveled that she'd managed to find shoes in the exact same color.

"Good morning, people," she began in a commanding voice. "It is unfortunate that the untimely demise of Melissa Plume has tainted an otherwise successful venture for this agency; nevertheless, the book festival was a job well done. Congratulations to you all." She cleared her throat. "Today is a new day and we must get back to business. Vicky, set up a meeting to fit everyone's schedule in order to do a post-festival assessment. And people, bring notes, comments, and suggestions." With that pronouncement she walked into her office.

I hurried after her, having been struck with a sudden inspiration. Bentley had many contacts in the publishing world. Perhaps she knew Ruben Felden, and may even have had dealings with him. If that were the case, Bentley might be able to help, and I could focus on finding the woman Makayla saw arguing with Melissa.

"Excuse me, Bentley," I called after her.

She turned at the threshold to her office. "Yes, Lila?"

"I wanted to ask you about an editor."

"Come in, then." She placed her briefcase on the desk, casting a mirror image of the attaché on its glass surface. Sunlight from the arched window shimmered on the chrome and glass in the office, warming the crispness of her Ansel Adams–inspired décor. She waved her hand at the chair opposite the desk as she sat down.

I perched on the edge of the seat. "Do you know an editor by the name of Ruben Felden?"

"I've worked with his publishing house but have never dealt with him directly. Why do you ask?" Abruptly she sat forward. "Ah, that's

Melissa Plume's publishing house. Is this related to what happened to her? Do you have some reason to believe Felden is involved?"

"I'm not sure. I believe he's what the police call a person of interest. Apparently he bears some kind of serious grudge against Melissa. I was planning to see if he could have been in Inspiration Valley this weekend, but then I thought about the connections you have and—"

"Say no more." Bentley stretched her palm out to me in the universal sign for stop. "I'll reach out to my contacts and get a complete dossier on Felden. If he had anything to do with staining *my* agency's reputation, he will answer for it."

"Let's not forget about seeking justice for Melissa Plume," I added.

"Of course." Bentley put her diamond-studded reading glasses on her nose and opened her laptop.

Obviously dismissed, I ventured into my own office and sank into the leather desk chair. I'd redecorated when I was promoted to agent, and this comfy seat was one of the first purchases I made. It was the perfect place to read, to type on the computer, to build up an author's hopes or possibly shatter their dreams. At this moment, however, I wasn't considering an author who had queried me, but rather one who had caused trouble—possibly of the fatal kind—for Melissa Plume. How could I find out more about the green-eyed, freckled woman? Had the police gotten any leads from the witnesses to the argument?

I punched in Sean's number on my cell phone, feeling only a slight twinge of guilt about interrupting him, and a shade more for ignoring the work on my desk.

"Hi, Sean," I jumped in as soon as he said hello. "Sorry to bother you when you're at work, but I was wondering if you found out anything more about the angry woman writer."

"You're not bothering me, Lila, although I can only talk for a minute." Sean sighed into the phone. "You're supposed to leave the investigating to us, remember?"

"I know, but I can't stop thinking about Melissa and her poor husband and son. I just want to help."

His tone softened. "You have a good heart. I can tell you that the witnesses we interviewed last night gave us no more information than Makayla did about that woman. We're currently interviewing Ms. Plume's list of clients to see if we can identify her."

"Is Mr. Delaney still in Inspiration Valley?" A nugget of an idea was growing in my mind. Perhaps Melissa's husband would know who the disgruntled author might be.

"Yes, he's still in town and is staying at the Magnolia B and B until he's able to make arrangements to ship his wife's . . . body . . . home."

Sadness squeezed my heart as I considered how difficult these few days must be for the bereaved Mr. Delaney. "I'd better let you go, Sean. Thanks for sharing the information."

After hanging up, I pondered how I could tactfully question Melissa's husband when the grief from his loss was so raw. Then it dawned on me—food. Food provided comfort, bridged gaps, and healed hurts. I'd bring him lunch.

Having made that decision, I managed to get a couple of hours of work done, struggling to stay focused while reading a manuscript about a romance and murder on a cruise ship, but getting through it nonetheless. At half past eleven, I phoned Stella, the proprietor of Magnolia Bed and Breakfast, to find out if Mr. Delaney was there.

"He sure is, hon," she declared. "Poor man. Spends hours just sitting on the porch and looking out at the front gate. I think he's hoping against hope that his wife is going to walk up that path. Bless his heart."

Upon hearing this, I wasted no time in getting to Catcher in the Rye. While waiting in line, I perused the menu on the board, trying to decide which sandwich would best give the message of comfort and support. The Pavarotti—Genoa salami, prosciutto, provolone, and roasted red peppers on toasted Italian—seemed a bit too intense. I briefly considered the Van Gogh—turkey, sliced Brie, and apples with honey mustard on a French baguette—but decided that the tanginess of the apples combined with the creaminess of the Brie and the bite of the mustard wasn't homey enough. Then I spotted the Mother Hubbard—a grilled ham and cheese on whole wheat—and I knew I'd found the right one.

When I paid for my order, the cashier handed me a card with the name Elizabeth Bennet. One of the delights of patronizing Big Ed's sandwich shop was seeing which fictional character I'd be assigned. Sometimes they weren't flattering and I'd sneak up to the pick-up counter in shame when Big Ed bellowed, "Miss Havisham" or "Nurse Ratched." I groaned aloud the day I'd received a card reading, *MEDUSA*, in bold block letters.

"Thanks," I told the cashier with a smile. "*Pride and Prejudice* is one of my favorite novels."

I mused over Elizabeth Bennet and Mr. Darcy's happy ending as I watched Big Ed slather grainy mustard on a sandwich. Wrapping it in wax paper, he shouted, "FRODO!"

A tiny gray-haired woman wearing a pink tracksuit stepped forward and reached up to toss the card with her fantasy identity into the basket on the counter. "Thanks, Ed," she said, taking the bag he held out. "I hope you were heavy on the mustard."

"You betcha, Winnie. The zing in that sandwich will have you zipping all the way to your Curiosity Shop." The portly sandwich maker winked at me. "And how are you today, Mizz Bennet?"

"I am well, good sir," I said in a formal British accent. "Pondering romance, as usual. Speaking of which, did you get a chance to talk to Nell at the festival this weekend? Her bakery kiosk was right next to yours."

Big Ed blushed, his plump cheeks flushing a dark shade of red. "No, we were too busy. Folks lined up all day long." He busied himself with preparing my sandwich order. "I'll ask her out on a proper date when I'm ready."

Watching Big Ed, I wondered why he didn't just let Nell know how he felt about her. If I'd learned anything over the past weekend it was that people don't always know how much time they have together. Logan Delaney had no idea that when he'd said good-bye to his wife as she left for the book festival, he'd never see her again. What words might he have spoken if he'd known?

I grabbed Big Ed's arm and, quoting Jane Austen, implored, " 'Why not seize the pleasure at once? How often is happiness destroyed by preparation, foolish preparation!' "

He stared at me in astonishment as he handed me my lunch, and then, seeing that my line was delivered in all seriousness, he paused to consider my words.

"You're right." He nodded solemnly. "I've wasted enough time makin' up excuses. It's been easier to love her from a distance. There's no risk in that, but I don't want to do that anymore. I want to love her up close and personal. Like Ms. Austen suggests, I'm ready to seize me some pleasure."

Chapter 8

I saw Logan Delaney before he saw me. Then again, I'm not sure he was seeing much of anything. Stella hadn't been exaggerating when she said that the grieving husband hadn't moved from the B and B's front porch. Despite the chill in the air, he was seated in a rocking chair in the far corner, dressed in a wrinkled button-down shirt and jeans. Even as I passed through the gate at the end of the brick path leading up to the porch, Logan just rocked and stared, his gaze passing through me as if I were a ghost.

Walking softly, as though a loud footfall would spook him, I maneuvered around an enormous urn overflowing with mums, pansies, and trailing ivy and took the chair next to his. A small glass table separated the two rockers, and I set the bag from Catcher in the Rye on its surface and unpacked Logan's lunch. I spread out a napkin to serve as a placemat, peeled back the paper from the grilled ham and cheese, and opened a bag of potato chips. I then twisted off the cap from a bottle of water and cleared my throat.

"Mr. Delaney, I'm Lila Wilkins." I willed him to look at me, but he didn't move a muscle. "I can't tell you how sorry I am for your loss. I met Melissa this past weekend and I thought she was lovely. I liked her from the get-go."

There was a twitch of Logan's mouth, as if the mention of his wife's name had the power to lift him from a near-catatonic state.

"I know there's not much anyone can offer you by way of comfort, but I wanted to tell you that she seemed like a woman who was happy with her life. She was full of laughter and quick-witted remarks and she inspired all the writers who were lucky enough to hear her speak."

Logan's rocker fell silent. He turned and swallowed hard, finally letting his eyes drift over my face. "You could be her sister," he whispered, his voice scratchy and raw.

I nodded. "Except that she was younger and more stylish than me. And I didn't know her well, but I know she loved you and she loved Silas."

Hearing his son's name, Logan's stiff posture collapsed. "How will I tell him?" he croaked. "What kind of life will he have without her? She was a wonderful mother. And my best friend. Silas and I . . . we adored her. I can't go on without her." He took a shaky breath. "I can't."

"You can and you will," I assured him. "And you'll start by eating this lunch. You and I are going to be part of a larger team working to find the person who did this to her. After that, you'll head home and hold Silas in your arms for a really long time."

Logan looked at the food blankly. "I'm not hungry."

"Of course you're not. You're numb all over. You want to be beyond feeling hunger and cold because she is. But you can't, Logan." I spoke as gently as I could. "Silas needs you." I reached over, drew one of Logan's hands to the table, and placed half a sandwich on his palm. I slowly closed his fingers over the sandwich. "Take one bite. That's all I ask. And in exchange I'll tell you what it's like to raise a child alone."

Logan lifted the food to his mouth, but his lips refused to part.

"Think of your son and eat."

I could see that Logan was on the brink of something. If he relented and took a bite, he'd be sacrificing the cocoon of denial he'd wrapped around himself. The agony would wash over him in wave after wave and he'd have no defense against the searing grief.

A tear rolled down his cheek as he opened his mouth, tore off a hunk of sandwich, and began to chew.

It was all I could do not to break down and cry, but I steeled myself and began to talk. "Trey was about Silas's age when my husband walked out. He'd had an affair, I'd caught him in the act, and he decided that his best course of action was to clean out our bank accounts and disappear."

Logan had already eaten half of the sandwich. His right hand grasped the water bottle and he drank deeply.

"We never saw him again, and not only did I have to explain to Trey that he suddenly had no father, but I had to hold myself together in order for my son to feel safe and secure." I sighed. It was still unpleasant to think back on those first six months of single parenthood. "Trey had nightmares for a whole year after that. He acted out. He broke things and tested limits and cried when he thought no one was looking."

Starting in on the second half of his sandwich, Logan met my eyes and nodded. He was taking in every word.

"It won't be easy," I told him honestly. "You'll want to hide in your room and sob, but you can't. Not until Silas is in bed asleep. You'll want to drink too much and eat too little. Stay inside on the most beautiful, sunny days. But you can't. You need to take Silas to the park and out for ice cream and to a grief counselor. And you'll discover that by living for your son, by getting up every morning and making him pancakes or eggs, by pouring him orange juice, and by packing his lunch for school, that you want to live." I smiled. "All along you'll think that you're saving your son, but in truth, your son will be saving you."

Logan had polished off his entire lunch. His cheeks weren't quite as drawn and his eyes were much more focused and alert. "Could I contact you for help? It sounds like you know what's around the corner for Silas and me."

"Call or email anytime." I handed him my business card. "And I didn't come just to bring you a sandwich. I want to help the authorities track down the monster who did this to Melissa." I paused, wondering if Logan was ready to field questions. "I heard that you also work in the publishing industry. Were you and Melissa with the same company?"

"No. I work for a much smaller house. We put out textbooks and books printed specifically for libraries." The corner of his mouth turned up slightly. "Of the two of us, Melissa definitely had the more exciting job."

He'd given me the perfect segue. "Did she talk to you about her authors?"

"Sure. Melissa and I always tucked Silas into bed, and then we'd go back to the kitchen and have a glass of wine and talk." His fingers trembled and he laced them tightly together. "It was my favorite time of the day."

It might seem callous, but I ignored his anguish and continued. "There was a woman at the book festival, an author, who was seen arguing with Melissa. She may have even threatened your wife. This woman had green eyes and was heavily freckled and rather busty. She was very angry and it seemed as though she and your wife knew each other."

"What a piece of work," Logan said with disapproval. "Her name's Coralee Silver and she's one of Melissa's paranormal authors. Melissa's focus has always been on books about family. Whether the family was insanely dysfunctional, living on a remote island, comprised of same-sex parents, or made up of vampires, it didn't matter to my wife. She was always on the lookout for a well-written story about what makes a family and what holds one together through life's peaks and valleys."

"And Coralee wrote such a tale?"

He nodded. "Yes. The manuscript Melissa purchased was about two Wiccans raising an abandoned werewolf cub. I know that sounds crazy, but it was a cool story. Melissa used to read me chapters from some of her authors' books while we drank wine after dinner." A shadow crossed his face, but he mustered up the courage to continue. "During the last round of revisions, Coralee added a bunch of really violent scenes to the novel. They were way too graphic for the target audience and Melissa insisted she remove them. Coralee wouldn't budge. She claimed that the blood and gore was an important part of the Wiccan/werewolf family bonding process and that Melissa was trying to stifle her creativity."

"That's it?" I was shocked. "Melissa merely

asked Coralee to remove a few scenes to ensure the book was saleable and Coralee wouldn't do it? Wow. I guess the situation had escalated by the time the two met here at the festival."

"I imagine so, because Melissa repeatedly warned Coralee that she was in breach of contract. The deadline had come and gone and Coralee refused to alter the manuscript, so right before Melissa left New York for here, she told Coralee the deal was off. The contract was canceled and my wife put the project out of her mind."

I thought of the thousands of authors who would kill to have been in Coralee's shoes. She had a contract, an advance, a great editor, and a reputable publishing house, and she threw it all away because she insisted on keeping scenes that hadn't been in the original manuscript. "What an idiot," I murmured.

Logan's expression had changed again. His eyes were brimming over with anger and he'd crushed the empty water bottle between his hands. "Do you think she had something to do with my wife's death?"

"If she did, you'll know soon enough. The police had no idea who Coralee was, but they will in a few seconds. Now they can track her down and question her, thanks to you." Rummaging in my purse, I located my cell phone and quickly called Sean.

"The mystery woman with the green eyes and

freckles?" I didn't even bother with a hello. I knew Sean would understand as soon as he heard that I was with Melissa's husband. "Her name is Coralee Silver." As succinctly as possible, I explained the connection between the irate author and the murdered editor.

"Please assure Mr. Delaney that we'll act on this information immediately," Sean stated, the excitement over a fresh lead evident in his voice. "And, Lila?"

Fearing that I was about to receive a harsh reprimand for interfering in a police investigation, I winced a bit and said, "Yes?"

"You're amazing. I don't know if you've been told that enough. If *I've* told you that enough. If you were here, I would show you just how grateful I am."

I could sense Sean's desire coming right through my phone speaker. It was like a burst of hot air. I would have loved to return the sentiment, to tell him how much I wanted to see him, to touch him, and to feel his lips brush against mine, but Logan's tortured face stopped the words in my throat. "I'll tell Mr. Delaney that you'll be in touch," I replied as casually as I could. "As for the rest of your statement, I'd be glad to discuss that with you in person. *Soon.*"

Back at Novel Idea, I addressed the onslaught of queries sitting in my email's inbox. I was surprised to see the number of subject lines reading "requested material," and wondered if word had spread among the writers present at the book festival that one could bypass Gate-keeper Vicky and reach any agent in our office simply by typing that magical phrase in the subject line.

Still, I recalled being interested in several pitches during my Friday session, including a wonderful romantic suspense and two cozy mystery series, and I couldn't wait to read those. However, I had over a dozen unsolicited queries to wade through first.

I did my best to respond to queries within four weeks, but this group had been sitting there for nearly six now and I wanted to get back to the authors today if possible. With my door closed and Handel playing from the free music station on my computer, I pushed all thoughts of Melissa Plume's death aside and devoted my full atten-tion to the queries.

Before I knew it, I'd sent fifteen rejection emails and two requests for the first fifty pages. I had made suggestions on eight of the rejection letters, recommending that the author increase or decrease the word count, clarify the project's hook, or paint his or her protagonist in a more engaging light. The other rejections elicited no comments. The projects felt flat and unexciting to me, and there was no way to verbalize that sentiment kindly, so those authors would receive a form rejection letter without a personalized note. Who knows? Another agent might fall in love with those queries, but I didn't feel a spark. So much of my job revolves around gut instincts— a sense of connection to the author's story. The best queries leave me hungry for more. The worst leave me completely unmoved.

I hit send on the last of the emails and then glanced at the clock, surprised to see that it was half past three.

"Coffee break!" I announced to the books on my shelves and headed downstairs.

Espresso Yourself was buzzing with the murmur of satisfied customers along with a group of artists who were boisterously hanging a new collection of paintings on the walls. They were large canvases and were distinctly modern in style. One painting, which was nearly as tall as Makayla, had been covered with a cherry red wash. A black square adorned the bottom half of the panel, and the work was entitled, "Jazz." I didn't get it, but then again, my knowledge of abstract art could fit inside a thimble.

"Not your cup of tea?" Makayla teased softly as I approached the counter. "I saw you tilting your head this way and that and frowning. Take a look at the one on the back wall. It's called 'Icarus.' I like it."

I turned to take in another oversize canvas

made up of swirls of blue, black, white, and gold and recalled the story of the boy with wax wings who'd flown too close to the sun and had ended up drowning in the sea as a result. "I can picture wings and waves. Sunlight and water. A range of emotions, too. The gold is like the freedom he must have felt during flight and the black is the fear that must have engulfed him as he began to fall." I shook my head in wonder. "There's so much going on in a few paint strokes. I don't like it as much as my lady at the fountain painting, but it's still amazing."

While Makayla fixed my latte, I filled her in on my lunchtime visit with Logan Delaney. I figured she had a right to know the identity of the mysterious green-eyed woman since she'd witnessed the fight between Melissa and Coralee. I was in the middle of explaining how Coralee was in breach of contract when a young man around Trey's age started shouting and pointing out the window.

"There's a giant banana across the street!" he shrieked and then burst into a peal of unsettling, high-pitched laughter. He was slight of build and dressed in a flannel shirt, jeans, and a knit ski hat whose flaps covered his ears. The blue and green flaps tapered into tails of braided yarn that dangled past the boy's shoulders. He tugged on them, repeatedly drawing attention to the "banana" out the window.

Scowling over having my narrative interrupted, I realized that he was gesturing at my scooter. Makayla and I exchanged perplexed looks, and she murmured, "Do you think he's drunk?"

I shrugged. "Maybe. If so, he's going to need a double shot of espresso or he'll be seeing an entire fruit basket on the train ride back to Dunston."

"I wanna peel the big banana!" the boy declared, heading for the door.

A young woman with a collection of star tattoos on her neck grabbed her friend by the arm. "Dude, that's a Vespa." She rolled her eyes in annoyance. "Get a grip. I just want to grab a café au lait and then we're out of here."

Makayla frowned. "I've never wanted to shoo off customers before, but these kids have been crowding my space for the last few weeks and they've all been raucous as magpies and messy as pigeons."

Studying the group of older teens, who appeared to be yet another wave of college students skipping classes, I remembered Trey telling me that Jasper had been charging coeds to meditate at the co-op. A couple of these kids were wearing caps embroidered with the Red Fox Mountain Co-op logo. Had they just come from there?

"I think I'll drop in on Trey tonight," I told Makayla. "Bring him some supper and see exactly what's changed up on Red Fox Mountain."

"Good," Makayla answered, handing me a

steaming hot pumpkin spice latte. "And if you could find a way to magically send these kids back to a college campus until they're thirty-year-old yuppies in business suits that would be super. Because they are crappy tippers."

With the late afternoon sun glaring in my eyes, I rode my scooter up the steep path toward the Red Fox Mountain Co-op. Scents of tree sap, pine, and fecund soil drifted past me, and I felt a tinge of remorse at disturbing the peaceful forest with my noisy little Vespa. It didn't last long, however, for at the top, the road leveled and the engine, not having to work so hard, rumbled quieter. Ahead, the wooden sign affixed to the willow branch arch proclaimed, *Welcome to The Red Fox Mountain Co-op.* I passed under it, emerging into a wide, flat clearing.

A red Honda Civic was parked near the chain-link fence surrounding the goat paddock. I pulled my Vespa in behind it and removed my helmet. It had been a few months since I'd been on the property, and at first glance the co-op appeared to be relatively unchanged. The grass on the circular plateau was neatly mowed, and the cluster of cabins to the right and the large barn behind the goat paddock were still unpainted. On the other side of the chain-link fence a few white goats bleated, their brown faces and floppy ears as charming as ever.

But as I continued to look around, I saw differences, too. No longer was there an old-fashioned push mower leaning against the fence. Instead, a shiny green riding mower stood by a shed. A new building had been erected behind the cabins with cream-colored aluminum siding and shiny glass windows. The most telling improvement, however, was the electrical poles and wires running up the mountain into the new structure. The co-op had prided itself on being solar- and human-powered, so this was an indication that something had changed in their basic philosophy.

On the porch of one of the cabins, two women sat in green Adirondack chairs with baskets of woven hemp at their feet. I waved at them, struck by another change—the weavers used to sit on crude stools. One raised her hand while the other sipped from a mug as she stared at me suspiciously.

Cabin windows glowed with interior lights. In the waning sun, the air became chilly. People wearing jackets and sweaters appeared from various parts of the property and headed toward individual cabins. I noticed that no one was setting the outdoor picnic tables for supper and wondered if the new building had been erected so the co-op members could enjoy meals inside during the colder months.

I looked for Trey among the residents but didn't

see him. When I glanced at the barn, thinking it might be milking time, he appeared at its door and began to shoo goats into the paddock. He saw me and waved, called out a hello, and continued to herd the goats outside.

When I opened the rear carrier on my scooter, the aromas of tomatoes, garlic, and basil wafted out. My mouth watered in anticipation of the lasagna I had purchased from How Green Was My Valley. The store had hired a new cook who'd emigrated from Florence, and her renditions of classic Italian dishes were scrumptious.

Trey appeared at the fence, his fingers curled around the wire. "What've you got there?" he asked, clearly pleased to see me even though we'd shared breakfast together at my house that morning.

I held up the bag. "Interested in some lasagna for supper? I thought we could eat together again tonight."

He grinned. "Awesome! If you cooked it, you know I'll definitely love it." He climbed the chain links with the agility of a monkey and jumped to the ground at my feet.

"You're such a sweet-talker, but it's takeout." I closed the carrier. "Where should we eat?"

"We can sit at one of the picnic tables." He glanced at my quilted jacket. "If you're not too cold."

I shook my head. "Nope, I'm good. But you

should put on something warmer." The mother in me always came out when I was with Trey, regardless of the fact that he was becoming a mature and independent young man.

He tugged at the hem of his sweatshirt. "I'm fine, Mom. Don't worry."

We sat down and I pulled plastic cutlery out of the bag while Trey opened the containers with the lasagna and Caesar salad.

I looked up at the sky. The blue hue of twilight created a stark contrast with the dying leaves and dark evergreens. It felt good to be sitting outside in the crisp November dusk. "They've made a lot of improvements," I said as I unfolded a paper napkin and placed it on my lap. I pointed to the aluminum-sided structure. "What's that new building?"

"Part of it is our communal area where we can gather in bad weather, but most of it's the"—he made quotation marks at the sides of his head with his fingers—"meditation center." He was quiet as he cut into his lasagna. "I don't know what they actually do in there, since I'm not allowed to go in." He speared the fork into the pasta and shoved it into his mouth, looking longingly at the building.

I placed my hand on his arm. "Aw, honey."

He chewed and shrugged. "I don't care. But this"—he pointed his fork at the pasta—"is delicious." He put another morsel into his mouth.

After swallowing a crunchy piece of romaine lettuce covered in Caesar dressing and grated Parmesan, I asked, "And they now have electricity?"

Trey nodded. "Only in the new building and some of the cabins. There are a couple of computers in the communal center, too. And a flat-screen TV."

"Wow." I savored a bite of lasagna. There was just enough garlic and basil to harmonize with the tomato sauce and melted cheeses, and the homemade pasta was a perfect texture. "Whatever happened to simple living? To the co-op being entirely human-powered? And how are they paying for all this? Is the market for goat and hemp products that lucrative?"

"Not that I know of. We're still getting the same prices for our stuff that we did when I first came here. And our yield isn't any greater." He put his fork down. "I don't know where the extra money is coming from, unless it's the meditation sessions. But the only people who come for those are college kids, and they can't pay that kind of money, can they?"

He seemed sincerely baffled, and I didn't know how to answer. The situation seemed at odds with everything I'd understood about the co-op. I had to admit, however, that observing the recent changes lit a spark of hope in my heart that Trey would become disillusioned enough by it that he'd decide to attend college after all. "I don't know, honey. I—"

"Hey, dude," a voice interrupted. "That smells, like, totally awesome. Got enough for us?"

The young man I'd seen in Espresso Yourself who'd been wearing the blue and green ski hat and who had shouted about a giant banana stood at the end of our table, the braided tails of his hat's ear flaps dangling over our supper. His friend, the girl with the star tattoos on her neck, had her arm in the crook of his elbow. Behind them stood another older teen, spiked hair dyed a fluorescent blue.

I smiled apologetically at them. "Sorry, I only brought enough for the two of us." I waved my hand in the direction of my Vespa. "But I rode in on my big banana over there."

"Huh?" The teen with the ski hat looked at the scooter and then at me. "What are you talking about?"

"I saw you in the coffee shop earlier, and you called my scooter a banana."

"I did not. I have no idea what you're talking about, lady."

The girl pulled on his arm. "Come on, Dex, let's go."

Dex freed his arm and looked at Trey. "You're, like, the goat dude, aren't you? Your name's Trey?"

Trey nodded and pointed to the meditation

center. "What exactly do you guys do in there? Were you meditating just now?"

He grinned. "Naw, not this time. We were just getting our groove on with a little—"

"Okay, guests, time to go. You know the agreement. Once it's suppertime at the co-op you've got to be out of here." Jasper Gyles, the leader of the Red Fox Co-op, approached our table with his sister, Iris, who looked as beautiful and ethereal as always.

In the manner of a shepherd herding his flock, Jasper directed the three teens toward the red Honda. I watched them, pondering the change in Jasper. Upon first meeting Jasper at the beginning of the summer, Trey had remarked that the co-op leader, who had bright blue eyes, a brown beard, and long wavy hair, bore a close resemblance to Jesus. But Jasper was beardless, wore his hair short, and was dressed in tidy jeans and an expensive leather jacket.

I turned back to the table. Iris was sitting beside Trey, nudged in close. Noticing me observing, Trey blushed and offered her the remainder of his salad. She shook her head, briefly touching his arm, then said to me, "Nice to see you again, Ms. Wilkins."

"It's good to see you, too, Iris. Would you like a biscotti?" I opened the container of crunchy, sweet almond biscuits. Trey reached out and took one. Iris shook her head.

"No, thank you."

"I see some changes here at the co-op," I said, taking a cookie and wishing I had a coffee to dip it in. "Are you pleased with the new direction?"

Before Iris could respond, Jasper appeared behind her and placed his hand on her shoulder. I noticed his fingers press into her flesh and she stiffened in response. "Ms. Wilkins," he said with a generous smile. "Welcome."

"Thank you, Jasper." I looked into his lake blue eyes. "I see that you are doing very well. Business must be brisk."

"Yes, we've diversified and it's been very lucrative. One can't stand still in the way of progress."

"But what about the simplistic approach you embraced when Trey first arrived?" I looked at Trey, who was giving me a wide-eyed signal to stop. Iris squirmed beside him. "Where you wanted to live a self-sustaining life, free of society's encumbrances? Now you have electricity, computers, TV, and a riding lawn tractor."

"Ah, well, people change. Philosophies change." He shrugged and walked to the end of the table, folding his arms across his chest. "It was getting a little tedious to work this place primarily on people power. We're all much happier now, aren't we?" He directed his gaze to Trey and Iris, who both nodded but said nothing.

"But how have you diversified to generate so

much more income?" I realized that this question was on the verge of being impolite, but my son was living here and I wanted to know what was going on.

Jasper frowned. "Oh, increasing our crop variety and expanding the market."

"And don't forget the meditation sessions," Trey blurted out. "You charge a lot for them, too, right?"

Iris nervously twisted a lock of her pale hair. Jasper turned in the direction of the new building. "Ah yes, the meditation sessions. They've proved to be very profitable." He reached his arm toward Iris and Trey. "Come, you two. The movie will be starting soon."

Iris stood. Putting her hand on Trey's shoulder, she said, "Let's go. The *Hunger Games* DVD arrived today." Turning to me, she said, "You don't mind if he goes, do you? We've been waiting for ages to watch this movie."

Jasper's blue eyes twinkled. "You see? Happier."

I glanced at Trey, who was obviously experiencing a series of emotions in response to this interchange. But the way he looked at Iris told me where he wanted to be. "Not at all," I said. "You go ahead. I need to drive down before it gets completely dark anyway."

"Thanks, Mom. And thanks for supper. It was awesome." Trey gave me a hearty hug. "Don't worry about me," he whispered in my ear, and then turned to Iris and held out his hand. She took it and together they followed Jasper. Trey looked over his shoulder once more in order to flash me a grin.

"Enjoy the movie!" I called and gathered the supper things. As I watched the threesome walk off toward the meditation center, I couldn't help but wonder what kind of "meditation" went on in that cream-colored building. My maternal instincts were telling me that whatever it was did not bode well for my son.

Chapter 9

Upon returning to my cottage on Walden Woods Circle, I lit a fire in the living room, poured myself a glass of merlot, and turned on my laptop. The undercurrent of anxiety and discomfort I'd sensed throughout the co-op had left me feeling unsettled. I had entrusted my son, the most important person in my life, to Jasper Gyles and the other adults running the co-op, and I worried that I'd made a grave mistake. Trey might have been content with life on Red Fox Mountain up until this point, but I wasn't sure either of us could be happy knowing the co-op's leader changed philosophies like Mister Rogers had once changed his shoes.

There was something particularly disturbing in Iris's body language, too. She'd always been such a free spirit, but tonight I'd seen her practically attached at the hip to Trey. He'd been chasing her all summer, and though she'd always been friendly to him, she hadn't encouraged his advances. Why did she suddenly want him by her side? I pictured the many small touches I'd witnessed in the short time I'd visited and wondered if Iris had been trying to reassure Trey or herself. Was she frightened? And if so, of what?

Troubled to be presented with another mystery when Melissa's murder was yet unsolved, I was determined to figure out what was going on at the co-op. What was the connection between money and meditation? To me, they were an odd combination.

I ran a Google search for "meditation at Red Fox Co-op," but nothing came up connecting the two. Red Fox had a website that was still under construction but gave no other information. Then I tried meditation styles and found articles on the different settings, body postures, and music one should use when trying to meditate. Having never been able to remain still for long unless I had a riveting book in my hands, I'd never tried to sit on the floor with my legs crossed and my eyes closed, attempting to block out all distractions as I focused on a single mental image.

Some techniques required monitoring one's breathing. Others called for chanting a mantra over and over again until the meditative state was acquired. Yet another recommended emptying one's mind of all thoughts and visions, thus achieving a state of blankness and absolute tranquility. As far as I could see, the only cost in creating an appropriate space would be the purchase of a few inspirational CDs or possibly some incense. Unless Jasper was charging exorbitant rates for a special chant or for guiding his guests into a state of tranquility and focus, then the profits he was making from the teens made no sense.

On a whim, I entered the search terms "college students" and "meditation" and scanned a select group of articles citing the connection between meditation and stress reduction. According to several reliable sources, the number of depressed, anxiety-ridden, and medicated coeds was on the rise and kids just like Trey were experimenting with all sorts of remedies, including drugs, to reduce their stress levels.

"Drugs," I muttered with a heavy heart, my fear for my son's welfare increasing. "What kind of drugs?" My fingers moved automatically over the keyboard, and I forgot all about my glass of wine as a list of the most popular illegal drugs used by coeds popped up on my screen. "Marijuana is the most widely spread," I read aloud from an article, somehow needing to hear the sound of a voice, even if it was only my own. "Also included are steroids, LSD, ecstasy, and Rohypnol. Prescription drugs most frequently abused are Ritalin and OxyContin."

I eased my laptop onto the sofa and walked over to the fire. Pushing at the burning wood with my fireplace poker, I stared at the shifting flames and wondered if Jasper was trafficking in illegal drugs. But it didn't seem likely. Sean had told me that he and other Dunston police officers conducted impromptu visits to the co-op, and each time Jasper had invited the law enforcement agents to look around. More often than not, the cops did a sweep of the cabins and tents, and on one occasion had brought a K-9 unit along. However, the co-op's structures and grounds had always been drug-free.

Still, something nagged at me. Over the course of the past few months, life had given me too many lessons proving that things weren't always as they appeared, and with Jasper's flippant attitude toward such an abrupt lifestyle change, I suspected him of hiding an ugly secret.

It had grown late and I was tired, but I continued to prod the burning logs, nudging orange sparks into life and ruminating over the changes at Red Fox Mountain. When my phone rang, the sound seemed to come from far away, and I realized with a start that my focus on the flickering fire had been so intent that I'd involuntarily reached a meditative state.

"Sorry to call at this time of night, but I just wanted to check in on you." Sean's voice flowed through the speaker, smooth and sweet as honey.

"I'm glad you did. It's been a strange evening, but before I tell you about my day, how has yours been? Any progress in the investigation?"

Sean sighed and I could sense his weariness and frustration. "We interviewed Coralee Silver.

She unabashedly admitted to arguing with Melissa and threatening her as well."

Suddenly, the poker felt too heavy in my hands. Dropping it on the hearth, I asked, "Did she . . . is she Melissa's killer?"

"No," Sean answered readily. "Believe me, there were several officers who would have liked Ms. Silver to have been the culprit. She is a rather unpleasant woman, to put it mildly. However, there is apparently one gentleman in town who finds her utterly winsome."

I groaned. "Let me guess. This guy's provided her with an alibi."

"You got it," he said.

Imagining Coralee's green eyes narrowing with hostility, her pointer finger raised in an intimidating gesture, and Melissa Plume's rightful indignation, I clenched my jaw tightly, fighting back a surge of anger. "Are you sure she's in the clear?"

Sean seemed reluctant to elaborate. "This is between you and me, Lila, but Ms. Silver's gentleman friend escorted her to the party Saturday evening and then rushed her out of the old town hall well before Melissa was killed."

"How do you know what time they left?"

Clearing his throat, Sean haltingly explained that not only did Coralee's date have a penchant for engaging in sexual encounters in public places, but he also enjoyed filming said encounters. The video included a time stamp.

"Oh my," was the only reply I could manage. "Please tell me they didn't pick the Fountain of the Nine Muses. That's my favorite place to eat lunch on a sunny day."

Laughing heartily, Sean assured me that while the fountain was safe, I might not want to enjoy any meals on a town center park bench for a while.

"I know you probably can't divulge the man's name, but at least tell me that he wasn't an author and that I'm not going to be reading about his evening with Coralee in a proposal one day." This was delivered in jest, but Sean took my statement at face value.

"He was attending the conference and is most definitely an aspiring author, but let's just say that you don't represent his genre." Sean seemed to be suppressing a chuckle. "Oh, this is exactly what I needed, Lila. For someone to lighten my mood."

I hesitated to bring up the subject of the co-op. Now that Coralee had been dismissed as a possible suspect, Sean and the rest of the officers on his team had to search out new leads. I told him that Bentley would undoubtedly dig up useful information on Ruben Felden, Melissa's disgruntled coworker, and then forged ahead and described my visit to Red Fox Mountain.

"Lila." This time, when Sean spoke my name, his tone carried a hint of warning. "We've been through this before. There isn't a speck of evidence indicating that Jasper or any other co-op member deals in illegal drugs. Granted, I haven't been up there since the meditation center was built, but I doubt it's stuffed with black lights and marijuana plants."

I groaned a little at the image.

"Organic products are all the rage right now," Sean continued. "Maybe he made a successful business deal and the goat's milk products are being subsidized by a company with a wide distribution. Up until this point, the co-op's goods have only been sold in Inspiration Valley and Dunston. Perhaps the demand is greater than those two towns and the co-op is reaping the benefits."

Sean's theory was certainly logical, but Jasper hadn't answered my question about the goat's milk products becoming more lucrative. Then again, he might have felt that the co-op's business practices were none of my concern. Still, it seemed odd that he wouldn't let Trey in on the windfall. Trey had designed the new packaging and was very involved with the goats. He knew the names of each and every animal and took great pride in the milk, cheese, soaps, and lotions created on-site.

"You may be right," I told Sean, but only because I wanted to pacify him. In my heart, I felt there was something shady about the secrecy of the meditation center and the unusual number of college students making regular treks up the mountain. I was not going to allow my son to continue living and working in a place where illicit activities were being conducted.

"I can tell that you're not convinced." Sean chuckled. "And I know you well enough not to bother saying to put the co-op out of your mind. I also believe that your instincts are as finely honed as a top chef's carving knife. If they're telling you something's amiss, then it probably is. But do me one favor."

Caught up by his words of praise, it took me a moment to respond. "Okay."

"Wait until I can come with you for a casual look-see around the mountain before you launch a full-scale investigation. Trey's a good kid with more common sense than most young men his age. Trust him to sort out what's going on and whether he wants to be a part of it. If he doesn't, he'll show up at your door none the worse for wear."

I considered Sean's advice. "All right, I'll back off for now. But only because I trust your judgment and, heaven help me, I trust Trey's, too. Besides, I'd rather focus all my spare energy helping you solve Melissa's murder."

Sean growled. "Lila! I told—"

"From the sidelines!" I added hurriedly. "Just civilian research, like the type I did discovering Coralee's identity. I want this to be over, Sean, for Logan and Silas to have closure. I have selfish reasons for wanting this case closed, too."

"You're the least selfish person on earth," he said with incredible tenderness.

"Not when it comes to you," I said softly. "I want you all to myself. All of you. To myself." The heat rose in my cheeks, and I knew that it wasn't generated by the fire burning in my hearth.

"When this is finished, you and I will truly begin. I promise, Lila."

That was a promise I could live with.

I spent Tuesday morning focusing solely on work. Armed with an extra-large cappuccino and one of Makayla's iced apple and date scones, I forged my way through proposals, queries, and contract reviews.

Just before noon, Vicky's voice emitted through my phone speaker. "Ms. Wilkins, you have a caller," she said. "The lady's name is Kate Sallinger. Says she's Melissa Plume's editor friend."

My heart skipped a beat. "Please put her through."

"Hi, Lila," Kate began, and though she tried to sound cheerful, there was an unmistakable heaviness to her voice.

"How are you holding up?" I asked her.

Her mournful sigh answered my question. "I spent yesterday in bed but thought I'd come in today and lose myself in work. Nothing could hold my attention until I picked up Calliope's manuscript. I'd started it before I heard about Melissa." She paused, as if speaking her friend's name had caused her physical pain and she needed a moment to recover. "I was in the office by seven this morning. Messed around with this and that until almost nine and then I picked up her book and, well, she made me forget about the real world for two hours."

"Sometimes that's the best thing a book can do for us," I said.

"Absolutely. I want the whole series, Lila." She continued by telling me what she was willing to offer for the first three books, and though it was an incredibly generous amount, I tried to negotiate even more. I wouldn't be much of an agent if I didn't push the envelope. Kate and I engaged in a good-natured bartering session until we were both satisfied, and then I told her I'd have to talk things over with Calliope and would call her back shortly.

Calliope typically spent the morning writing and always muted her phone when she worked, but by some miracle she answered my call. She shouted with unadulterated joy when I told her about Kate's offer.

"I feel like it's the *first* time!" she shrieked. "I remember when I got that call like it was yesterday. I thought I could just float away I was so happy. And now it's happening again, because this is a whole new series and one that I wanted, that I *needed,* to write. Thank you, Lila! You're a gem!"

Her pleasure was contagious, and part of me longed to jump up and down in excitement like a little kid on Christmas morning. This was my biggest deal yet—the kind of deal people in the industry dream about. I knew that I'd buy the issue of *Publishers Weekly* announcing the sale, take out the page listing the details, and have it framed.

"You deserve this, Calliope," I told my client. "You're an amazing writer, and your willingness to be flexible saved the series. Now go out and celebrate."

"Not a chance," she countered merrily. "I am on such a high right now that I could hammer out a thousand words before lunch. Tell Kate that I *so* look forward to working with her." She hesitated. "And please send her my condolences as well. I heard about what happened to Melissa Plume. It's *absolutely* terrible."

I swallowed, feeling as though a shadow had just invaded my office. I assured Calliope that I would pass her messages on, called Kate back, and then sat quietly at my desk for a moment. My elation over the deal had been dampened, but not extinguished. What I needed was to share the news with someone, to spread my excitement around the office. Unfortunately, as I wandered down the hall in search of coworkers, I discovered everyone had already headed out to lunch, and the idea of eating a celebratory meal alone held no appeal.

"There you are, Lila! You've certainly been holed up today," trilled Flora. She pulled the restroom door shut behind her and smiled at me. "Have you had anything to eat yet?"

"No," I said, returning her smile. "And I'd love to take you to lunch if you're free. I've made my first big deal and I want to eat a whopping cheeseburger followed by a massively decadent dessert."

Flora nodded with gusto. "Say no more, my dear! You can tell me all about it on the way to the James Joyce Pub. They make the best burgers in town."

The James Joyce Pub was situated near the end of High Street and was connected indoors by a large archway to the Constant Reader, a new and used bookstore. One could browse for books with a beer in hand, or sit in the pub enjoying a steak-and-mushroom pie while engrossed in a newly purchased novel. Although very "unSouthern," this little bit of Ireland in Inspiration Valley fit well into the community and was always busy.

Walking in the brisk November air, we had carried on an enthusiastic discussion about Calliope's deal. We entered through the Constant Reader, eager to be immersed in its bookish ambience on our way to the restaurant. As soon as we set foot inside, that delicious musty scent of old books filled our nostrils, and we made our way to the pub through pathways flanked by shelves. In my buoyant frame of mind, I reveled at the sight of so many volumes cramming the shelves. Romance, adventure, mystery, fantasy; they seemed to be competing with one another for our attention, promising us hours of pleasure.

"Ah." Flora inhaled deeply. "Whenever I'm here I dream about living in a book. I could be anyone I wanted. Travel anywhere. Explore a glorious garden or dive to the bottom of the ocean in search of sunken treasure." She ran her fingers along the spine of a thick tome, its brown leather weathered gray and the gold lettering faded.

"I know what you mean," I said, pulling out a small anthology of poetry. Its worn dark blue cover featured a drawing of a woman sitting under a tree, papers clasped to her breast. I leafed through the pages. " 'The love of learning, the sequestered nooks, and all the sweet serenity of books,' " I said, quoting Longfellow.

Flora smiled. "Exactly, my dear. Now, shall we go eat?"

I replaced the book and followed her into the pub. There wasn't an empty stool at the polished wooden bar, and we made our way past booths filled with people enjoying their lunch. Flora waved at a red-haired waitress carrying a tray laden with plates of food. She brightened when she saw Flora.

"Hi, Flora. I think there's a free table on the patio," she said cheerfully and began unloading platters at a booth where four businessmen sat, sharing a pitcher of amber ale.

"Do we want to sit outside?" I asked Flora. "It's a bit cool."

"Their patio heaters are very efficient. Brian and I had dinner here just last week and it was lovely sitting out there." She pushed open the door to go outside. "And it's nice and sunny today."

Flora was right. It wasn't at all cold on the patio. Four tall heaters glowing orange cast their warm rays on the diners, keeping the temperature very comfortable. Several people had even removed their coats, and if I used my imagination, I could pretend we were eating outdoors in late summer. We sat down at the one empty table beneath a large chestnut tree whose branches were bare except for the occasional golden yellow leaf. As I hung my jacket on the back of the chair, the waitress brought us glasses of water and menus.

Flora moved the menu to the edge of the table. "Thanks, Kathleen, but I don't need to see the menu. I'll just have my usual."

The waitress grinned, her green eyes twinkling. "Irish stew and soda bread?" When Flora nodded, Kathleen turned to me. "I'll give you a few minutes to decide."

"I understand you make a great burger here," I said, holding the menu but not opening it.

"Best in the Valley."

"I'm celebrating, so I'll take a cheeseburger with the works." I handed the menu back to her and told Flora more about my phone calls with Kate and Calliope.

When the food arrived, the aromas were tantalizing. Flora's stew was loaded with beef chunks, potatoes, and vegetables, all submerged in a thick gravy. The crust of the accompanying soda bread was a firm golden brown while the inside appeared dense and soft. "That looks and smells *really* good," I said, eyeing her plate and wondering if I should have ordered the stew.

"So does your cheeseburger," she replied and proceeded to butter a slice of her bread. "You won't regret your choice."

I didn't. The burger was cooked just right and seasoned to perfection. It was topped with a slice of sharp cheddar and sautéed mushrooms and onions, and balanced with sweet slices of tomatoes and fresh leaves of lettuce. The fries on the side were thick, fresh cut, and crisp. I ate with gusto.

I was dipping my last fry into the dollop of mayonnaise on my plate when Flora smiled at someone near the door and raised her hand in greeting. "Yoo-hoo!" she called and then turned back to me. "Here's someone I'd like you to meet."

Following her glance, I saw a tall, slim woman coming toward us carrying a leather overnight bag. Her dark hair was casually pulled back with a clip, and she wore jeans and a gorgeous, intricately knit cardigan. As she approached the table, Flora stood.

"Tilly! I didn't know you were still in town." She hugged the woman and then gestured in my direction. "This is Lila Wilkins, a wonderful agent in our firm. She's just landed her first big deal. Lila, this is Tilly Smythe. She's a client of mine and writes the most wonderful YA series about the adventures of an orphan boy trying to discover the identity of his parents. Her last two books hit the bestseller list, and we think the series could become as popular as Harry Potter."

"Fingers crossed," the woman said as she shook my hand. "It's very nice to meet you, Lila." She glanced around the patio. "There aren't any free tables anywhere in this restaurant. I thought I'd pop in for a quick lunch before catching the train back to Dunston, but—"

"Oh, join us, Tilly. We were just about to order dessert." Flora had already grabbed an empty chair from a four-top table occupied by three diners.

After Tilly sat down, I asked, "Could you tell me a bit more about your series?"

"Sure. The books feature a fourteen-year-old

boy named Danny who was orphaned as a young child and doesn't know what happened to his parents. So he travels around the country trying to find them and gets caught up in a host of adventures. It's also a fantasy, because he meets odd characters along the way, like elves and people who fly and talking mountain lions. Each book is set in a different place. The one I'm working on now, the fourth book, takes place in South Dakota. Danny joins up with a wolf pack that communicates in a special language. And for some reason, which is yet to be revealed, Danny can understand them."

As Tilly spoke, her enthusiasm for the project was evident. However, she appeared somewhat distracted and was continuously looking over her shoulder throughout her narrative. There was something familiar about her, and I had the sense that I knew her from somewhere, but I couldn't place her.

"Have we met before?" I asked.

She shook her head. "I don't think so. But I was at the book festival over the weekend, so you may have seen me there."

I didn't recall encountering her at the town hall, but parts of the weekend were a blur, so it was possible. There was definitely something memorable about Tilly—I felt like I'd looked into her eyes before. And despite her friendliness, those dark eyes unsettled me.

When the waitress returned to our table, Tilly ordered a salad while Flora chose an apple cobbler for dessert. I decided to have a Baileys mousse pie with a coffee.

"What are you still doing in town?" Flora asked Tilly. "I thought you were heading back right after the festival."

"I spent a few days with my friend, Ginny Callaway, the metal sculptor. I've known her since high school and we've been catching up. Plus, I've been exploring the town in depth, thinking I might set one of Danny's adventures here. I'm finding inspiration in Inspiration Valley." She chuckled and pulled out of her bag a spiral-bound notebook with a hot pink cover, fanning its pages. "See, I've been taking notes and have a loose outline for the book already." She suddenly turned her head toward the door, her shoulders rigid.

At that moment, the waitress brought our food. My Baileys mousse pie was sky-high, with a mound of cream on top. If I finished it, I'd probably have to undo the top button of my skirt, but I dug into the treat anyway. It was chocolaty smooth, with a hint of alcoholic creaminess. Well worth that top button!

Tilly nibbled at her salad anxiously and then leaned forward. "Do you consider this town safe?" she asked.

Flora looked puzzled. "Of course. I've lived

here most of my life, and I think it's the safest place in the world."

"But there was that murder at the festival," Tilly countered. "And I get this feeling . . ." She shot a nervous look over her shoulder again.

I touched her hand. "Tilly, the police are pretty certain that Melissa's murder is related to either her personal or professional life back in New York. It probably had nothing to do with Inspiration Valley."

"But I get the sense that someone is watching me here." She began to shred her napkin. "I know it sounds crazy, and I never actually see anyone, but it feels like I'm being followed."

I was suddenly struck by a thought. "Did you know Melissa Plume? Did you two ever meet?"

She shook her head. "I'd never even heard of her before she was murdered."

Flora pulled out her credit card and waved it at the waitress. "You're probably feeling spooked because of the murder. It spooked me, too. You're safe in this town. And put away your wallets. This lunch is on me."

"Thank you, Flora. That's kind of you. Oh, I'd better get going," Tilly said, checking her watch. "Sorry to rush off, but the next train leaves in ten minutes, and if I cut out the back I'll just catch it." She picked up her valise and went through the gated exit bordering the grassy field that led to the station.

"Is she usually that high-strung?" I asked Flora as I watched Tilly hurry toward the train station.

Flora shook her head. "Not in my experience. She's always been a calm, easygoing person."

"Well, something out of the ordinary is going on with her," I commented, noticing she'd left her pink notebook on the table. Perhaps some of Althea was rubbing off on me, because I was filled with a sense of dread that Tilly's anxiety was not unfounded.

Chapter 10

I felt rather deflated for the rest of the day. My big sale had allowed me an hour or two of elation, but by the time I left the agency that afternoon, oppressive thoughts sat on my shoulders like a sodden cloak. Melissa. Trey. Tilly. I was worrying about a woman I'd just met, for crying out loud, but her discomfort was almost palpable. And more than a little contagious.

A month ago, I would have brushed aside her odd behavior and decided that she was just another eccentric writer, but not now. Too much had happened for me to ignore any instinctual warning flags, and since Flora had assured me that Tilly was normally very even-keeled, her trepidation had definitely set off my "something is amiss" radar.

Even my yellow cottage, toasty warm and smelling of cinnamon candles, didn't cheer me up. I cooked myself supper, listened to a voicemail from Sean saying that he was thinking of me but wouldn't be able to stop by, and fell asleep leafing through *Apples for Jam*, one of my favorite cookbooks.

Thankfully, I had so much work waiting for me

at Novel Idea on Wednesday morning that there was no time to brood. I'd barely begun reading my emails when Zach burst into my office, a wide smile on his boyishly handsome face.

"Come get your sugar on!" he shouted, disrupting the tranquil atmosphere. "We celebrate with coffee and carbs around here. One of Novel Idea's agency mottos is that if you haven't gone up a clothing size by the end of the year, then you're not making enough deals." He patted his flat stomach and winked. "Except for *me,* of course. I've got to stay fit if I'm going to rope in the top athletes. If any of them saw how fast I'm going to devour one of Nell's bear claws, they'd make me do suicide drills on the sidewalk before signing a contract. Let's go before Franklin picks all the best stuff." He gallantly offered me his arm and I walked around from behind my desk and took it.

I found the rest of my coworkers in the kitchen. They'd ordered a pastry platter from Sixpence Bakery and a tray of lattes from Espresso Yourself. Outside the window over the sink, the sky began to darken, threatening a bone-chilling thunderstorm, but I paid it no mind. It's amazing how a cup of strong coffee, a pumpkin muffin top drizzled with icing, and the kindheartedness of friends can make any day feel like summer.

My coworkers entertained me with stories of their first major deals and our laughter filled the office. Even Vicky joined in and let her self-discipline slide enough to enjoy half an apple Danish. I looked around the room and smiled. For the hundredth time, I thought how lucky I'd been to land this job. No matter what happened, I loved what I did and was truly fortunate to work alongside such delightful people.

Thus invigorated, I returned to my laptop and stuffed inbox.

The first email that caught my eye contained the subject line "requested material," and I immediately recognized the sender's name. It was from Ashley Buckland, the writer who'd pitched the cozy mystery series featuring stay-at-home dads turned amateur sleuths.

I began with the query letter and was immediately hooked. Not only was the letter organized and polished, but the writer's witty, humorous voice also shone through each and every line.

"If the manuscript is anything like the query, this is going to be a fun book to read," I mused aloud and opened the document.

The first fifty pages were an entertaining romp through the domestic trials and tribulations of a winsome stay-at-home dad. Ashley began his story with his protagonist, Will MacGillicuddy, accidentally pouring bleach over a load of his family's colored clothes, nearly losing a finger to the food processor, and walking in circles in a superstore in search of his child's favorite cereal.

Will collides into the shopping cart of another overwhelmed father, and after transporting their screaming children to the park, the two dads form the Men at Home support group.

I laughed many times over the course of those fifty pages and found Ashley to be a skilled writer. He treated real-life parenting experiences with humor, but also with sensitivity and a genuine depth of feeling. By the point at which one of the stay-at-home group's six members is murdered, I had become so fond of the characters that I wanted to shout, "No, not him! I liked him!"

There were plenty of potential suspects, the murder was handled with tasteful compassion, and as I read Ashley's synopsis of how the rest of the book would unfold, I knew it was a winner. The title, *Deadly Diapers*, needed work, but I was ready to request the full manuscript, and I sent Ashley an email telling him that I'd like to see the rest of the book.

I'd been so engrossed with Buckland's writing that my coffee had gotten cold, so I returned to the kitchen to warm it up in the microwave. Jude was doing the same thing and we exchanged a laugh over the coincidence.

"It's amazing how quickly an hour can pass when someone sends you an intriguing proposal," Jude said. "I hope my guy responds quickly to my request for the full manuscript, because if I don't act fast, someone else is going to snap him up. This author's got a really gritty, edgy voice and his material is dark and gripping and a little warped. I love it." Jude removed his coffee cup from the microwave and gestured for me to hand him mine. "Please, allow me," he added, his seductive mouth curving up in a smile.

As I passed him the cup he intentionally covered my fingers with his. For a moment, I was transported to the summer evening in which Jude's mouth had found mine. We'd kissed once, with what I'd foolishly believed was genuine passion, until we were interrupted. Now Sean was my man and Jude knew it, but neither of us could deny that a physical attraction still lingered between us. It had been months since my body had reacted to his presence, but the air crackled around our fingertips and I nearly sighed in relief when he finally let go.

Vicky came into the kitchen for a second cup of tea, and as soon as my coffee was reheated, I scurried out of the room like a teenage girl caught making out with her boyfriend in the backseat of the family car.

"I'm only responding to Jude because I miss Sean," I mumbled once I'd reached the sanctuary of my office. My hot cheeks and clammy palms belied the truth of this statement. Jude was gorgeous. He was smart. He was sweet. And he was a womanizer. He was never going to be good for me. I didn't want to expend another ounce of energy thinking about him.

Sitting primly in my chair, I focused on another email containing requested material. These were the first three chapters of T. J. West's cozy mystery. His was set in a charming lakeside town, and I remembered the vivid setting as well as the plucky heroine—a widow who ran the town's bed and breakfast. West called himself a medical professional, but he had attended culinary school and was a self-professed handyman. As a result, his cozy was replete with do-it-yourself home repair tips and included a tantalizing recipe section. He'd emailed a few recipes for me to peruse, and my stomach gurgled in appreciation as I scanned over the directions for preparing vegetable barley soup, bacon-wrapped maple pork loin, and gingerbread cake.

I spent the remainder of the morning reading West's first three chapters. I had my doubts that a male writer could successfully pull off the voice of a feisty young widow, but West did it in spades. Not only did he create a rich, interesting heroine, but there were also sprinkles of romance and a splash of humor in those first three chapters. The only mistake he made resided within his synopsis. At the pitch session he'd mentioned that a child's toy would play a role in the murderer's capture. I'd responded by advising him to alter that clue, but he hadn't made the change. Cozy readers don't like children to be closely associated to a murder case, and while Ashley Buckland's Men at Home series included kids, they were never present when violence occurred. Buckland's kids remained in the background, which was where they belonged.

I was just explaining this in an email to T. J. West when my fingers froze over the keyboard. Turning back to his synopsis, I reread the brief description of the child's toy. "A beloved yellow teddy bear," were the exact words.

Instantly, the photograph of the plush Winnie the Pooh clasped in Melissa's dead hand flashed in front of my eyes.

"No," I whispered to my computer screen, my eyes locked on T. J. West's email address. "You're a harmless mystery writer. You have nothing to do with that picture of Silas's bear. It's just a crazy coincidence and proof that I need a lunch break."

I sent off the email, shouldered my purse, and was trying to decide whether to grab a sandwich at Catcher in the Rye or head to the hot food bar at How Green Was My Valley when Vicky's voice came over my phone's speaker.

"Ms. Wilkins, Ms. Burlington-Duke would like a word with you," she said succinctly.

"Right now?"

There was the briefest of pauses. "Ms. Burlington-Duke did not specify a time, but I was under the impression she meant for you to appear in her office within the next five minutes."

"Then I'm on my way. Thanks."

Vicky didn't reply, and I decided to bring my purse into my boss's office. Maybe Bentley would realize that I was on my way out and would keep our impromptu meeting short and sweet.

No such luck.

Bentley was on the phone when I poked my head into her office, but she raised a regal finger, silently ordering me to wait until she was done. She then wiggled the same finger in a downward motion, indicating that I should take a seat. She obviously didn't care if I overheard her conversation.

Twirling the tip of a resplendent mustard-hued Hermès scarf, Bentley frowned as she listened to the person on the other end of the line. Finally, she sighed in impatience and stated, "While I am happy to do my part in reporting my findings, I don't expect to be inconvenienced in this manner. Please inform Officer Griffiths that I am willing to discuss this matter via telephone or email, but should he wish to speak to someone in person, he should contact Lila Wilkins, one of my agents here at Novel Idea. Good day."

A man spluttered indignantly at the other end of the line before Bentley severed the connection.

"With buffoons such as that on the force it's no wonder the crime rate has escalated." Bentley flicked an imaginary speck of dust from her black suit and replaced the opal and diamond earring she'd removed during her call. "I was merely trying to pass on information regarding Ruben Felden, but that Neanderthal didn't seem to know the first thing about the Melissa Plume case or which of his fellow officers did."

My hunger forgotten, I dumped my purse on the floor and gave Bentley my undivided attention. "I'd be glad to deliver the report on your behalf," I assured her hastily.

"Good." She handed me a piece of paper. "This is Mr. Felden's flight itinerary, faxed to me by his assistant a few minutes ago."

I examined the neat bullet points typed on the sheet. According to this document, Ruben Felden had flown to Chicago on Friday and returned late last night. "If this checks out, then he's off the suspect list," I said. "Did his assistant happen to mention why he went to Chicago?"

"Yes, she was most helpful." Bentley paused and a look of disapproval crossed her face. "Though if she'd discussed *my* affairs so openly with a stranger, I'd have her fired on the spot."

"Of course. But what did she tell you?" I prompted.

"Ruben's aunt has been in declining health for the past few months. He received a call at work Friday morning that she was fading quickly, so he rushed from the office and took the first flight out. His aunt died on Saturday and Ruben was very distressed by her passing. Too distressed to call his assistant on Monday to say that he'd be absent. She found his itinerary through his work email."

I glanced at the itinerary. The scant lines in my hand represented another loss. Albeit a natural death, Melissa's coworker had obviously cared for his aunt and I felt a pang of sympathy for him.

As if reading my thoughts, Bentley said, "Apparently the aunt raised him and worked two jobs in order to pay for his college education. He stayed in Chicago for the funeral and to pack up some of her belongings before returning to New York."

"Poor man," I murmured.

Bentley wasn't interested in the editor's sorrows. "Ruben's assistant told me that he'd indeed been angry with Melissa. One of their authors, an established writer of bestselling women's fiction whose name the assistant actually refused to divulge, originally signed with Ruben. However, she was uncomfortable having a man edit her work and begged Melissa to take over her contract."

"But Melissa couldn't do that, could she?"

"No, that would have been completely inappropriate. However, the editorial director of the publishing house could, and in the interest of keeping this author happy, transferred the contract to Melissa."

I could see how such a decision would serve to wound Ruben's pride and told Bentley as much.

She shrugged dispassionately. "This is a business, Lila. And a tough one at that. Eventually, Ruben would have recognized that keeping this author content and pumping out bestselling novels was worth more to the company than his ego."

"Sounds like Ruben Felden hasn't had the best of times lately," I mused. "But if his flight confirmation checks out, then at least he won't be considered a murder suspect. I'll tell Sean—uh, Officer Griffiths—what you've told me and drop this fax off at the station later this afternoon." I thanked Bentley for finding out about Ruben and headed off to lunch.

After loading a plate with roast chicken, mashed potatoes, and honey-glazed carrots at the grocery store's hot food bar, I selected a small café table near the windows and tried to read a few query letters. However, I started thinking about Melissa's murder instead. My look-alike hadn't been killed by a disgruntled coworker or her husband. More than ever, I was certain that Kirk Mason was responsible.

I recalled how I'd felt when he'd dropped the black feather on my table during the pitch session. He wore menace like it was yet another body piercing, and I'd been instinctively afraid of him.

If I'd had enough sense to feel fear, then why had a woman as smart and savvy as Melissa followed him into a dark and deserted corridor? Even though she'd received the photograph of her son's teddy bear, what had driven her to meet an obviously unstable man all alone? A significant piece of the puzzle was missing, but I didn't know what more I could do other than relay the information about Ruben to Sean.

My meal devoured, I dialed his number. Once more I was disappointed and to be honest, a little irritated to be put through to his voicemail. I gave him an abbreviated account of Ruben's activities during the weekend Melissa had been killed and said that I'd be happy to drop the fax off at the station, but I'd rather do so when I knew he'd be there.

Returning to the office, I tried to be as industrious as I'd been during the morning, but failed. As if in tune with my recollections of Kirk Mason, the slate gray sky darkened into a shade of charcoal and it began to rain. I sat at my desk, wondering how I'd concentrate on query letters when I felt so distant from the people I cared about. Trey was busy at the co-op, Sean was tied up with the case, and lately, my mother only called me when she didn't have clients to see.

And yet, my case of the blues was nothing in comparison to what Melissa's husband and son were experiencing. For them, the immediate future was like the sky over Inspiration Valley: sunless, bleak, and filled with tears.

By midafternoon I had a crick in my neck. I stretched my arms high, reaching for the ceiling to unfurl the tension, when Flora knocked on my open door.

"Oh, Lila, I'm sorry to interrupt. Could you do me a favor?" She held up a spiral-bound notebook that I recognized as Tilly's by its bright pink cover. "I called Tilly to tell her I had this and she's frantic to have it back today. I'd run it over, but I can't leave my desk as I'm waiting for an important phone call. Do you mind?" She pointed to a Post-it note stuck on the cover. "That's her address."

"Sure, Flora. I welcome the distraction." Taking the notebook from her, I said, "I can't really ride my Vespa there in the rain, though. I'll call my mother and see if I can borrow her truck." I could also take the opportunity to drop the fax off at the police station, and at the same time sit with the sketch artist to render a likeness of Kirk Mason. Perhaps Sean would have returned by then.

My mother answered the phone at the first ring and agreed to pick me up at the agency. "I was about to leave for Dunston myself. I'll be there in two shakes of a lamb's tail and you can tag along to see that policeman of yours." Once again, Amazing Althea was close to the mark. It occurred to me that, since I'd moved to Inspiration Valley, my skepticism about her powers had lessened. If only those powers could help us nail Melissa's murderer.

"Thanks, Mama. I have some errands to run while we're in Dunston. Is that okay?"

"That works out fine, honey. You can take the truck after droppin' me at ol' Miz Margaret's. She's bedridden now but still needs my guidance." She coughed importantly. "You can collect me when I'm done and then we can go to Bill's Bar and Grill. I'll be needin' plenty of Jimmy Beam's special brand of reenergizer after readin' for Miz Margaret."

She sounded cheerful about the supper plan, and I realized she was probably delighted to have a designated driver.

The rain had stopped by the time we reached Dunston, although the sky remained stubbornly gray. I delivered my mother to Miss Margaret, my ears buzzing with her predictions and advice, and headed for the Dunston police station. Even though I was dating Sean, I'd only visited this place twice.

Climbing the steps, I recalled the first time I'd been here, when Trey had been in trouble for destroying school property, and subsequently when I came to give an official statement regarding violence and death. I shuddered at the memories, and then, as if by divine intervention, the clouds in the sky drifted apart and the afternoon sun shone brightly overhead.

Those incidents were behind me, and today I was here to deliver a document that would exonerate one man and hopefully bring the police closer to arresting a guilty one. I squared my shoulders and pushed open the door.

The young policewoman at the front desk smiled as I approached. "Can I help you?"

"Is Officer Griffiths in?"

She shook her head. "Sorry. He's out on a case. Do you want me to call his partner?"

"No, could you just please give this to him?" I handed her the envelope containing the fax from Ruben Felden's office. "Tell him Lila brought it by. I also need to meet with the sketch artist."

"Oh, *you're* Lila! Griffiths has been smiling much more since you two got together." Giving me a sisterly wink, she stood and said, "Follow me."

I drove out of the parking lot in good spirits, despite revisiting the image of Kirk Mason, thanks to the policewoman's words and the sun now shining through the clouds. Being on the streets in Dunston felt unaccountably strange, considering it had been a mere six months since I'd left. I felt so settled in Inspiration Valley that it was as if my Dunston life belonged to an entirely different person. My situation was very different now, with Trey out of the house, me in my cozy yellow cottage, and my job as a literary agent. Perhaps Dunston had just been a stepping-stone to the life I was meant to live.

I turned onto a tawny-colored pebbled driveway in front of a pretty white house and parked the truck. This was a lovely treed neighborhood with beautiful houses and well-maintained gardens bursting with blossoms of chrysanthemums, zinnias, ageratum, and roses. Autumn-colored leaves added vibrancy to the green manicured lawns. The large homes had varied façades, some with red brick, others with colored siding; all were affluent. As I stepped out of Althea's rusty pickup, I felt a little conspicuous.

The path that led to Tilly's house was pebbled like her driveway, and it ended at steps leading up to a welcoming porch. One end was screened in, with windows half open and white wicker furniture with puffy floral cushions arranged around a small table. I could imagine how delightful it would be to sit there and read. Large windows framed by forest green shutters looked out onto the veranda, and as I glanced in one, I noticed Tilly sitting at a desk typing away on a computer.

Wanting to avoid appearing as if I were eavesdropping, I quickly approached the door and rang the bell.

"Hello!" Tilly exclaimed when she'd opened the door. "Flora told me you'd stop by. Thank you so much for bringing my notebook. I don't know how I could have left it behind."

"No problem. I had other errands in Dunston," I said, handing her the pink-covered book, which she accepted and immediately hugged tightly to her chest.

"Would you like to come in? I was just about to have some hot cocoa, and I baked oatmeal cookies this morning."

I shook my head. "I don't want to keep you from your work . . ."

"Please, I was ready for a break anyway. Besides, the kids will be home from school soon and I try not to write when they're here." She held the door open wide and gestured inside.

As I didn't need to pick Althea up for another half hour, I decided to accept Tilly's offer. "Well, those cookies do sound tempting," I said as I stepped across the threshold. Tilly peered anxiously down the street before shutting the door.

Inside, light poured in from the windows, reflecting off glistening wood floors laid with intricately woven rugs. I followed her to the kitchen, where the scent of baked cookies hung in the air. I immediately felt at home. The cream-colored walls were covered in framed children's artwork, which coordinated very well with the beautifully grained cherry cabinets, stainless steel appliances, and coffee-colored granite counter-tops. A vase with a brilliant bouquet of gerbera daisies sat in the center of the table.

"How many kids do you have?" I asked, inspecting a vibrant painting of fish in the sea.

"Two. Peter and Emma are twins; they're nine. They've been the joy of my life," she said as she placed two milk-filled mugs in the microwave. "Would you like some whipped cream on your hot chocolate?"

"Yes, please." I nodded. "I know what you mean. I have one son who's almost eighteen, and he has enriched my life in innumerable ways." I smiled ruefully. "Of course, there were the teenage years . . ." I let my sentence hang in the air.

Tilly laughed. "Oh, I'm not saying there aren't challenges. But my kids fulfill me." Having arranged a tray with two mugs and a plate of cookies, she picked it up and asked, "Shall we sit in the screened porch? It's warm enough now that the sun's out. Then we can see the school bus coming."

I held the door for her, and we nestled into the wicker chairs as we sipped our hot chocolate. I inhaled the fresh air and listened to the sparrows twittering in the tree behind me.

"It's lovely out here," I said.

She nodded. "I know. I can't believe how lucky

I am. I have a wonderful husband, two fantastic kids, an amazing home. And now, to top it off, a successful writing career. I don't know what I did to deserve all this."

"You must be a good person," I suggested, gazing at her. Her dark eyes filled me with the same disquiet I'd felt when I first met her at the pub. What was it about her that unsettled me?

A shadow crossed her face. "I used to be different." She glanced over her shoulder, her features pinched. "Remember yesterday when I said I felt like I was being watched? I still feel like that. Did you see anybody on your way here? Other than that group of moms waiting for the school bus?"

I scanned the street, paying particular attention to the clusters of trees and shady bushes. At the corner three women stood chatting. A black cat walked up the brick driveway across the street. "No."

"I don't know if I'm becoming paranoid or if my suspicions are rational. Either way, I can't shake this creepy feeling."

I was uncertain how to respond. I didn't know her well enough to determine if her paranoia was unfounded. Instead of speaking, I took a bite of my cookie.

Tilly put her mug down and continued. "I keep seeing the same man wherever I go. I don't know who he is, but I saw him at the book festival, too.

He looks nice enough, I guess. He has short hair, glasses, and dresses neatly." She shrugged. "It's probably a coincidence. I see lots of the same people around here. Dunston isn't that big."

At that moment, a yellow school bus pulled up at the corner, and a group of children poured down the steps, dispersing with their mothers. A boy and a girl, both wearing backpacks, ran toward us. The boy was waving a sheet of paper as he bounded up the steps.

"Mom, look at my math test!" He handed her the page on which a big, red "100%" had been written. He bounced from one foot to the other.

"Wow, Peter, that's awesome!" She gave it back to him. "Want to put it on the fridge?"

He nodded vigorously and ran inside, slamming the door behind him. The girl stepped close to her mother's chair.

"Who's this lady, Mom?" she asked. Wearing embroidered jeans and a pink flowered T-shirt, the girl's brown chin-length hair was pulled away from her face with a pink barrette. The resemblance to her mother was uncanny. She had the same dark eyes that seemed inexplicably familiar to me.

"This is Miss Lila, Emma. She's a friend of Miss Flora. You remember Miss Flora? She helps sell my books."

Emma nodded and extended her arm toward me. "Pleased to meet you, Miss Lila."

"And I'm happy to meet you, too," I said, shaking her warm little hand.

She shrugged off her backpack, dropping it to the floor, and reached for a cookie. "Can I?" she asked, directing her gaze to her mother.

"Of course." Tilly put her arm around Emma's shoulders and hugged her.

I stood. "I should go. I know what after-school time is like. Thanks for the hot chocolate and cookies. They were delicious."

"It was my pleasure." Tilly walked me down the steps to the truck with Emma trailing behind her. "Thanks for bringing my notebook to me."

The driver's door creaked as I opened it. "This is my mother's truck," I said, feeling the need to explain why I was driving a bright turquoise vehicle bearing magnetic signs proclaiming the Amazing Althea. I climbed in, and Tilly and Emma headed back to the house.

Pulling the seat belt across my chest, I waved at them as they went inside. Tilly had an idyllic life. Not only were her books taking off, but she had a beautiful home, a successful marriage, and adorable children. Why was her contentment being marred by a sudden case of paranoia? *Was* someone watching her? Or did she have deeper psychological issues?

Unable to answer these questions, I backed the truck out of the driveway. Pushing the gear stick to drive, my peripheral vision caught a flash of black from behind a thick oak tree near where the school bus had stopped. I glanced over, but saw nothing. Slowly, I drove in the direction of the tree, keeping a sharp eye out for any sign of movement.

I pulled up at the curb in the spot where the school bus had dropped off the children and opened the driver's door. "Who's there?" I called. No one answered. I jumped out of the truck and approached the tree. The sky darkened as a cloud drifted over the sun, and the large oak loomed ominously overhead. I scrutinized the tall laurel hedge beside it.

A door slammed, making me jump, and I quickly turned in the direction of the sound. Two boys walked out of a nearby house carrying skateboards. A rustling in the shrubbery behind me caught my attention, and I whipped back around in time to catch a glimpse of a shadow disappearing around the corner of the street. My heart pumping wildly, I ran to the intersection.

Scanning the sidewalks, I saw only children playing, a woman walking a poodle, and a large tabby cat sauntering on the curb, its tail twitching. There was no sinister presence. Yet someone had been hiding in the bushes. I felt it in my bones. Tilly wasn't just being paranoid. She *was* being watched.

Chapter 11

Usually my mother smiled from ear to ear when presented with the country fried steak platter from Bill's Bar and Grill, but she quietly thanked our server and then sat staring at her food with indifference.

"Not hungry?" I asked, eyeing the gravy-smothered mass on her plate with mild distaste. I'd never cared for the dish that had put this place on the map and always opted for the spicy catfish po'boy, which came with a side of slaw and a mound of sweet potato fries.

Picking up her fork, my mother pressed the metal tines against the pads of her fingertips. I could tell that her mind was on other things besides her food. "I'm afraid I've brought a dark cloud to supper, hon."

Noting that she had ordered a mixture of lemonade and iced tea in lieu of whiskey, my concern grew. I'd planned on telling her about my visit to Tilly's and that I thought I might have seen a figure lurking near the writer's home, but seeing that my mother was not herself, I decided not to mention the worrisome subject.

She was gazing blankly at some point in the middle distance, and I gently waved my hand in front of her face to bring her back to the present. "Did something happen during your reading?"

"Only at the end," she said after blinking a few times. "I laid out the cards and asked Miz Margaret to think of a question she'd like answered. Most of the time, she's frettin' over one of her kids. I think havin' them live so far away is tough on her. She's awfully lonely, and if you ask me, they don't call her near enough."

I pictured the elderly, housebound woman sitting expectantly by the phone and shook my head in sympathy. "That's sad. She has a care-giver though, right?"

My mother nodded. "Sure. The kids send money and hire plenty of help for her. They're right good about that, but there are other ways of carin' for folks. The most important ways." She put her palm over her heart. "If one of those kids doesn't step up, that old gal is gonna keep fadin'. She's gettin' real depressed." After sprinkling some pepper on her fried steak, she continued. "But there were good signs in her cards today. Her son, I think, is gonna get her trained to use a computer so they can email. He's always on his BlackBerry and he'll reach out to her a couple of times a day once this happens."

"That sounds like a great solution for both of them," I said, hoping my mother would perk up.

"Go on and take a bite. Your food is getting cold."

Absently, she did so. "The problem came at the end of the readin'. Once I knew good news was on the way for Miz Margaret, I'm ashamed to admit that my thoughts wandered. I started thinkin' about Trey and about that woman who got killed. The one who looked so much like you that my blood practically turned to ice when I saw her picture in the paper. She—"

"Her name was Melissa Plume," I interjected. I didn't want her to be referred to as "that woman" or "the victim." My mother hadn't meant any harm, but it was important to me that Melissa be remembered as an individual and not just a cold and impersonal noun.

"Melissa." She spoke her name with respect. "I was layin' cards down into the Future position, but they weren't meant to speak to Miz Margaret's future because I was focusin' on you and Trey."

I hated to ask, but it was clear that my mother needed to tell me about those cards. "What were they? Our Future cards?"

"The immediate Future was the Tower. It's a card of ill omen," she explained heavily. "Shows a tall tower that's been hit by lightning. People are runnin' for their lives or fallin' from the heights. It's a warnin', Lila, probably to both you and Trey. And it's serious."

I didn't like the sound of that. The shadow I'd

seen near Tilly's house seemed to fill the room. Despite the din of the other diners and the innocuous setting, I felt vulnerable.

"The Emperor came next. It's not a scary card. He influences folks. Can be a benevolent father figure or a mentor. But this Emperor was in reverse. He's manipulating his authority and that made me think of Jasper. And he can be dangerous, like the man who took Melissa's life. I reckon both of those men have discovered a new and dark power in themselves. It's twisted them, made them wicked—each in their own way." She put down her fork and grabbed my hand. "They've got to be stopped before the Tower's omen comes to pass."

Whether I believed in the cards or not didn't matter. My mother did and she was obviously in distress. I glanced around for our waiter. If ever Amazing Althea needed a shot of Jim Beam, it was now. As I searched the room, my gaze fell upon a familiar figure seated at the bar.

I'd only met him once, but I remembered the average-looking man from our pitch session at the book festival. It was T. J. West, the author whose proposal I'd read and responded to earlier in the day. I studied his plain countenance and steel-rimmed glasses, the tidiness of his short hair, blue button-down shirt, and brown slacks. He seemed to fit Tilly's brief description of the man she kept seeing around Dunston. Then again, hundreds of men could qualify as dressing "neatly" and looking "nice enough."

And yet, West had mentioned a teddy bear in his synopsis. He'd written about a murdered mother and placed a teddy bear next to her dead body. Was that truly coincidental or had West known Melissa Plume? Was it possible that he was now stalking Tilly?

With a shudder, I suddenly recalled how the cozy writer wouldn't tell me his real name, referring to himself only by his pseudonym. That was definitely strange. I probably would have pushed the point had the ceiling not started leaking in the middle of his pitch.

Having seen me craning my neck, our waiter headed over to the table, successfully distracting me from a host of confusing thoughts. I ordered a whiskey for my mother and then decided to go and say hello to T. J. West. I leaned in toward her and told her that someone I knew was sitting at the bar. "Do you mind if I talk to him for a second? It's important."

My mother gave me a wan smile. "Of course not, shug. I'm gonna eat this meal if it kills me. You know how I can't stand to see food go to waste."

"And I'm taking what you said about the cards to heart," I quickly assured her. "Perhaps there's more I can do to help catch Melissa's killer. And you're right about Trey. It's high time we put our heads together and find out what exactly is going on at the co-op. I've been worried about that boy, but if you sense real danger, then I've got to do more than worry. I've got to act."

Because my mother was satisfied that I was responding to her warning instead of ignoring it, she encouraged me to go speak with West. I cast a quick glance toward the bar again and saw that he was gone.

When I didn't move, my mother looked at me quizzically. "Did he slip away while we were gabbin'?"

I tried to conceal the alarm I felt over his sudden disappearance. From my vantage point, I could see that West hadn't finished either his beer or his cheeseburger but had deposited cash next to a crumpled napkin. His barstool hadn't been pushed in and his fork and knife had been tossed unceremoniously on his plate. All these signs indicated that he'd been in a rush to leave.

Picking at my own sandwich, I tried to concentrate on my mother's plan to lure Trey away from the co-op by sending him on a tour of Europe. She offered me a big chunk of her savings to make this happen, and though I was deeply touched by the offer, I shook my head in refusal.

"He has to give up Red Fox Mountain voluntarily," I insisted. "And there's no argument for him to do that until we discover what's amiss. However, I have an idea of how to address this issue. It will require Trey's involvement, so the decision will ultimately be his."

I put forth a scheme to infiltrate the co-op by hiring one of Trey's former high school class-mates. I'd give this boy money to pay for a meditation session with Jasper, and he could then report back to us about what really went on inside the restricted building.

My mother wasn't pleased. Her mouth formed a severe frown. "Lila, we could be sendin' that boy into a precarious situation. Would you want Trey to agree to such a crazy plan? I doubt it."

Her comment gave me pause. I'd certainly be upset if a strange woman hired my son to investi-gate a potentially unstable commune leader. On the other hand, our actions might prevent other college students from falling victim to Jasper's power. I didn't know how he was attracting these kids, but he was doing something to encourage them to skip class, hike up the mountain, and pay an exorbitant fee for a few minutes of reflection.

"I wouldn't want an adult in a position of authority to take advantage of Trey, either, and that's what Jasper is doing. I'm certain of it. Think of all the kids that have been funneling into Inspiration Valley. If you can think of anything else I can do to protect them, I'm open to ideas."

But she couldn't come up with an alternative and we agreed that I should talk strategy with Trey first thing in the morning.

"He's gonna stop by the agency tomorrow anyway," my mother assured me, looking much less troubled now that we were taking action. "He's been missin' you lately. I have, too. I liked it when we were all under the same roof."

I smiled at her. "It was nice, but we all need our own space. I love my cottage and I'm still hoping that Trey will head off to college in January. He can't defer his admission beyond that." I gazed fondly at my mother. "But we should do *this* more often. Have a regular girls' night. Just you and me. I don't want any distance to come between us because I moved a few miles down the road. You're important to me, Mama."

At this poignant moment my cell phone buzzed. I'd set it to vibrate before entering the restaurant, but when I saw Sean's number floating in the rectangular screen, I excused myself and rushed to the foyer to answer his call.

"Hi, stranger," I said.

His sigh echoed through my phone's speaker. "Stranger, huh? It's been too long, hasn't it? Sometimes I hate this job because the bad guys just won't turn themselves in like I wish they would. If they'd only cooperate, you and I could go out for a nice, leisurely dinner. We could talk about anything other than police work over an enormous steak and a really good bottle of wine."

"I have a decent merlot at home," I offered. "Are you still on the clock?"

"Yes." His regret was tangible.

Thinking fast, I said, "If I told you that I hadn't left Dunston yet and that I had information that might be relevant to the case, could you meet me at Bill's Bar and Grill?"

"Absolutely." The delight in Sean's voice was unmistakable. "See you in five minutes."

Grinning like a fool, I went back inside and was surprised to see my mother pouring the contents of her whiskey tumbler into a take-out cup. "I'll drink this when I get home," she said with a smirk. "You don't need me hangin' around like a third wheel. You and your hunky policeman need some alone time."

Despite my protests over her swift departure and the fact that she was carrying whiskey home in a foam cup, my mother called for the check, handed the waiter a few bills, and kissed me on the cheek.

"Call me after you see Trey tomorrow," she commanded and then headed out into the night.

I resumed my seat and finished my sandwich. Suddenly, I was starving, and I didn't want to wolf my food down in front of Sean. As it turned out, he'd already eaten so we both ordered decaf cappuccinos.

Behaving like a pair of smitten teenagers, we held hands across the table and couldn't stop smiling at each other. I drank in the blue of Sean's eyes and reveled in the touch of his fingertips. He told me about his day and we both shared a laugh over a joke one of his fellow officers had told him over lunch. He then thanked me for the fax and assured me that Ruben's story checked out. The bereaved editor had definitely been in Chicago and dozens of people could attest to this fact.

I was relieved on Ruben's behalf, but the mention of his name brought an end to our jovial mood. We tried to cling to it as long as possible, but as soon as I raised the subject of Tilly and her stalker, Sean's eyes lost their merry twinkle and became dark with concern.

"And you saw someone near her house? A man or a woman?"

I shook my head. "I can't be that specific. It was a movement. A shadow. But I'm pretty sure someone was there. Tilly thinks she's been followed since the book festival." I wondered if I should mention that T. J. West fit Tilly's description of the man she'd repeatedly seen around town. However, I decided that it would be unfair to put West on Sean's radar without a scrap of evidence that he'd done something wrong.

"Is there a connection between Tilly and Melissa?" Sean asked, his gaze keen. I could practically hear his mind churning. "They're both in the book business."

"I don't know," I said. "Tilly's books aren't put out by Melissa's publishing company, but the fact that they were both at the book festival

232

might mean something. Flora's her agent, so you could get Tilly's professional history from her."

"I'm going to take you home now," Sean said with a tinge of regret. "But we'll go by Tilly's house first. I want to make sure that no one is lurking around before we leave Dunston."

At that moment I felt such a strong rush of affection for my dedicated policeman that I stood, leaned over the table, and kissed him on the mouth. People turned and smiled at us and Sean looked pleasantly surprised.

"What was that for?"

"For being Tilly's knight in shining armor, even though she doesn't know it. Most people would think she's just another eccentric artist with a flair for drama, but you only care about her being scared. You're ready to leap to her defense within seconds of hearing her plight." I caressed his cheek, feeling the stubble along his strong jawline. "I am a lucky woman."

Sean sighed happily. "This makes all the bad coffee, night shifts, stakeouts, paperwork, and lousy pay worthwhile. Let's go chase the shadows away from Tilly's place. And after that, I'll check *your* closet for monsters before tucking you into bed."

In Tilly's neighborhood, the streetlamps cast a warm incandescence onto the sidewalks and road. Some of the houses were dark, but most of them had lights on, giving the community a welcoming feel despite the darkness of the night.

Scrutinizing the shadows while he drove, Sean pulled up in front of Tilly's house and parked. He kissed me and said quietly, "Wait here while I look around." Patrolling up and down the sidewalk, he peered around trees and bushes and scanned the houses on the other side of the street. He ventured up Tilly's driveway and surveyed the hedge at the side of the garage.

Colored lights from a flat-screen TV shimmered through the bay window at the front of the house. I could see Tilly on the couch with Peter leaning against her. Her husband relaxed on a recliner with Emma on his lap. The tableau filled me with a sense of nostalgia, transporting me to a time when Trey was Peter's age. We used to cuddle up on the couch just like Tilly and her son, watching reruns of *Murder, She Wrote*. Trey would snuggle in closer during suspenseful scenes, and we'd make a game of trying to figure out "whodunit" before Jessica Fletcher.

"Well, it all seems peaceful around the neighborhood." Sean's entry into the car pulled me back to the present. "There doesn't seem to be anything suspicious; no one is lurking in the bushes. I think you can rest easy tonight." Sean touched my knee and then started the car.

"Especially with you nearby," I said, leaning over to kiss his cheek.

By contrast, everything was dark when we drove up the driveway of my cozy yellow cottage. I had left no lights on that morning when I went to work and hadn't been home since.

"Looks a little gloomy," I observed. "After Tilly's."

"We'll soon have it glowing." Sean reached for my hand and gave it a gentle squeeze before opening his door. I pulled my door handle, and suddenly his police radio squawked, crackling an indiscernible code. With an apologetic look in my direction, he responded to the dispatcher. "My ETA is twenty minutes." He then cradled my face in his hands, gently brushing his lips against mine. "I'm so sorry, Lila. I really need to go."

Disappointed, I nodded and tried not to show my frustration at how his job always seemed to interfere with our plans. "I understand." I sighed. "At least we were able to have cappuccinos together."

In the office that Thursday, I threw myself into work while waiting for Trey to arrive. At the same time, I tried to avoid the thoughts that had troubled my sleep during the night. I loved being with Sean, and we were good together, but the demands of his job were preventing us from taking our connection to the next level. It was true that the qualities that made him such a special man—his compassion and kindness, his strength and loyalty—were also what made him a great cop. Still, I was beginning to wonder about the future of our relationship.

I was reading a unique proposal for a paranormal mystery about a woman who'd sprouted wings when there was a knock on the door.

"Mom?" Trey stepped over the threshold. "I hope I'm not interrupting. Nana said you'd be expecting me."

I smiled broadly at the other man in my life and walked around my desk to hug him. "Not at all, Trey. You can interrupt me anytime." I was about to suggest that we go downstairs to Espresso Yourself, but then thought better of it, since I was planning to propose a clandestine operation to my son. "Can I get you a coffee from the kitchen?" I asked instead.

"No, thanks. I've stopped drinking caffeine. It's totally addictive, you know."

Raising my eyebrows at what were probably Iris's words coming out of my son's mouth, I gestured toward my guest chair. "So what's up?" I asked as I lowered myself into my own seat.

"Oh, nothing specific. Just wanted to hang out with you for a bit . . ." His voice trailed off. "I'm feeling kind of unsure about things at the co-op. Like, how long I want to stay there? And if it's really what I want to do with my life."

I tried to keep my expression neutral in order

to not reveal how much this delighted me. If he were beginning to question his future at the co-op, then perhaps he would seriously consider going to college in January. "Have things changed that much for you? You were so fulfilled at first," I ventured.

"*Some* things are good," he said, his cheeks flushing pink, and I knew he was thinking of Iris. "But like I told you before, the meditation center is off-limits to me and that makes me feel like an outsider. I mean, I'm either a member or I'm not, right?"

I nodded. "I can imagine how being excluded would make it seem that way." Folding my hands on the desk, I leaned forward. "I have an idea of how we can figure out what's going on there."

"You do?" He looked up, his eyes bright. "It wouldn't get me or anyone else in trouble, would it?"

I knew his unvoiced concern was for Iris. "I can't imagine that it would. What if I hired one of your Dunston friends to go to Red Fox for a meditation session? I'd give him the money to pay for it, and he'd report back to us on what happens in there." I could see the wheels turning in Trey's mind as I spoke. "That way you could discover if it's in keeping with your philosophies and if you'd still want to stay there. Or not," I added quietly.

"You mean he'd, like, go undercover?"

"I guess you could say that."

He sat back in his chair. "It might work. But, Mom, those meditation sessions are pretty expensive. A couple of hundred bucks." He looked up at the ceiling, as if answers were written there. "I bet Jeff would do it. You remember Jeff Morgan, right?"

I did remember Jeff. He was one of the boys with whom Trey had gotten into trouble last spring for destroying school property. "Didn't he go away to college?"

"Nah. He said he decided not to go in the end, but I don't think he got accepted anywhere. Anyway, his dad gave him a job at the car dealership and then Jeff moved out and now he's living with his girlfriend." He nodded vigorously. "Yeah, Jeff'd definitely do it. How much would you pay him?"

"What would he expect?"

"I bet he'd do it for a hundred bucks." Trey looked at me with concern. "Can you afford three hundred dollars to do this, Mom?"

"Trey, I'd do anything to help you. You know that, right?"

He smiled sheepishly. "Yeah, I know."

"And it's worth it if it helps you to figure your life out."

Trey looked at his watch and stood. "I gotta go. I have a delivery to make in Dunston. I'll talk to Jeff while I'm there."

I walked him to the door and he turned to give me a big bear hug. "Thanks, Mom, for listening. And for having my back."

"You're welcome, Trey." I watched him as he headed for the lobby, feeling pride in how he was maturing. Abruptly, he stopped and turned.

"I forgot to ask about that college admissions deferment—how long is it good for?"

Despite my excitement over his question, I calmly replied, "Only until January. Are you thinking you might go after all?"

"Just considering all my options." He grinned and then was gone.

The next morning I entered Espresso Yourself in better spirits than I'd been in for a while. Having slept soundly the previous night and knowing that Trey was reconsidering his future had me feeling cautiously optimistic.

Makayla had just handed a coffee to a customer when she saw me. "Morning, girl. You're looking chipper as a chipmunk today."

"I am feeling good. Good enough to have a cranberry orange scone with my latte."

She reached for a cup. "Take a seat. I'll come and have breakfast with you."

When she brought our beverages and scones to the table, she handed me a copy of the *Dunston Herald*. "See this headline? Bad stuff happening in Dunston."

I unfolded the paper as she sat down. **Local Author Murdered!** screamed out from the front page. I felt as if my heart stopped beating for a second and I gaped at Makayla. "Do you know who?"

She shook her head. "Read me what it says."

Yesterday morning, local author Tilly Smythe was found murdered in her home.

My hands started to shake. "Makayla, I know her! I was at her house the other day." Taking a deep breath, I continued reading:

Her cleaning lady, Ms. Anna Clyde, arrived at the house at eleven a.m. and discovered Mrs. Smythe's body in the kitchen. According to a preliminary report from the medical examiner's office, the cause of death was strangulation. There was no sign of forced entry and no unknown persons were sighted in the neighborhood. Smythe, aged forty-four, was clutching a stuffed toy that might have been left behind by her assailant. Ms. Clyde did not recognize the teddy bear. "It doesn't belong to either of the children," she claimed emphatically.

I couldn't read any further. My eyes kept traveling over the words "clutching a stuffed toy." It was impossible to ignore the similarity of this morbid detail to T. J. West's proposal in which his victim had a teddy bear lying next to her. Nor could I ignore that Tilly had been seeing a man matching his description all over town. I myself had observed him at the bar in Dunston, and now his abrupt disappearance seemed especially suspicious. I suddenly found it difficult to breathe and dropped the newspaper. It fluttered to the table.

"Honey, you've gone white as a fish belly," Makayla said with concern. "Are you okay?"

I could barely get the words out. "I . . . I think I know who killed her," I croaked.

Makayla's eyes widened. "Who?"

"A writer. A harmless murder mystery writer. Or so I thought." I put my hands over my mouth as the horror of the situation hit me full force. Makayla wrapped her arm around my waist to steady me. "I was wrong," I murmured, staring at the newspaper and its dire headline. "God help me, but my mistake may have cost Tilly Smythe her life."

Chapter 12

Feeling sick to my stomach, I grabbed the newspaper and left a stunned Makayla sitting at the café table while I raced upstairs to my office. Vicky said something to me as I rushed by, but I ignored her.

There was a pounding in my head, like a rush of floodwaters, and it almost overpowered my ability to function. My whole body was trembling as I fell into my desk chair and dialed Sean's number.

"Please," I prayed into the receiver. "Please pick up."

He did, but his first words were a curt "I can't talk to you right now."

"You have to! It's about Tilly's murder," was my abrupt response. Suddenly, I released all the anger I felt over my own blindness at Sean. "I think I know who killed her, but if you're too busy to listen, let me speak to another officer!"

I could hear an intake of breath on the other end and I tensed, expecting Sean to lash out at me. Instead, he softly said, "Excuse me for a moment," to someone nearby and I realized that he hadn't been alone. The sound of a door closing came through the speaker and then Sean spoke again. "I was just about to interview Tilly's husband, Lila. I shouldn't have answered my phone, but . . . well, now that I have, tell me what you know."

The image of Tilly's husband, sitting grief-stricken and stunned beyond all reason in one of the department's interview rooms, filled me with shame. What was I doing, picking a fight with the one man who'd go to the ends of the earth to see that justice was served?

"I'm sorry," I said. My apology was not just for behaving like a petulant child, but also for not mentioning T. J. West to Sean the night before last. I knew there was no hope for atonement, as the damage was already done, but I could at least give the police a solid lead. "Tilly mentioned seeing a man around town. He fits the description of a writer I met during a pitch session at the book festival. Sean, the guy's manuscript contains details freakishly similar to Tilly's murder. I only know what I read in the *Dunston Herald*, but it was enough to give me chills."

"What's the writer's name?" Sean asked, his tone professional and direct.

"He only gave me his pseudonym, which is T. J. West. I have his email address and I'll ask Vicky to look up his mailing address. West must have put one on his registration form or we wouldn't have been able to send him materials for the book festival. Vicky probably has his credit card number or a copy of his check on file as well."

Sean sucked in a quick breath. "Can you email me this man's book? Right away?"

"I'll do better than that. I'll drive it to the station this minute. That way, I can show you the scene I mentioned without your having to hunt for it."

There was a pregnant pause and I feared that Sean didn't want me around right now. I couldn't begin to fathom what the last twenty-four hours had been like for him. I wondered when he'd first heard about Tilly's murder and was both surprised and hurt that I'd had to learn of her death by reading about it in the newspaper. Why hadn't he told me? How could he let me discover what happened to her like this? Did he care so little for me?

"Okay," he finally answered. "But I'm reluctant to have you come to Dunston. You've been through enough lately and I want to spare you any more pain."

I felt a rush of warmth. Sean hadn't called because he'd been trying to protect me. He knew that Melissa's death had taken its toll on me, but I was stronger than he realized and there was no chance of my standing aside. Not now. Not when I felt responsible for what happened to Tilly. "Sean, if I'd told you about West sooner, Tilly might be still alive. I deserve to feel pain. I'm coming in."

"You don't know that. I've told you before that it's dangerous to jump to conclusions." He instilled his voice with tenderness. "And, Lila?"

"Yes?"

"I know you're upset, so drive carefully," he cautioned gently. "That Vespa should only go so fast over mountain roads."

After promising to arrive in one piece, I printed out T. J. West's first three chapters, synopsis, and a copy of his original email. I then rushed out to Vicky's desk and asked her to look up the writer's address.

"It'll have to wait until I finish my current task. Ms. Burlington-Duke would like me to make a few phone calls for her." Vicky gave a satisfied tug to her charcoal gray cardigan.

Her self-possession rattled me. "Those phone calls can wait. This writer might be a murderer. He may very well have killed two women. Wives and mothers. So I need that address and I need it now." I was practically snarling.

Vicky studied me for a second, swiveled in her chair, and pulled open a file cabinet drawer. "His name?" Her tone was calm and even.

"T. J. West."

Her nimble fingers raced over meticulously labeled manila folders. She withdrew one and, without opening it, handed it to me. "Thank you," I said, shoving the folder into my laptop case. "And I'm sorry for how I spoke to you just now. I feel helpless and responsible and scared, like I have no control over anything."

Vicky gave me such a warm smile that the tears I'd been desperately trying to hold back nearly spilled onto my cheeks. "Don't worry, dear. You just do what you need to do." She hesitated and then reached into a desk drawer and drew forth a stainless steel flask. "I keep it for emergencies. Would you like a sip?"

I gaped in astonishment. Puritan Vicky, who wore starched blouses and orthopedic shoes, who drank herbal tea and refused to eat complex carbs, who ran the agency with the efficiency of a drill sergeant, kept a flask in her desk! The revelation forever endeared her to me and I managed a weak smile before politely refusing her offer.

"Everyone has secrets," I mumbled as I jogged down the steps and outside to where my scooter was parked. I didn't know the extent of T. J. West's secrets, but I knew that if anyone could unearth them and expose them to the light, it was Officer Sean Griffiths.

When I arrived at the police station, I had little sense of how long it had taken me to drive from Inspiration Valley to Dunston. My mind had been consumed with replaying the brief but pleasant moments I'd spent with Tilly. Over and over again, I pictured her face and the way her expression had vacillated between anxiety and then, upon seeing her children, joy.

I was still caught up in reflections of that afternoon when the police officer manning the front desk gave me a sober greeting and then told a pretty female cop standing nearby to take me back to Sean. She led me through a warren of corridors and dropped me off in a small conference room. A computer and a mug of black coffee were the only objects on the surface of the table, and sitting in a corner on the floor was a cardboard file box. I had just taken a seat and dug Vicky's file folder from my bag when Sean entered the room.

He looked terrible. His hair was uncombed, his cheeks and chin were dark with stubble, and his uniform was wrinkled. I wondered if he'd slept in it until his eyes met mine and I saw how bloodshot they were. He probably hadn't had a wink of sleep last night.

Murder weighed heavily on this man. And he saw all angles of it from the bodies stretched out on a coroner's slab, to the effect it had on loved ones, to the ripples it created in a community. He faced the ugliest parts of human nature without backing down. I was ashamed that I'd been feeling neglected because of Sean's job. What choice did he have with killers on the loose?

"Let me see what you've got," he said, wasting no time on pleasantries.

I showed him the address West had printed on his registration form, and Sean hurriedly examined the paper and then stuck his head into the hall and shouted, "Hastings! I need you to run an address for me!"

The other cop took the sheet, gave me a curious glance, and then said, "You want me to bring this joker in?"

Sean shook his head. "T. J. West isn't his real name. Get me that first. And let's see if he has any priors. I want an idea of what we're dealing with here. There's no telling if this is even our guy, so we'll spend a few minutes on a background check before we kick his front door down."

"Got it," Hastings said and hustled off.

"Now." Sean pointed at the short stack of papers I'd placed on the conference table. "Read me the murder scene."

I did as he asked, and while I read, he compared the details of T. J. West's fictional killing with the photographs and written reports from Tilly's real-life homicide.

"We've got a dead mother and a teddy bear. It's suspicious, but not enough to make me surround this guy's house with a SWAT team," Sean said when I was done. "West's victim was struck on the head by a blunt object. Mrs. Smythe was strangled."

I grabbed the pages and clutched them tightly in my hand. "But *Melissa* was hit with a brick. This description might not be a perfect match for

Tilly's death, yet it fits Melissa's. West has been around both women. And the teddy bear? That can't be pure coincidence."

"We can't assume that Melissa and Tilly were murdered by the same person, Lila, not without solid evidence, although it is certainly suspicious that two real-life murders as well as a fictional one involve a child's toy. We're going over to West's place, don't you worry. Still, I prefer not to charge in, guns blazing, without having all the facts first." His tone was patient, yet tinged with a hint of reproof.

But my guilt over possibly being complicit in Tilly's murder only served to increase the urgency of the situation. My hands clenched into tight fists around West's manuscript and I was on the verge of losing my composure and balling up each and every page. Luckily, Hastings burst into the room and waved a printout at Sean.

"Guy's real name is Thomas Jefferson Wipple and he's in a town house by the movie theater. One moving violation. That's it."

Sean raised his brows. "Thomas Jefferson Wipple? No wonder he used a pseudonym." Turning to me, he said, "We're going to pay Mr. Wipple a visit. Do you want to wait for me or go back to Inspiration Valley?"

"I'm not going anywhere," I said. Sean dipped his chin in acknowledgment and strode out of the room.

Left to my own devices, I spent the time rereading West's first fifty pages. It certainly didn't seem like the prose of a coldhearted killer. Even though my opinion on the author was completely tainted by this point, I still found his writing skillful, amusing, and entertaining. Could West really be capable of this kind of duplicity? It was hard to imagine that someone who could draw the character of the plucky widow with such sensitivity also harbored the ability to commit murder.

When I'd finished reading, I helped myself to the desktop computer and did a Google search on Thomas Jefferson Wipple. There were very few results. One was from the white pages and displayed his age, address, and phone number. For an additional fee, I could acquire his email address as well. I shook my head. There was no such thing as privacy anymore.

Another page listed forty-nine-year-old Thomas Jefferson as an active member of the Dunston Rotary Club, and a third site showed a photo of him participating in a walkathon benefiting the Make-A-Wish Foundation along with a group of other Dunston General Hospital employees. This led me to a search of the hospital's staff page, and I was able to locate Thomas Jefferson within a few clicks of the mouse. He was a registered nurse.

I sat back in the chair, confounded. Could this male nurse who wrote cozy mysteries and worked to improve his community truly be a murderer? It seemed impossible, and yet I knew it wasn't. Over the summer, I'd learned firsthand about the masks people wear and how there are those among us who are masters at the art of deception. Victor Hugo had once written, "Virtue has a veil, vice a mask," and while we all try to conceal our faults behind a façade, West had adopted a public life that made him look like a saint. But behind the polished veneer, he could very well be a killer.

A cop with a shock of red hair suddenly appeared in the threshold, thankfully keeping me from waxing philosophical any longer. "Griffiths here?" he asked.

"No, and I'm not sure when he'll be back," I said.

"I'm collecting cash for pizza. It's almost lunchtime and I know he hasn't eaten a thing since last night."

No wonder Sean looked so peaked. He'd had neither sleep nor food for far too long. Grabbing for my purse, I handed the redheaded officer a twenty. "Please get him a whole pie. And maybe a salad?"

The cop's mouth fell open in surprise, as if I'd ordered something utterly foreign. "A salad? Uh, yeah, I guess I can do that. Anything for you?"

I gave him a wan smile. "No appetite right now, but thanks."

Sean returned before I could make additional

headway in searching for tidbits on Thomas Jefferson Wipple. I found nothing to connect him to Melissa or to Tilly. Only Dunston united the three people.

"It's not him," Sean was quick to assure me. He sank down into a chair, his face ashen with exhaustion. "In fact, Mr. Wipple is as nice as they come. And he was quite disturbed to hear about the murders. Says he works with women all day and couldn't stand the thought of something happening to one of them. He was in the middle of a twelve-hour shift when Mrs. Smythe died and was at the book festival's costume party with a group of friends when Ms. Plume was murdered." Sean rubbed his eyes. "And it would have been difficult for him to sneak out seeing as he was dressed up as the Scarlet Pimpernel."

It was hard for me to contain my relief. The man I thought of as T. J. West hadn't been stalking Tilly. He wasn't a killer, but a kind and sensitive writer and caregiver. I no longer had to bear a feeling of responsibility for Tilly's death. I could also direct my anger where it belonged. "Kirk Mason." I spoke his name with loathing.

"The phantom festivalgoer who seems to have dropped off the face of the earth!" Sean threw out his hands in exasperation. "I've had men watching his house for days and there's no sign of him."

I narrowed my eyes. "Wait, are you telling me

252

that you've identified Kirk Mason?" Picturing his long, lean body, the dark eyes, and his silver piercings winking in the light, fear fed my anger.

Sean shifted uneasily in his chair. "Yes, but there was no sense in sharing that information with you. I didn't want you to be alarmed that we'd found his residence unoccupied, indicating that he was still at large."

Indignation uncoiled within me. "I had to read about Tilly's death in the paper and now *this?* I'd rather you were more forthcoming instead of trying to keep me in the dark. You think you're protecting me, but not knowing what's going on makes me feel much more vulnerable. Kirk Mason's probably killed two women, Sean. I don't want to be in the dark when it concerns him!"

"I read you loud and clear, but we don't have any evidence that the two murders are connected," Sean replied hastily, and then he took a deep breath and reached for my hand. "You're right, Lila. If Mason is the murderer he poses a threat to you. After all, you know what he looks like. That drawing you worked on with the sketch artist has been distributed, but no one we've spoken with has seen him. The guy doesn't have a driver's license. I have no idea how he gets around, but, unfortunately, if he was the shadow outside Tilly's house the day you were there, he might think that you're hunting him. Which, in a way, you are."

I tried to keep my alarm in check, but my fingers started trembling and Sean gripped them tighter.

"An officer has been watching you from a safe distance since yesterday morning," Sean assured me softly. "No one's getting near you, sweetheart."

Nodding, I looked away. Didn't Sean think I'd like to know that I was officially under police protection? How many other secrets was he keeping from me? I peered at Sean's concerned face and realized my ire was misdirected. I should focus my anger on Mason. If it weren't for him, Sean and I wouldn't be at odds and two women wouldn't have lost their lives. "What does Kirk Mason do? Does he have a job?"

"He's a software engineer," Sean said. "Apparently, he creates programs for smartphones. Works from home and brings in a nice salary. He recently completed some big project and informed his employers that he was taking the week off. He left his cell phone behind, and the neighbors don't know where he went or the names of any of his friends or family members."

"Can't you search his house?" I asked.

Sean shrugged his shoulders and frowned. "We don't have any evidence. I can't obtain a warrant without probable cause, and right now, all I have is a name." He let go of my hand and rubbed his temples. "I've called airlines, rental car companies, and dozens of North Carolina residents with the last name 'Mason.' This guy is like smoke. I can't pin him down."

We fell silent, and I sensed that Sean and I were both feeling angry, helpless, and frustrated. It was the Information Age. People couldn't just disappear, could they? As I struggled over this question, the smell of hot pizza wafted through the air. "Delivery for Griffiths!" The redheaded cop who'd taken my twenty carried a pizza box in one hand and a plastic take-out bag in the other. "Meat lovers' supreme and a Greek salad, per the lady's orders. Enjoy."

Sean pried back the box lid and inhaled, his eyes brightening for the first time since I'd arrived at the station. "You are a queen among women, Lila."

He fell on his lunch, devouring a slice laden with sausage, ham, pepperoni, bacon, mushrooms, and green peppers. Once his initial hunger had abated, he wiped his mouth with a paper napkin. "Dig in," he offered, sliding the box toward me.

"Maybe later," I said. "While you were gone, I did a Google search on Wipple and I also tried to come up with a list of things Melissa and Tilly had in common. They were both involved in the world of books and they both had ties to Dunston."

Popping open a can of Coke, Sean hesitated before taking a drink. "If the murders *are* connected, then there has to be something more linking the two women besides books."

My mind rifled through the limited facts I had on the two women. "Tilly wrote books about a kid in search of his parents," I began. "And Melissa specialized in signing authors who wrote about families. What if that's the common denominator?"

He considered my theory. "So you think that an element in Tilly's writing is pertinent to Melissa in some way, and that this theme or subject matter led to both of their murders? That seems a little dubious. We don't have any evidence pointing to the fact that their deaths are linked. The MO is different, the—"

"But the teddy bears!" I blurted.

Sean shook his head. "That's not enough."

I ripped off a piece of crust and absently nibbled at its crisp brown edge. "It may not be enough to be conclusive, but I feel it in here." I pointed to my chest. "Melissa and Tilly were murdered by the same person. I know it. We just need to dig deeper to find the reason."

Sean opened the salad container. "Many cases are solved because gut instincts lead us to a discovery of the facts, Lila, and your instincts are better than most. I, too, have a feeling there's a connection between these women, but we need evidence to solve cases, not just hunches."

I sat on the edge of my chair and considered the possibilities. "The other day, Tilly vaguely alluded to being a different person once. What if, in her past, she knew the murderer? And what if Melissa had some kind of connection with him, too? Maybe, years ago, the three of them were linked somehow."

His lunch all but forgotten, Sean got up and brought the file box to the table. With a fresh burst of energy, he lifted the lid. "When Melissa lived in Dunston twenty years ago, she worked with the Department of Social Services. The person I interviewed at the agency didn't work there when Melissa did, so she couldn't tell me much. I do have an appointment to see one of Melissa's former coworkers this afternoon, though. In the meantime, I got these old case files, which I've been reviewing to see if I might find something." He indicated the box full of manila folders. "It appears that Melissa had lots of high-risk kids in her caseload." He lifted out a pile of folders. "I still have to go through this bunch."

"I can help," I offered as I reached for part of the pile. Sean clasped my wrist.

"This is confidential information, Lila. You can't see these files."

I pulled back my hand and sighed. "I understand, but with my help, you could get through twice as many. I wouldn't breathe a word about what I see. To anybody."

Our eyes held each other's briefly, and then he shook his head. "I'm sorry. I can't." He handed me his pen and notepad. "But you could write down the similarities I discover as I read them. That would be helpful."

"Okay," I replied as I opened to a blank page and clicked the pen.

He leafed through the folders and intermittently read aloud tidbits of information that seemed random and unconnected to the case. I dutifully recorded them, not discerning any kind of pattern. The details he revealed were vague, yet it struck me that many of the children were victims of unfortunate or violent circumstances, requiring removal from their homes and being taken from their mothers.

I wondered how these kids, who would all be adults now, had turned out. Had their placement in foster care or adoptive homes allowed them to grow into responsible adults with fulfilling lives? I doubted that was the case for all of them, and it was entirely possible the murderer was one of these unfortunate souls who had suffered within the system and blamed Melissa for his misery. But then, how did Tilly fit into that picture?

"Something happened between Ms. Plume and the killer that caused him to snap," Sean said, drawing me out of my musings. "Hitting a woman with a brick in a semipublic place is indicative of a rash act, one that was likely triggered by emotion. This feels more like a crime of passion than a premeditated act of violence."

I nodded. "And the reason for his rage might be in one of those," I said, pointing to the few remaining folders.

Sean nodded as he put a folder aside and flipped open the next, silently reading its contents. Suddenly his eyes widened in amazement. "Oh my god, Lila, this could be something!"

I caught my breath. "What?"

"Melissa was seeking a permanent home for this young boy named Justyn. Apparently, he'd already been passed around a few different foster homes because of behavioral problems. But here's what caught my eye." He shifted in his seat. I leaned forward as he began to read:

Justyn had been abandoned as a newborn, left in a plastic laundry basket on the steps of a church with only a note indicating his name. He was wrapped in a sweatshirt, and tucked beside him was a small teddy bear.

Sean looked up from the page, his cheeks flushed. "A teddy bear, Lila."

My pulse began to race. "That's too much of a coincidence, isn't it?" We were getting close; I knew it.

"Maybe." He scanned the rest of the page. "A few weeks later the police found his birth mother, a fifteen-year-old crack addict named

Mattie, in Dunston. She was living in squalor in a condemned three-story apartment building on Fuller Street. Melissa got her into rehab, but when she turned eighteen she disappeared, having relinquished all parental rights for Justyn." He scraped back his chair. "This is definitely worth looking into." Closing the file, he stood. A small square photograph slipped out of the folder and fluttered to the floor.

We both bent to retrieve the photo, but I got to it first. I picked it up and found myself staring into the face of a young boy who looked to be about eight or nine. He had curly black hair and unsettling, piercing eyes. The child's gaze seared into mine, and I was instantly transported to the moment at the festival when a much older Justyn had laid a black feather on my table. No, not Justyn. I knew the true identity of the man with the sinister gaze.

"Sean, this photo . . ." I handed it to him, dumbfounded by what it revealed. "Justyn is Kirk Mason!"

Chapter 13

Sean examined the photograph of the boy with the intense stare carefully, but I could tell he wasn't convinced.

"I know you're looking at a picture of a little kid," I said. "And Kirk Mason may be in his late twenties, but those are his eyes. I'd know them anywhere." I pointed at Justyn's face for emphasis, and suddenly, my mind took me back to the book festival. There I was, standing in the shadowy corridor of the old town hall while the looming figure of the young man with the dark eyes crept toward me. Those eyes were hypnotizing. They were like twin black holes, swallowing all traces of light and hope.

I couldn't climb out of the memory until I heard Sean say my name and felt his hand on mine. And when I fixed my gaze on Justyn's photograph again, another realization struck me. "Oh, Lord. Is it possible?" I turned from Sean and sat down in front of the computer. "There's something I need to see." Typing "Tilly Smythe" into Google's search box, I struck the return key and waited for the results. Within seconds, I'd enlarged the image used on her latest book jacket so that it filled the screen. "Look. Tilly has the same eyes. I knew there was something hauntingly familiar about them, but I couldn't make the connection at the time."

Stunned, Sean raised the photo of Justyn, held it alongside Tilly's, and said, "He's got her nose and mouth shape, too. The resemblance can't be chalked up as mere coincidence."

Sean pulled out his notebook and flipped to a page covered with writing. "There's a gap in Tilly's history. We can trace where she lived, worked, and traveled all the way back to her early twenties, but before that, she doesn't seem to exist. Not on paper, anyway."

Things began to click into place. I compared the two faces before me. "She's the right age . . ."

"To be Justyn's mother." Sean completed my thought.

The possibility filled up the room, compelling us to fall silent.

Questions ricocheted like pinballs in my head, but I kept coming back to one truth: We needed evidence or none of our brilliant deductions would bring the murderer to justice.

"What happened during your interview with Tilly's husband?" I asked Sean. "Couldn't he tell you anything about her childhood?"

"Not really. Said she was an only child and her parents had passed away before he and Tilly met. She told him she'd grown up in a trailer park on the outskirts of Dunston and that her childhood wasn't a pleasant one and she didn't want to talk about it." Sean shrugged. "So they didn't. Tilly has a blog and I've read through a bunch of her posts. More than once she says that her life with her husband and kids has allowed her to erase bad memories from her past and given her leave to focus on being happy."

A vision of Tilly waiting for her children's school bus rose up before me, and I distinctly remembered the way her face glowed with joy when she saw her son and daughter racing toward her. "I believe she was happy. Until Mason began to stalk her, that is."

Glancing at his watch, Sean gathered the files together and stuffed them back into the cardboard box. He tucked the box under his right arm and said, "I'm going to head over to the Department of Social Services. If any of our theories are going to be substantiated, it'll take a caseworker with a long, accurate memory to provide us with the details we need. I'll call you if there's a break in the case."

I shook my head. "No way. Like you said, these are our theories. I'm a part of this case, Sean, and unless it's illegal, I think I've earned the right to come along with you on this interview."

"What about your work?" he asked, and I knew he was grabbing at straws.

"I'll explain my absence to Bentley if neces-

263

sary." Grabbing my purse, I put on my most obstinate expression, and he shrugged, gesturing for me to follow him out the door. "So the woman you're meeting today used to work with Melissa?"

He nodded, moving down the hall with quick, determined strides. "Her name's Glenda and she was at home sick when I visited the offices earlier this week. From what I hear, she's been battling the flu for over two weeks. But she's back today, and the moment she heard that I'd been asking about Melissa's case files, Glenda called me. I was at West's house at the time, but she assured me that she was prepared to help and invited me to drop by this afternoon."

Outside the station, a cold November breeze snuck beneath my collar and a riot of shriveled brown leaves whooshed by on eddies of crisp air. I was going to have to buy a thicker coat or I'd freeze riding around on my Vespa during the winter months.

I scuttled into the passenger seat of Sean's police cruiser, relieved to escape the biting wind. We didn't speak as he drove through town toward the government complex, and the silence between us was both familiar and comfortable.

The lull of the road moving under the car wheels and the slow blur of buildings passing beyond my window allowed my mind to zero in on the connection between Justyn and Tilly. Tilly had told me that she was a different woman now than she'd been in the past. Did that mean that she was ashamed of things she'd done when she was a young woman? And if so, what were those things? How could she abandon her baby, leaving him helpless and alone? There was a note stating that his name was Justyn, but no explanation, just a blanket and a teddy bear to keep him company as she turned her back on him for the rest of his life.

Ten minutes into my ruminations, Sean pulled in front of a sprawling brick building in the midst of a dozen similar structures and grabbed the cardboard box from the backseat. He led me to a bland waiting room filled with outdated magazines, nervous adults, and several subdued children. Approaching the harried-looking receptionist, he showed her his badge and explained that I was assisting him with a case. While I flushed with pride over having been called Sean's assistant, the woman gestured to a closed door to her left.

"Go on through," she said in a weary but courteous voice. "Glenda's down the hall. Last door on your right."

Glenda was seated behind a desk in a minuscule office crammed with filing cabinets, photographs of smiling children, and an ancient computer. She was a homely woman with mousy brown hair and eyes the hue of roasted chestnuts. Her voice was soft and gentle and she welcomed us warmly.

"I called after I heard my friend Jillian mention Melissa's name," she said after introductions had been made. "I had no idea what happened to Melissa until two days ago. I've been out of the office for two weeks now, fighting this awful stomach bug. I've been watching all these classic movies on TV to try to take my mind off how bad I've been feeling, so I didn't see the news reports." She shook her head sorrowfully. "In a way, I'm glad I didn't, because now I can remember her as she was. Melissa was a lovely person. Devoted to her job, her friends, and her family. At least, that's my impression. We didn't keep in touch after she moved to New York, but she couldn't have changed too much. I can't understand why anyone would have done this to her."

"We believe a clue lies in one of Melissa's case files." Sean opened the cardboard box and grabbed Justyn's folder while I delighted in his use of "we." Placing the file on Glenda's desk, he opened the cover and pointed at Justyn's photograph. "Can you tell us anything about this boy?"

I watched Glenda bring the image closer to her face and then check the name listed in the file. She nodded empathically. "He paid us a visit. It would have been about three weeks ago. He filled out a request form to get information on his birth mother. You see, we're not allowed to give anyone so much as a first name without permission, so I had to make sure Justyn's mother was willing to make contact with him. He told me he remembered a nice woman from this office named Lissa or Melissa or something. Because he was a young boy when she helped him, he wasn't sure of her name. Well, I've been here forever and we've only had one Melissa here."

She replaced the photograph on her desk and stared at it as she continued. "The majority of our records are computerized, and I could have just looked his mother up on the spot, but Melissa's and most of the files from that far back are still downstairs in Records. Hard copies only, I'm afraid." She sighed. "We just don't have the resources to enter them into the database. We're underfunded and understaffed."

"The delights of being a civil servant," Sean said, earning him a droll smile from Glenda.

"Oh yeah," she chortled. "Goes right along with our company jet and twelve weeks of paid vacation." Her eyes were once again drawn to Justyn's photo and she immediately sobered. "I called down to Records with the young man's request and explained that this was one of Melissa Plume's cases. I didn't think I'd done any harm by mentioning her name, but now . . ." Her eyes grew moist and she gave Sean a pathetic, searching look.

"You're not at fault, Glenda. Please go on," Sean said soothingly.

Recovering her poise, Glenda sat up a little taller in her chair. "My coworker in Records said that the name the young man had given wasn't listed in our files, and when I turned to ask him about it, he'd disappeared. I wonder if he ran off because he heard what my colleague said. She's one of those loud talkers." She gave a hapless shrug. "Though he put Justyn on the form, the last name he gave us wasn't in our records and neither was his address. Maybe he knew he'd have to tell me the truth about his identity and he just . . . couldn't." She swallowed hard.

"Go on," Sean prompted.

"When I found out that Melissa was murdered, I started wondering if the young man's deception had some significance." Glenda looked at Sean hopefully. "Or it could be that he was just scared. It's not easy for some of these kids to face their birth mothers, especially if they've spent their whole lives dreaming about the moment they'll meet for the first time."

I shook my head in sympathy. "Talk about a high-pressure situation."

"Exactly," Glenda agreed and then quickly brightened. "But I've seen some beautiful reunions in my time. And I've also seen foster parents fall in love with a child in need of a home and discover the family they've always longed for. Family's in the heart, not the blood. That's what I always say."

Sean opened a notebook and subtly cleared his throat, hoping to get back to the subject at hand. "According to Justyn's case file, his last name was Kershaw, but do you remember the fake surname he used on his request form?"

"No," Glenda replied with genuine regret. "After he left, I threw it out. I figured if he really wanted to contact his birth mother he'd be back."

"A fair assumption," Sean said kindly. "Could you describe his appearance?"

Glenda let loose a small snort. "Sure could. He was tall and thin, but didn't look scrawny. 'Lean' is a better word. Dark hair and eyes." She raised her hand to her brow. "Bunch of piercings here. Silver hoops and a few barbell thingies, too. I'm not sure what they're called. Dressed all black from his shirt right on down to his boots. And he seemed uncomfortable in his own skin. Real tense. On edge."

"I'd like to show you a sketch. Does this look like the man you saw?" He removed the drawing made the day I'd worked with the sketch artist at the Dunston police station.

Glenda didn't even have it in her hands before she was nodding vigorously. "That's him all right."

"Thank you. That's very helpful." I was amazed by how calm Sean sounded. My heart was beating triple time in my chest. Glenda had just identified Kirk Mason!

"I'll see what I can find out about Justyn Kershaw," Sean said, reclaiming the sketch and tucking it inside his file folder. I was relieved when he closed the cover on Mason's angry glare. "But if I come up empty-handed, I might need your assistance again."

Glenda's glance flicked to the photo of Justyn as a boy, and I saw her eyes fill with pity. "I'll do anything in my power to help, Officer."

"What about Justyn's birth mother, Mattie Kershaw?" Sean asked. "I read that she was a drug addict and had been arrested several times for illegal possession and misdemeanor shop-lifting charges. But can you tell me anything else about her?"

"I wish I could, but she was assigned to Melissa. The only thing I could add to what she wrote in her files probably won't be of any interest to you," Glenda said.

I might have been overstepping my bounds, but I leaned forward in my chair and smiled encouragingly at Glenda. "So far, everything you've told us has been important. I bet this detail will be, too."

She gave me a grateful look in return. "It was a long time ago, but I remember Melissa telling me that she was really struggling over how to help this lost young girl named Matilda. I know she went by Mattie, but Matilda was her real name. However, Melissa called her something else entirely. Only to me, of course. Only in private."

Sean's pen hovered over his notebook. "And what was that?"

"Troublesome Tilly," Glenda replied. Grinning a little, her face took on a wistful expression as she traveled to another time in which she and Melissa discussed their cases with each other.

Sean and I exchanged astonished glances. Here, at last, someone had confirmed the connection between Melissa, Tilly, and Justyn.

Except that Justyn had transformed into someone else. He didn't exist as Justyn Kershaw any longer, but was posing as Kirk Mason. And under that guise, he had become a murderer.

I entered Novel Idea rubbing my hands together to warm them. Not only would I have to buy a thicker coat, but I'd also need to invest in gloves. I was beginning to think that my little yellow Sunshine was not the most practical vehicle for the coming months.

Acknowledging Vicky's greeting, I made my way to the kitchen to pour myself a hot coffee. Wrapping my fingers around the heated mug, I walked to my office, pondering the questions that Sean and I had bounced around on the drive back to the station: Why would Kirk Mason kill Melissa? Hadn't she done all she could to help him when he was young Justyn? After all this

271

time, what trigger had caused him to hit her over the head with a brick? And what about Tilly? Why, after seeking his birth mother, would he murder her once he'd found her? Had that been his intent all along in searching for her? And the most chilling question: Would he kill again? Was there someone else he wanted to punish?

Completely engrossed, I entered my office and was startled to see Trey sitting at the desk, his friend Jeff in the guest chair.

"Mom." Trey jumped to his feet. "Where've you been? We've been waiting for almost a half hour."

"I'm sorry, Trey, I got caught up in something." I looked over at Jeff, who also rose to his feet. "Hi, Jeff."

"Hey, Ms. W." Surprisingly, he wore a suit, although the tie was askew and a shirttail hung over his belt. His hair was trimmed and he was clean-shaven—quite a change from the long-haired, rebellious boy who'd worn only black T-shirts with skulls imprinted on them.

"You're looking quite professional," I said.

He pulled at his shirt collar. "Yeah, we all have to wear these monkey suits at the dealership." He shifted his weight from one foot to the other. "I came by to get the money, and I've gotta get back to work soon or my dad'll kill me."

"Okay." I pulled out my wallet. "I assume Trey has told you what we need you to do?"

"Go to the co-op and buy a meditation session and report back to you." He grinned broadly. "I'm up for that. And you'll pay me a hundred bucks, right?" He darted a swift glance at Trey.

"That's what we agreed," Trey said. "And you can't let on that you know me. Just find out what they're doing and get out of there."

Jeff slung his arm over Trey's wide shoulders. "No worries, my man. I'm a master at deception."

In that moment, I recognized the teenager who'd always been around whenever Trey got into trouble. I was suddenly reluctant to hand over the three hundred dollars, wondering if this was a wise decision. "Jeff, don't do anything foolish. Just act like a customer, pay them their money, and get whatever they offer for it. If you feel the slightest bit uncomfortable, then leave. You get to keep the money either way."

Jeff's eyes widened. "Ah, Ms. W, there's no need to worry. I'm happy to get whatever they offer for two hundred bucks. I have an idea about what they're doing there anyway."

"You do?" Trey looked incredulous. "What?"

"I'm not saying 'til I find out for sure." He held out his hand.

I placed two hundred and fifty dollars into it. "You *could* share your suspicions, Jeff."

"Naw, that wouldn't be cool." He counted out the bills. "I don't want to waste your money, Ms. W."

"There's two hundred dollars for the meditation session, plus fifty for now. You'll get the other fifty when you report back to me. Deal?"

"Sure thing. And hey, could I interest you in buying a good used car?"

Briefly, I recalled how cold I was riding my scooter today, but then I shook my head and smiled. "Sorry. I already have a good set of wheels."

"Thought I'd give it a try." He headed for the door. "C'mon, Trey, I gotta get back."

Trey grinned and gave me a little salute. "See ya, Mom."

I watched them saunter down the hall, feeling uneasy about sending Jeff into a situation that could involve something unsavory at best and illegal at the worst. I closed my eyes and silently wished for him to return unharmed.

I'd barely dug into the proposals on my desk when my phone buzzed. Vicky's authoritative voice came on the line.

"Lila, Ms. Burlington-Duke wants to see you at once. And a messenger just dropped off a package addressed to you."

I hurried to the lobby, wondering what the delivery was and who might have sent it. Vicky held out a thick courier's envelope.

"You'd better go directly to Ms. Burlington-Duke's office. She's asked for you several times today and is most displeased that you haven't been available this afternoon. I tried to provide reasonable excuses on your behalf, but . . ." She shrugged. "I didn't know where you were all that time."

"I was at the police station sharing what I knew about T. J. West, remember?" I tried not to squirm under her frank scrutiny. "Thankfully, he's innocent. But I'll tell Bentley all of this in person. I appreciate how you covered for me." Grabbing the envelope, I hastened down the hall.

Unable to contain my curiosity, I examined the return address on the packet and saw that Thomas Wipple had sent it. I ripped back the tab and pulled out a stack of papers. They were the first three chapters of T. J. West's bed and breakfast cozy. Hopefully they'd been rewritten to incorporate my suggestions, because if so, I'd offer him representation. I knew I'd have no trouble finding a publisher for his engaging series, as long as he took out the reference to the teddy bear and anything else that involved a child in the murder.

At that moment, a picture of Justyn came to mind. I saw him as a small infant, sleeping beside a worn teddy bear in his laundry basket. Then I envisaged Tilly, lying dead and clutching a plush bear. That murder wasn't fiction. And neither was Melissa's.

I shook my head in an attempt to scatter those

thoughts and shoved the pages back into the envelope. Reading them would have to wait. Having reached Bentley's door, I took a deep breath and knocked.

"Enter."

I stepped into her office. "You wanted to see me?" I said, approaching her large, glass-topped desk.

Bentley's fingers clicked rapidly on her laptop, her long, cardinal red nails the exact color of the tailored suit she wore. I waited. When she finished, she peered over her diamond-studded half-moon glasses. "Lila. I'm pleased to see that you do, in fact, still work at this agency."

"I'm sorry. I was delivering a file to the police and became involved in the investigation . . ." My voice trailed off and I waved the envelope in my hand. "I have been working, though. I'm close to signing a new client."

"That's good to hear. I know you have a vested interest in the current police investigation, but please remember that you are a literary agent, not a detective." The hint of a smile crossed her face. "Although I do recall that you have a certain knack for detecting." She removed her glasses, and they dangled like a pendant on a gold-jeweled chain around her neck. "Just try to spend more time at the office."

"I will," I said, properly chastened.

"I wanted to see you because I have a project to assign you. To you and Jude, actually." She picked up her phone and pressed a button. "Vicky, please send Jude to my office."

"What kind of project?" I asked when she replaced the receiver.

"Let's wait until Jude arrives, shall we? In the meantime, why don't you fill me in on what the police have discovered about the two murders." She frowned. "An editor and an author. What is the world coming to? Are the killings connected?"

"It's possible." I sifted through all that I'd learned, trying to decide what I could and couldn't tell my boss. Just as I opened my mouth to speak again, Jude burst into the room. His eyes twinkled when he saw me.

"Ah, *two* lovely ladies wanting to meet with me."

"Take a seat, Jude." Bentley leaned her elbows on her desk and tented her fingers. "The publisher for *The Alexandria Society* wants a sequel. Of course, since Marlette Robbins is no longer alive, he obviously won't be able to write it. I need you and Lila to put your heads together to find someone suitable for the project."

"A ghostwriter?" I asked, remembering Marlette's unique voice and wondering if we'd be able to find someone to fill his shoes.

"Exactly. Between Jude's stable of suspense authors and your burgeoning group of mystery writers, I'm confident you'll be able to come up with a few names. Now, the publisher has put together an outline, so whomever you think is up for the job needs to submit a proposal based on their framework." She handed each of us a printed sheet of paper.

Jude folded it in half. "I'm happy to be working on this with Lila," he said, flashing me a smile. "But I've got a full plate at the moment. I've just sold a thriller to a small publisher, and I'm about to sign another author whose book is destined to become a blockbuster. However, it needs some polishing before I shop it around."

Bentley sat back in her chair. "Your current projects take priority, but the publisher is eager to enter into discussions, so see that you get to it as soon as possible." She set her glasses back on her nose and proceeded to type on her computer.

Thus dismissed, Jude and I exchanged curious glances and left the room.

"I need a coffee," he said. "How about you?"

I nodded and scanned the publisher's outline as I accompanied him to the kitchen. It was a vague summary of the proposed plot, with little detail about the setting or characters. The potential ghostwriter would have to read *The Alexandria Society* in order to obtain the necessary background information. But I couldn't think about the project now. "I'm glad you told Bentley that you were too busy to work on this immediately," I said as I held out a mug for Jude to fill. "My brain is so full at the moment that I wouldn't be able to focus on this."

"Yes, I understand you've gotten yourself involved in the murder investigations of that New York editor and the writer in Dunston. Is that because you have a secret desire to be a detective?" He drew closer. "Or because of your friendship with that cop, Griffiths?"

"Jude, the deaths of those two women are a serious matter. I want justice for them both, and if there is any way that I can contribute to the police arresting whoever was responsible, then I'm going to do that." I put my coffee down and crossed my arms. "Don't kid around about it."

Jude immediately stepped back and adopted a contrite expression. "I'm sorry. You're right. These killings have hit too close to home. The author was one of Flora's, wasn't she? Doesn't this harken back to last summer?" He leaned back against the counter and sipped his coffee.

I stirred cream into mine, regretting that I'd dwelled on the subject. "Tell me about the author you're about to sign," I said, hoping to lighten the mood.

Immediately, Jude perked up. "He's coming in this afternoon." He checked his watch. "In about ten minutes, actually. Vicky's prepared the final contract for his signature and then we'll be ready to rock and roll. This guy can write, Lila. He's dark and sinister, to be sure, but there's a definite market for his stuff. I know of two publishers who will probably engage in a bidding war over this book."

"Wow. That's great."

"And I have you to thank for it. You brought me his proposal last week."

"Really? Which one?" I often brought queries to Jude when they were more suited to his tastes, and since I didn't read them in great detail, they seldom stuck in my mind. Thinking back, I tried to recall what I had given him. All of a sudden I felt a chill and grabbed Jude's arm, causing him to slosh his coffee.

"Hey, careful," he admonished, wiping at the spill with his hand.

"Are you referring to that query I gave you just before the book festival?" My voice shook.

"That's the one. The author is—"

"Kirk Mason?" I spit out the name in horror. "Jude! You're about to sign a contract with a murderer!"

Chapter 14

Jude laughed once, and then seeing that I was deadly serious, set his coffee cup down on the counter and grabbed my hands.

"Lila, what on earth are you talking about?"

I was glad he had a tight hold of my trembling fingers, because his grip seemed to be the only thing keeping me on my feet. Fear had turned my mouth dry and I searched for words, for the nouns and verbs and conjunctions I needed to explain myself, but they had become elusive, flitting out of my head like spooked starlings.

"Look at me," Jude commanded gently. "I don't understand what you mean."

Numbly, my gaze wandered over his shoulder to the rooftops beyond the kitchen window. The sun was barely visible behind an oncoming bank of dark thunderclouds. It would be storming soon. And with the storm and the lightless gloom, Kirk Mason would arrive. A shadow among the shadows.

"He wrote about a building used as a field hospital," I stated mechanically. "I remember the stained floorboards and the character's fascination with blood. That author's name was Kirk

Mason. It's a pseudonym, Jude. The guy's real name is Justyn and he's a killer. He hit Melissa with a brick and strangled Tilly Smythe in the middle of her own kitchen. I'm sorry that I didn't share my suspicions with you earlier. I had no idea you'd end up offering him representation." My voice became low and cold. "And now he's coming here. We have to be careful. We could all be in danger."

I didn't wait for Jude to respond but pulled my hands away from his and rushed into my office. Grabbing the phone, I called Sean, my heart threatening to beat right out of my chest. Where was Mason right now? Was he outside the building? In the lobby? Or was he already climbing the stairs?

"Sean!" I cried the moment I heard his voice. "Kirk Mason is heading to the agency. Jude offered him representation and he's scheduled to appear in person and sign his contract. He's coming. Please, you've got to help me!"

"Okay, Lila, stay calm. I'm already moving," Sean assured me. "You should leave the building."

"I can't do that. Neither can anyone else. There's a chance we'd run into him on our way out, though I'm the only one who poses a genuine threat to him." I made a quick mental scan of the offices, closets, and conference room. "I could hide in a locked office, but you could pop the locks with a penknife."

"You need to stay out of sight," Sean directed and began to talk rapidly, as if he were thinking out loud. "I had concluded that Mason attended the book festival because Melissa was there, and that his proposed serial killer novel was just a ruse. I had no idea Mason was really a writer. Is it possible he'd risk life in prison to become a published author? That he's that invested in signing this contract?"

Sean's questions gave me pause. People would go to great lengths to see their work on the bookstore shelf, but Mason had committed two murders. Surely he knew the police were closing in on him. Was he truly foolish enough to show up at my agency, chancing an encounter with the woman who'd been suspicious of him upon first glance?

I swallowed hard. "I don't think his main purpose is to sign a contract, Sean. He's coming for me. And I have no weapons except for a stapler and a really heavy dictionary." I laughed a bit hysterically, my panic increasing as the seconds ticked by. I tried to come up with a logical solution to this new threat, but fear had robbed me of my good sense and I couldn't think straight.

"Hold on, Lila," Sean said and issued terse orders at his fellow officers. Then, a car engine rumbled and I knew that he was in motion. My cop was riding in on his black-and-white metal horse to rescue me, but would he be in time?

"Sean, I'll call you back. I need to get out of my office."

After making sure no one else was in the corridor, I dashed into the office next to mine and was met by Flora's congenial grin. "Hello, dear."

"Flora, this is going to sound crazy, but I need you to pretend that I'm not here."

Her smile grew broader. "Oh, I completely understand. Sometimes, we just need to check out for a spell. Me? I like to get lost in a Harry Potter novel or recite some of Shel Silverstein's poetry. Edgar Allan Poe once said, 'Those who dream by day are cognizant of many things which escape those who dream only by night.' I completely agree," she declared, and then the twinkle faded from her eyes and she sighed. "A little journey into fantasy is good for the soul, especially during trying times such as these."

Her references to Poe and Tilly's murder unnerved me even further. I was about to warn her about Kirk Mason when I heard noises in the office reception area. There was no time! I whipped open the door of the white wardrobe tucked into the corner of the room. Flora's coat, polka-dot rain boots, and flowered umbrella were stored inside, leaving just enough room for me. "Act like you never saw me, Flora. Please!" I stepped into the narrow closet, faltering for a brief second because I hadn't cautioned her about

Kirk Mason. But then I determined that there was no reason for him to harm her. She hadn't set the police on his trail. *I'd* done that.

Clutching my cell phone to my chest, I closed the door and waited.

I must have been mistaken in thinking that the sounds in the lobby had been Kirk Mason, because I didn't hear his voice. Straining to listen for him or Jude, all I heard in the dark was the creaking of Flora's chair as she eased her weight into it followed by the *click, click* of her nails against the computer's keyboard. Suddenly, the sound of music floated from the direction of her desk. It was a soothing piano sonata, and I was grateful for Flora's good taste. The soft notes and languid rhythm allowed me to relax the tiniest fraction, and my fingers became steady enough to send a text to Sean. I told him where I was hiding and asked how long it would take before he could reach Novel Idea.

He responded immediately, which let me know that someone else was driving, and promised that his partner was going as fast as he could over the mountain roads and they'd be in Inspiration Valley in ten to fifteen minutes.

Fifteen minutes! Never had such a brief stretch of time seemed so long. Fifteen minutes in the dark. Fifteen minutes of helplessness and terror. I had to do something to occupy my mind. No matter what happened, I wasn't going to let Kirk

Mason reduce me to a quivering mess for another second.

I pressed the photo album icon on my phone's screen and scrolled through the pictures I'd taken in July. There was Althea in her garden, plucking a fat tomato from a plant a foot taller than her. She grinned widely and I knew she was already planning to use the fresh tomato in a Caprese salad. I could picture the herb garden behind her house, where several varieties of basil perfumed the summer air.

Next, there were eight shots from the Red Fox Mountain Co-op. The first showed Trey feeding an apple to a goat. In the second, he and Iris had paused in the middle of weaving a hammock out of hemp to wave for the camera.

I touched his face with my index finger, praying that I'd see him again soon, and that when I did, he'd give me one of his famous bear hugs. I moved on to a picture Trey had taken of me standing in front of my yellow cottage on moving day. What I'd give to be inside my cozy little house right now!

Having scrolled through my photos, I checked the clock on my cell phone. Only three minutes had passed since Sean's last text. How long would this nightmare last?

Suddenly, I heard a knock on Flora's door. I stiffened as she called out, "Come on in!"

"Where's Lila?" Jude asked.

Flora turned her music down. "I'm sorry, dear. She told me she needed a break. Could I help you with something?"

I held my breath and wished Jude would leave before Kirk showed up to sign his contract. A bead of sweat was trickling down my forehead, but I dared not move to wipe it off. I wanted to be invisible and inaudible, to not exist for a slice of time so that I could avoid coming face-to-face with a murderer.

"She thinks my new client is some homicidal maniac." Jude's voice was somewhat irritated. "And I want her to meet him so she can see for herself that he's as nice as can be. The only thing sinister about him is his writing, and *that's* going to make Mason and me a little wealthier. Kirk Mason's our newest author. Oh, here he is now. Can I introduce you?"

To my horror, Flora said, "Of course. Let me just get up so I can shake Mr. Mason's hand."

As my forehead and palms grew clammy, I glanced at my cell phone. Sean was at least ten minutes away. Squeezing my eyes shut, I listened intently. Would Mason sense my presence in the room? Would Flora give me away? I didn't dare breathe.

Flora didn't betray my hiding place, but my cell phone did. I'd foolishly left the ringer on, and the energetic notes of a salsa melody burst out of the speaker. Fumbling for the mute button, I saw Trey's name on the call display.

"Call you back," I whispered and severed the connection.

Too late. With a creak, the wardrobe door eased open and Jude's face mercifully blocked most of the glare from Flora's ceiling light as well as the figure of the man in black.

"What are you doing in there?" he asked in surprise.

Instead of answering, I steeled myself and inched sideways, looking around Jude's shoulder at the tall, slim bald man standing next to Flora. He stared at me in puzzlement and I couldn't even blink, such was my own astonishment.

"Kirk Mason?" I croaked, taking in his black leather jacket and slightly lined, middle-aged face. He had no piercings and his eyes were a lovely shade of sky blue.

He nodded but made no move toward me. "Yes, ma'am. That's me."

I looked from Jude to Kirk and back to Jude again. "Is Kirk Mason his pen name?"

"No, it isn't. My client, Mr. Kirk Mason, is not the man you saw at the book festival, Lila. Kirk here was called out of town on an emergency and missed his pitch appointment. I'm sure you've also taken note of the physical dissimilarities between this man and the man you believe to be Kirk Mason."

"Didn't he know the police were looking for

him? Where was he all this time?" I gazed at the man named Kirk Mason.

His cheeks flushed and he cleared his throat. "I spent the week in Tennessee, at the bedside of a dear friend who was very ill. I went there rather suddenly, neglecting to tell people where I was." He shrugged. "I had no idea anyone would be looking for me."

A smile played around the corners of Jude's mouth and he held out his hand. "May I help you out of the broom closet, milady?"

Stepping out of the wardrobe on wobbly legs, I tried to summon a sheepish grin for Kirk Mason, but failed. I'm sure the fact that I'd been hiding in a closet and then mercilessly stared at him had made Mr. Mason feel more than a little uncomfortable. However, I did not possess enough mental acuity to explain myself to him. Tilly's orphan son Justyn was the killer, and now I had no idea what his real name was or how the police would ever be able to hunt him down. One thing was clear, however: This man was not Justyn. He was no murderer. He was a gentleman writer by the name of Kirk Mason.

"Welcome to Novel Idea. I'm Lila Wilkins," I said to him in a dry rasp. "Please forgive me. I'm . . . dealing with some personal issues." I moved to the door and then turned back to Jude. "Why don't you buy Mr. Mason a cup of coffee downstairs? My treat."

Jude cocked his head quizzically. "I was going to introduce him to Franklin and Zach first."

I tapped my watch face and gave him a loaded look. "My friend Sean is on his way here. And he won't be alone. This might be a really good time for Mr. Mason to meet the lovely Makayla."

Comprehension dawned on Jude's face. "I could certainly use a caffeine hit. How about you, Kirk? Care to take a trip down the stairs to Espresso Yourself?"

"I'm a café au lait man, myself, so I'd love to check out the coffee shop. Thanks, Lila." A pair of dimples appeared on Kirk's cheeks as he smiled.

The moment Jude had ushered his new client down the hall, I tried contacting Sean, but my call went straight to voicemail. That could only mean that he was on foot, probably racing into the building just as Jude and Kirk were descending the stairs.

"Feel better now, dear?" Flora inquired with concern.

Flashing her a grateful smile, I declared, "I might need to climb back into your wardrobe in a few minutes!" I then shot out of her office and barreled toward the landing where Vicky sat primly at her desk, sipping hot tea and humming softly to herself as she applied address labels to a stack of envelopes.

Jude must have really hustled Kirk into Espresso Yourself, because by the time I'd set my foot on the first step, they were nowhere in sight. At that moment, the lobby door was flung open and the sound of hurried footfalls echoed up the stairwell.

Sean moved up the stairs like a high school track athlete, calling out, "Lila!" as soon as he saw me.

In that single syllable I heard a lifetime's worth of worry and fear and, yes, love. Within seconds, he had reached the top and, keeping one hand on his holster, drew me into his chest with the other. "Where is he?"

"It wasn't him," I answered quickly as three other officers bounded up the stairs, their bodies tense and coiled like a trio of panthers preparing to spring.

"What?" Sean demanded, pulling away in order to face me.

"The Kirk Mason who showed up here today is not Justyn. He's a middle-aged man with a bald head and dimples."

Sean stared at me with disbelief. "You've got some explaining to do, Lila."

"I know, I know." I raked my hands through my hair.

"Griffiths?" One of Sean's fellow officers approached us. "You want me to do a sweep?"

He shook his head. "Negative. I'd like you to drive around the downtown district and see if you can spot our man. I'm thinking a ten-block radius. You've got a copy of the sketch, right?"

It seemed pretty transparent to me that he was trying to get rid of the other cops, but they responded to his order without question and hurried off, their utility belts clanking as they jogged down the stairs.

"Your office. *Now*." Sean gave me a little nudge, propelling me forward. Vicky watched us with a curious gleam in her eye, but she remained mercifully silent.

Because I didn't want to have my desk between us while we talked, I dragged my chair across the floor and pulled close enough to his that our knees touched.

"When did you first hear the name Kirk Mason?" he asked.

I searched my memory carefully before answering. "When I read his query letter, which really wasn't a query but a sample of his work. It was very dark and I don't know how his book chapter ended up in my in tray, so I passed it on to Jude."

"Go on," Sean prompted.

"And then Kirk Mason registered for the book festival using an incomplete address and requested an appointment at the agent pitch session," I continued.

"A session that you shared with Jude, correct?"

Nodding, I said, "Yes. But he was there, Sean. Tall, creepy, wearing all-black . . . and he left that raven's feather on my desk. And then, he came after me in the empty hallway. Even Jude thought he was Kirk Mason."

"*Justyn* was at the pitch session. *Justyn* came after you, Lila. A *writer* named Kirk Mason had an appointment for a pitch session, but he was unable to attend that day. Therefore, he wasn't the man in black." Sean hesitated and then forced himself to finish. "You made an assumption based on a stranger's writing sample."

The truth of his words hit me full force, and I put my hand over my mouth as if I could call back my error. "You're right. Oh, Lord, you're right! I never had evidence linking Kirk Mason's brief passage to the man who sent chills up my spine every time I looked at him. I heard Jude mention Kirk Mason after the pitch sessions, and later, that statement led me to believe that the writer was Melissa's killer. I'm sorry, Sean. I pointed you in the wrong direction from the beginning." My eyes grew moist. "Did my mistake create the opportunity for Justyn to murder Tilly?"

Sean grabbed my arm. "No. Even if you hadn't given us Kirk Mason's name, we wouldn't have known exactly who to pursue, Lila. We still don't! We've got a black-and-white sketch and a first name. This bastard has eluded us from the start. He's like a shadow. And it's not your job to catch shadows. It's mine." He stood up and held me tightly, and I let my tears fall. I'd been so scared a few minutes ago and all for nothing.

Too distracted to do any more work, I decided to call it a day despite Bentley's decree that I should spend more time at the office. I headed for the exit with Sean, after informing Vicky that I'd be in to work very early the next morning to make up for today's absences. Although tomorrow would be Saturday, most of us planned to come in to the office anyway, to get caught up with extra work we had pushed aside during preparations for the festival.

As we stepped onto the sidewalk, a light flashed in my eyes. Then another. Someone was taking photographs of us. I clutched Sean's arm.

A freckle-faced young man with a Nikon slung around his neck advanced toward us, clutching a pen and notepad. "Can you give me a statement about what happened up there?"

"No comment." Sean immediately stepped in front of me, obscuring the photographer's view. While I appreciated the gesture, I wanted to know who the reporter was and peered around Sean's head to see.

"Aw, come on! Four cops go rushing into the town's literary agency and you can't tell me why? The public deserves to know what's going on." He showed us his press card, indicating that he worked for the *Dunston Herald*. I didn't recognize him from my time there. He stuck the card back in his pocket. "I can ask around, you know, but I'll probably get a distorted view of the situation. Wouldn't it be better for me to hear the story from a reliable source?"

I whispered in Sean's ear, "We should talk to this guy. If Justyn's name appears in the paper, people who know him might come forth with information."

The journalist's eyes widened and he wrote something in his notepad. "Justyn? Who's Justyn?"

Sean sighed and turned to me. "You go on home, Lila. I'll deal with this guy." He moved as if to kiss me but then seemed to think better of it and squeezed my hand instead. "I'll call you when my shift is over."

I managed to make it back home before the rain began. Since I couldn't walk outside, I donned gray sweatpants and a T-shirt and headed for my treadmill. The opening bars of "I Will Survive" blared out of the CD player as I started to build up my stride. After two minutes of warm-up, I ran faster and faster. Breathing hard, I let myself be hypnotized by the rhythm.

But the cadence of my pounding feet could not completely still my mind. Throughout the monotony of my jogging, I couldn't shake the recollection of how frightened I had been in mistakenly thinking that Justyn—in my mind,

Kirk Mason—was coming to my office to kill me. Whatever might have happened at the agency this afternoon, I'd been certain that I'd finally see an end to the horrors of the past week. I had believed our questions would be answered and the mystery solved.

But it was far from over.

And no matter what Sean said, my blunder in believing that Kirk Mason was Justyn had misdirected the police. I had to rectify that somehow, to figure out who and where Justyn was. I needed to redeem myself, not just in Sean's eyes but also in my own.

Out of breath and sweaty, I felt better now that I'd resolved to take action. Slowing my pace, I stopped the machine, wiped my brow, and gulped some water. The relentless thudding of the bass on my exercise CD was aggravating now that I was no longer running, and I turned off the stereo. But the thumping continued. Puzzled, I stared at the speakers.

"Mom! Are you home?" Trey's muffled voice came down the hallway and I realized that he'd been banging on the front door. I hurried to open it, finding my son standing on the porch with Jeff. Both boys were flushed and bright-eyed.

"We have a report," Jeff said importantly.

"Come on in." I stood aside to let them in the house. "Sorry, I'm a bit sweaty. I was just working out."

"So that's why you didn't hear us ringing the bell. Were you getting your disco on again?" Trey followed Jeff inside, then led the way to the kitchen. "We went to your office, but the secretary said you'd gone home." He opened the fridge and peered in. "Don't you have any sodas?"

I shook my head. "Just orange juice and milk."

As Trey poured juice into two glasses, Jeff shook off his jacket. "We found out what they're up to at the co-op," he said with a broad grin.

" 'Begin at the beginning and go on till you come to the end,' " I said, quoting Lewis Carroll.

"Huh?" Jeff looked perplexed.

"Don't mind her." Trey rolled his eyes. "She's always quoting books. I happen to know that's from *Alice in Wonderland*, because she used to say it to me when I was a kid and she wanted to know everything about my day." He handed Jeff his drink.

I smiled at my son. "Good memory, Trey. Now, tell me what you found out about Red Fox. What are those meditation sessions exactly?"

Jeff chugged his juice and pulled a small plastic bag out of his pocket. It was filled with dark brown, shriveled nuggets attached to black stem-like threads. They looked vaguely familiar, but I couldn't quite identify them.

"What's in the bag?" I asked. "And what does it have to do with the co-op?"

"These are 'shrooms, ma'am." Jeff held them up.

" 'Shrooms?" I repeated, mystified at first, and then horrified. "You mean *hallucinogenic* mushrooms?"

"Yup. For two hundred bucks, you get this little bag and a session on how to use them safely." He tossed the bag on the table. "I didn't try them 'cause I know that's not what you wanted me to do. I didn't want to break the law, either. These things scare me. But I pretended to chew on some so Jasper wouldn't catch on."

Understanding that I'd sent Jeff into a truly compromising situation, I was overcome with a wave of guilt. Weakened, I sat down.

"Can you believe it, Mom?" Trey touched the plastic packet of mushrooms. "I'm helping them cultivate edible mushrooms for the grocery store, and all this time they've been growing these! 'Shrooms aren't innocent like weed. They're *dangerous*."

My mouth went dry as the implication of their discovery sank in. I moved to the sink and poured a glass of water. "All drugs are dangerous, Trey." I took a sip.

"Whatever." Trey clearly wasn't looking for a lecture. "Tell her what happened, Jeff."

Jeff took out a sheet of paper. "Well, Jasper recited a bunch of rules before we could unzip our bags." He read from the page.

Start with a small amount. Only take them if you don't have anything important coming up for twenty-four hours. Trip in a relaxed environment with people you know and trust.

He snorted. "Like I trust Jasper! Anyway, you can read the rest yourself." He handed me the list.

I scanned over the warnings about side effects, bad trips, and advice on only trusting mushrooms from a reliable source to ensure they are not poisonous. I noticed that there was absolutely no reference to the Red Fox Co-op anywhere on the sheet. Worriedly, I glanced at Jeff. "You really didn't try them?"

"Honest, Ms. W. I pocketed the bag to bring to you and just started acting weird like everybody else there. They were bouncing around the room, laughing at everything. Jasper was the only one who stayed straight, but I did a pretty good job of fooling him, I think." He shook his head. "Still, it was scary seeing what the 'shrooms were doing to the other kids. Turned them into total idiots."

I reached over and briefly touched his hand. "I'm sorry to have put you through that. It was irresponsible of me to send you into a situation that could have caused you harm." The culpability I felt over giving money to a young man to buy drugs was overwhelming. "I'm just glad you're all right."

He ran his fingers through his hair and shrugged. "Yeah, I'm good." His cheeks flushed. "I'm kinda glad I saw what it was all about. Definitely turned me off 'shrooms."

"Well, I suppose that's one good thing to come out of this experience," I said, picking up my purse from the counter. "And I owe you fifty dollars." I handed him the money.

Jeff stuck the bills in his pocket. "Thanks." He stood and reached for the bag of dried mushrooms, then pulled his hand back. "I guess you want to keep those, huh?"

I looked from him to Trey. "What do you boys think we should do with them?"

"I'm going to bring them to the police," Trey said emphatically. "Jasper's gone completely against the co-op's philosophy with these, and he should be stopped."

Panic lit Jeff's eyes. "You won't tell them that I bought them, will you?"

"Totally not. I'll just say they were grown at Red Fox." Trey glanced my way. "Okay, Mom?"

"I think that's the best way to handle this, Trey. You can keep everyone else out of it." I wondered what Sean would say if he knew I'd paid Jeff to investigate the meditation center. "You boys want to stay for supper?"

Jeff picked up his jacket. "Thanks, but no. My

girlfriend is cooking me a meatloaf tonight. I gotta go."

When Trey shut the door behind his friend, he eyed me worriedly. "Jasper really screwed up. I wonder how it'll affect the co-op. And Iris."

"Jasper's trouble is of his own making. Unfortunately, a person's actions have repercussions on those around them." I touched his arm. "I'm proud of you for making the decision to take this to the police. It might mean the closing of the co-op, and if that happens, your life will change, too."

As he nodded his agreement, I was struck by how much he'd matured during his months at Red Fox. It was gratifying to know that my son had such a strong moral code. Trey was so unlike Justyn, whose upbringing had been devoid of stability and good values. I couldn't help but wonder what that young man's life would have been like had his childhood been different. His circumstances didn't give him the right to commit heinous acts of violence, but I pitied him for the hollowness that existed within his twisted soul.

"I think I'll go to the police right now, Mom," Trey announced, calling me from my morose thoughts. "There's a meditation session scheduled for eight tonight, and if the cops know, they could raid it or something. And since I walked down to Nana's and borrowed her truck, they'll expect to see me coming back on foot. Alone. But that's not gonna happen." He shook his head in disgust. "The sooner Jasper gets thrown in jail, the better. He's a liar and a hypocrite and yet, I looked up to him. Well, that's all over now. I'm not under his spell anymore."

I reached out and touched his shoulder.

Trey looked at me, his mouth curving into a grin. "And I've got to admit, I really miss hot showers."

Chapter 15

After Trey left, I walked into the kitchen and opened the refrigerator, searching for inspiration. It had been a long day, and with no one to cook for, I decided to fix myself a quick and comforting meal. I dumped a can of tomato soup in a saucepan, put it on the stove, and laid out bread, sliced cheese, and butter on the counter.

Ten minutes later, I was dining on a perfectly grilled cheddar and provolone sandwich along with a steaming bowl of tomato soup. Not one to eat anything out of a can without doctoring it first, I'd added fresh basil, garlic, and a generous sprinkle of black pepper to the soup.

I tried to focus on the pleasant aromas in my kitchen and the taste of my delicious supper, but it was difficult, so I reached for an advanced reader's copy of a young adult fantasy Flora had given me. The author was one of Flora's clients, and she'd loaned me the ARC because I'd read the first four books in the series and was dying to know if the shape-shifting hero would end up falling for the mermaid or the forest nymph.

However, I just couldn't seem to concentrate on the novel. In between reading the same sentence over and over, I wondered if Trey had already spoken to the police. And had he asked for Sean or decided not to get his mother's love interest involved? It was incredibly difficult to let Trey bear this burden on his own, but I knew he needed to do this without me.

Only an hour remained before Jasper would begin his next meditation session, and it was quickly becoming an unpleasant night for a crowd of college students to be traipsing up the mountain. The cold, starless sky was striped with dark clouds, and the moon was a pale sliver above the treetops. A nasty wind had sprung up, whipping the last of the leaves off the branches outside my kitchen window and pulling the petals from the chrysanthemums on my front porch.

I gazed outside for several minutes, trying to imagine how a drug raid went down. I'd seen them on television shows, those crime dramas featuring teams of heavily armed men and women kicking in doors and storming into squalid tenements or warehouses, but this was not TV. And how would my son fit into the scenario? Would he wait at the station or lead the police to the meditation center in my mother's turquoise pickup truck? Would he accuse Jasper of being a criminal to his face or would the cops insist Trey stay in the background while they confronted the co-op's leader?

My conjectures only served to increase my anxiety, so I got a fire going in the living room and poured myself some wine. After taking a single sip, I set it down again. It was doing nothing to relax me and I doubted anything could until Sean or Trey called with news. But my phone remained stubbornly silent.

Looking for a way to pass the time, I switched on the television, turned to a mindless reality dancing show, and flipped through a small press publisher's winter catalogue. I loved reading about the upcoming releases. The tantalizing blurbs, alluring cover art, and promises of hours spent absorbed in a captivating story helped distract me from the day's events.

Shortly before nine o'clock, the ringing of my phone startled me into dropping the catalogue and nearly knocking over my wine in my eagerness to talk to my son. However, it wasn't Trey on the other end of the line. It was my mother.

"I know you've been pacin' the floorboards all evenin'. Probably nursin' a glass of wine instead of tossin' back a shot of whiskey. When are you gonna learn how to cure a bad case of the nerves?"

"Mama!" I barked. "What's going on?"

"Trey's here with me. That girl, Iris, too. They're right as rain." She lowered her voice. "Trey's a bit shaky, but he's puttin' on a good show in front of the young lady. She's a pretty thing, but she's had a hard time of it and looks like she'll keel over any second. I fixed them some sandwiches and left them in the living room. Trey wanted to call you right away, but I knew you'd want me to settle him down some first."

I thanked her, grateful that my mother lived close to the co-op and would take excellent care of Trey. "So did the cops find the 'shrooms?"

"They sure did. Your good-lookin' policeman wasn't with them, though. Guess he's got his hands full lookin' for another bad man. Anyhow, a handful of kids are gonna have to call up their mommies and daddies and confess to bein' real stupid, but the adults of Red Fox are in much bigger trouble."

I sighed in relief. "Then Jasper's been arrested?"

"No, hon. Jasper slipped away in the dark. The police went after him, but he knows those mountain trails better than anybody."

This was not what I wanted to hear. "Does he have any idea that Trey was responsible for the raid?"

"Yes, indeed, he certainly does. Trey told him off good. He didn't want to go into too many details with me, seein' as Iris is Jasper's sister and all, but I could tell that he'd needed to speak his piece and he spoke it." She cleared her throat. "Unfortunately, Jasper skedaddled right after that."

I groaned in frustration.

My mother was quick to assure me that Trey was perfectly safe. "There'll be cops crawling all over these parts for ages. Nobody's gonna come and go from Red Fox without their say-so." She sighed. "There were good folks up at the co-op, too, Lila. They're all gonna leave as soon as the cops let them. Head farther west with the goats and all their gear. When they do, I'll lose some of my favorite clients."

"It's sad," I agreed. "But I can't pretend that I'm not relieved. The thought of Trey spending the winter up there was giving me nightmares. Those portable heaters only do so much, and what would happen if he got sick? Or injured?"

"Don't say anythin' like that to him, ya hear?" she cautioned. "This is a raw wound. No need to rub salt in it."

I spluttered. "Give me some credit. It's not like I'm glad that Trey's happiness was shattered by a charlatan. My poor boy. His own dad ran off when he was a baby and then this pseudo–father figure betrayed his trust. I hope he won't be affected too adversely."

"The young are tougher than we think. They bounce back better from these sorts of things than older folks do. Why, Trey's already mentioned college. He's tryin' to convince Iris to visit the campus with him and meet with some folks there about applyin'." My mother made a sympathetic noise. "Guess her brother took off with all the cash, though. Don't know how she can pay for school unless the cops run him down."

Could Jasper successfully evade the police? He was on foot, and it was cold, especially at night. He didn't have clothes or shelter. Even if he found refuge in a cave, he'd eventually have to come down from the mountain in search of food.

"Maybe you should all come stay with me after tonight," I suggested.

"No, no," she quickly replied. "We're fine here. Jasper's long gone. But *you* should join us. The sooner the better."

I didn't like the edge to her voice. "What makes you say that?"

My mother answered in a hushed tone. "The mirror. Remember when you broke that mirror on moving day?"

My shoulders sagged. I really didn't want to rehash my mother's dramatic reaction upon seeing the glass scattered across the floor of my front hall. "Yes, I do. I also remember your ominous prediction that trouble was headed my way. And you were right—it's hardly been a peaceful autumn—but why are you bringing that up now?"

"When I picked up one of the pieces, I saw a shadow lurkin' near your new house and knew it meant you harm. Today, when I was readin' the cards, I saw that tall, dark figure again. It's angry and full of blame. It's gonna lash out. And soon. You shouldn't be alone."

"I'll be fine," I assured her, even though I felt

prickles of dread. Still, I'd already made a fool of myself once by hiding in Flora's closet at the office. I wasn't going to run and hide somewhere else now. I wished her a good night and then hung up, staring at the television screen without taking in the images. My mother's mention of a tall, dark figure immediately made me think of Justyn, but Sean was out there, vigilantly searching for Justyn while most of the inhabitants of Dunston slept. I wanted to talk to him, to see if he'd heard anything about the co-op bust from one of his fellow officers, but I didn't want to disturb him. Knowing he was on the hunt for a killer put my mind at ease. Suddenly exhausted, I turned off the TV and went to bed.

That night, my dreams were fractured and unsettled. Once again, I was huddled inside Flora's closet. I heard several voices bouncing around her office, but in the illogical way of dreams, they belonged to people who didn't work at Novel Idea. They included the reporter from the *Dunston Herald* who'd wanted to interview me after the Kirk Mason mix-up, a girl I'd known in grade school, and Big Ed from the Catcher in the Rye sandwich shop. Feeling unthreatened by this group, I opened the wardrobe door to find the carpet littered with thousands of shards of broken glass. I was about to gingerly step down from the closet in my bare feet when I saw a reflection in one of the jagged pieces. It was Justyn's face. His dark eyes were filled with hatred, and his mouth was curled into a murderous sneer. Suddenly, his face was everywhere, glaring out at me from every shard.

I woke with a start. Instead of being scared, I was furious. I was not going to be haunted by this man. *I* was going to haunt *him*. In the half-light of the early morning, I believed that I knew exactly where to find the killer.

Showing up at Espresso Yourself well before my regular time, I was relieved to see that the coffee shop wasn't busy yet. It usually drew a pretty good crowd on weekend mornings. I waved to Makayla from a relatively private café table in the corner and watched as she slid a tray of apple scones into the oven to bake and then walked around the counter to join me. She had a coffee cup in one hand and a newspaper in the other.

"Girl, you're famous. It's not quite the front page, but it's mighty close." Makayla tossed today's edition of the *Dunston Herald* onto the table. Her face was etched with concern as she placed my latte next to the paper.

My eye was immediately drawn to a large photograph showing Sean and me. The caption read:

Officer Sean Griffiths and literary agent Lila Wilkins leaving the Novel Idea offices after a false alarm.

"Oh no," I murmured, fearing what the article would say. It was a short piece and mostly rehashed the details of Melissa's and Tilly's deaths while adding several quotes from frightened residents of both Dunston and Inspiration Valley. Unfortunately, the intrepid reporter had interviewed Kirk Mason, who'd told him all about yesterday's case of mistaken identity and my foolish deduction that he was the murderer. I sighed in dismay. Why would he have shared the story with the reporter? Did he hope it would gain him notoriety and therefore increase his chances of having a publisher buy his book? And couldn't Jude have kept from going into such detail about the murder case with his new client? I'd have to have words with my coworker when I saw him next.

Makayla waited until I'd finished reading before putting her hand over mine. "I don't like this, Lila. There's your face and name in black and white for all the world to see. Now everybody knows where you work and it'd be a snap of the fingers to find out where you live. You gotta tell me—and don't you dare go sugarcoating your answer—if there's any chance this guy could come looking for you."

Staring at the photo in the paper again, I recalled my mother's warning about the tall, dark figure and weighed the possibility that Justyn would view me as a threat. We'd come face-to-face in an empty hallway during the book festival, and since then, it was likely that he'd seen me with both of his victims prior to their deaths. If he got hold of this article, he'd undoubtedly feel enraged that another woman was trying to manipulate the course of his future.

Meeting Makayla's eyes, I said, "Yes, I believe he might come after me. I don't think he spent all of his anger killing Melissa and Tilly. In my opinion, he's released a darkness inside of himself that he can't call back. It controls him now."

Makayla raised her arms skyward. "Lord have mercy, why do you end up in the middle of such wicked plots? Can't you and Sean just live in a nice, steamy romance novel and stay away from the true crime stories?"

"Rest assured," I said with a calm determination that was only partially genuine, "I have a plan."

She rolled her eyes. "Somehow, that makes me even more anxious."

"Well, I hope you're still willing to help me. I think I know where Justyn is, but I don't want to investigate this place alone."

"What about Sean?" Makayla asked.

I shook my head. "It's just a theory. If I'm right, we'll call him and he can zip on over and make the arrest. But I don't want to waste his time if I'm wrong. I already did that once by calling him in on a wild-goose chase yesterday. I won't be like the boy who cried wolf."

"All right, I'm in."

Squeezing my friend's hand in gratitude, I said, "Great. And can we take your car? I don't think my scooter is the best vehicle for a stakeout."

Makayla laughed, a sound as lovely as the ringing of church bells. "And don't forget that I've got cup holders. We're not playing at Starsky and Hutch without our lattes."

I was at my desk before any of my coworkers arrived at Novel Idea. Leaving my door open, I put on some Mozart sonatas and reached for the packet from Thomas Wipple that I'd received yesterday. I was barely into the first page when Vicky walked past my door.

"You're hard at work early, especially for a Saturday!" she proclaimed. "It's a rare day that someone gets to the office before me."

I smiled in response and continued reading, pleased to see that T. J. West had removed the teddy bear from the victim's arms and deleted any reference to children in the murder. The writing was even more engaging than in his first submission, and I felt that unique thrill that told me I could sell this project.

After sending Thomas Wipple an email requesting the complete manuscript, I tackled the overflowing pile of papers in my in-tray. Bentley breezed past, nodding her head in my direction. Gratified that she'd witnessed my dedication to the job, I turned my attention to a proposal for a cozy mystery whose protagonist was a pastry chef in a large restaurant. In the midst of pondering whether the writer might be better suited to cookbook writing than fiction, the phone rang.

"Hi, Mom," Trey said, sounding weary. "I guess Nana told you about last night? It was not a good scene—all those cops and freaked-out co-op people running all over the place. Plus, I really laid into Jasper. I probably shouldn't have, and a cop tried to hold me back, but I was just so mad."

"I understand, honey. You felt betrayed."

"Yeah. And not just me." He sighed heavily. "Did Nana tell you that Iris stayed with us last night? She has a lot to figure out now. Jasper's disappeared and the co-op's closing. She's got a cousin or something in Connecticut she could go to, but . . ."

"Things will fall into place, Trey. Somehow they always do." My heart went out to my son, who seemed to be shouldering burdens too heavy for such a young man. "What are your plans for today?"

Immediately his voice perked up. "Nana's lending us her truck and Iris and I are driving to UNC Wilmington to check out the campus and the town. If Iris likes it, she can go online and request an application. We've already looked at the website a bunch of times. I'm hoping to start in January, and Iris can take classes part-time until she's officially accepted."

Buoyant after that phone call, I found it difficult to concentrate on writing a response to the pastry chef writer. I was tempted to pick up the phone again to call Sean and tell him the good news about Trey's decision. And I wanted the official update on the co-op raid and whether or not Jasper had been captured. However, this morning Sean had texted me to say he was thinking of me and Trey, but he'd be busy all day and didn't know when he'd be able to call, so I chose not to bother him. Besides, if I did get through to him, I might let something slip about my excursion with Makayla tonight, and he'd want to talk me out of it. Instead, I turned my attention back to my work and endeavored to stay focused.

My diligence paid off, and by the end of the day I was caught up on correspondence and filing, I had made several phone calls, and the stack of proposals in my in-tray had disappeared. Satisfied that I'd made up for the time I'd taken away from work recently, I left the office feeling guilt-free.

Makayla was already sitting in her car in front of the building. When I slid into the passenger seat, she held up a paper bag. "Sandwiches from Big Ed's for the stakeout—a couple of Columbos.

Seemed fitting, somehow. Turkey, hummus, cucumber, and spinach on a whole-grain kaiser."

I shot her a grateful smile. "Thanks. I was so focused on our outing that I didn't think about dinner."

"So where are we off to, Starsky?"

"Fuller Street in Dunston. When Tilly—I mean Mattie—gave birth to Justyn, she lived on this road. At least that's where she was found shortly after she abandoned him. It was listed in Justyn's Social Services file." I briefly wondered what Sean would say if he knew I was acting on information from Melissa's case files. Ignoring the thought, I continued. "Most of the buildings in that part of Dunston are in a state of disrepair, if not condemned."

"And yet that's where we're headed," Makayla said ruefully.

"The police haven't been able to find Justyn anywhere else," I said. "Wouldn't it make sense, if Justyn is revisiting his past and punishing people for their supposed crimes, that he'd hang out in the place where his misery began?"

Makayla nodded as she drove out of town. "Sounds like a good theory. But it's also possible that we're on a wild-goose chase."

"I know. But what if we aren't? We could break this case and get him off the street before he hurts anyone else."

"At the very least, we have good sandwiches

and coffee to keep us going." Makayla flashed me a wide smile. "And if things get real boring, we can sing 'Ninety-Nine Bottles of Beer.'"

I groaned. "Please, no! With a son who was a Boy Scout, I've had enough of that song to last a lifetime."

Makayla laughed. "Okay, no singing, den mother. Let's go stalk our bad guy."

Dusk had fallen by the time we arrived at our destination. In the shadowy light, a dilapidated two-story apartment building lurked eerily between an empty lot and a mountain of debris from the demolished buildings nearby. It was small and narrow, and I doubted there could be more than six or eight apartments inside. Makayla parked across from it, alongside a small house with peeled paint and a sagging roof, and turned off the engine.

"Man, they could really use some neighborhood improvement here. You sure you want to do this?"

I nodded and pointed across the street to the apartment building. "That one's not completely boarded up. See the door? It's been propped open with a cinder block. I bet that's where Justyn was born." I gripped the car door handle. "Let's check it out."

Makayla grabbed my arm. "Girl, have you gone and lost your mind? If he's in there, you'd be an easier target than a lame duck. And if he's not, well, the whole building could fall down around you. I've seen playing card houses that look more stable!"

"But we won't know it's the right place if we don't check it out. I just need to see if there's any sign that someone's taken up residence in this building—any evidence that Justyn's been here." I held up my bag. "I have no intention of confronting him, but if he is inside, I came prepared. I've got a can of pepper spray and my phone has 911 on speed dial. We'll just peek in the doorway, okay?"

Makayla exhaled and reached into the glove compartment. "Okay, but I'm also taking my flashlight and this handy pocketknife I keep in the car. We are not going in that place blind and unarmed. Sorry, Lila, but your pepper spray just isn't enough to make me feel good about this."

As we crossed the road, the streetlights came on, casting a dim and eerie glow on the building entry. I stuck my head in, but all I could see was darkness. I pushed on the door and it creaked open. Suddenly, it swung in all the way and I lost my balance, tumbling inside.

"Damn it," I whispered in anger and pain as my leg fell through a piece of rough and jagged wood. I knew it was wood from the feel of a dozen splinters piercing my skin at once.

"You all right?" Makayla aimed her flashlight at me.

I shielded my eyes from the glare. "Yes, be careful you don't fall. Can you point the light at the ground?"

The beam illuminated a rickety ramp made of plywood, which had been placed where the steps had once been. The wood was partially rotted, and my leg was wedged in up to my thigh. No matter how hard I tried, I could not get enough leverage to push myself up and out of it.

"Oh, girl, it looks like I need to come inside after all." Makayla gingerly climbed down the ramp and used her knife to pry away enough of the wood to free my leg. It was bruised and there were several fragments of wood beneath my skin, which was painful, but I was otherwise unharmed.

We had made enough noise that if there was someone inside the building, they would certainly have heard us. But all was silent. The place felt utterly empty, and as if by mutual agreement, we turned down the short corridor. To the right were stairs, and beyond that were four open doorways. Makayla cast her light down the hall and we followed its beacon, looking in each apartment as we passed. The sound of our footsteps bounced off the cement floor. A freakish sense of déjà vu settled on me as I recalled the gloomy corridor in the town hall where I had previously encountered Justyn, and I had to make an effort to stay calm.

"Watch you don't trip on that," Makayla whispered as she aimed her light on a crumbled pile of bricks. "This place is nasty. I don't want to breathe in here. It smells like dirty diapers and week-old trash. Probably full of rats, too."

I shuddered. "It doesn't seem like anyone's been in these apartments for a long time. Let's go. This place gives me the creeps."

We'd just spun around when the door to the street suddenly opened, briefly illuminating our decrepit surroundings. Almost immediately, the light was obscured by a shadow. Silhouetted in the entrance stood a tall, thin man in a long black trench coat. I instantly recognized the body shape and dark glare. It was Justyn!

My heart pounded and I sucked in a quick, fearful breath. Makayla seized my wrist in terror. "That's him, isn't it?" she hissed in my ear.

I nodded. He kicked away the brick that served as a doorpost, and the door slammed behind him as he shone his own flashlight at us.

"Do I know you?" he demanded. I squinted as he directed the beam at my eyes. "*You*," he growled, then jumped down past the broken ramp and strode menacingly toward us.

"Hold it right there, mister." Makayla blinded him with her flashlight. She brandished her knife in her other hand.

Justyn narrowed his eyes and his eyebrow rings glinted. "Oh, what a cute little knife."

Without warning, he charged at Makayla, knocking her on her back. The flashlight fell out of her hand, clattered onto the concrete, and rolled in the direction of the entrance. Makayla became a dark heap on the floor.

"Makayla!" I reached down to help her, but Justyn's hard fingers dug into the soft tissue of my forearm and I cried out.

"Why are you getting up in my business?" he snarled close to my face, his foul breath assaulting my nostrils. "I'm done with all you interfering bitches."

He dragged me toward the stairs. I tried to pull back, tried to pry his fingers from my arm, but his grip was viselike. I kicked at him and twisted my body this way and that, but he was incredibly strong for one so wiry.

"Let me go!" I screamed. "Help!"

Without warning, his hold on me loosened and he crumpled to the ground. Makayla stood over him, holding a brick. She dropped it and grabbed my hand. "Let's get out of here and call the police."

"You hit him with a brick?" I asked dazedly. "Did you know that that's how he killed—"

"Come *on!*" she commanded, yanking my arm. I hobbled, trying to keep up with her as we ran to her car. My leg was throbbing.

Once we were safely locked inside, our hearts pounding, we assessed my injury.

"That looks nasty," Makayla declared. "All those splinters."

Ignoring the pain, I opened my cell phone to call Sean.

"Sean!" I exclaimed when he answered. "We found him! We've got Justyn. For real this time."

"Slow down, Lila. What are you saying? And who's 'we'?"

I took a deep breath and described what had happened.

"So he's still in the building?"

"Makayla hit him with a brick. He's unconscious." I sent an apprehensive glance at Makayla. "Or dead. You need to come now."

"Stay in the car with the doors locked," he commanded, his voice tight with anger and worry.

When I hung up, Makayla spoke in an unsteady voice. "I don't think I hit him hard enough to kill him."

I squeezed her hand. "Even if you did, it was self-defense. He was going to murder us, I'm certain of it."

We sat like that, silent and holding trembling hands, until sirens heralded two police cruisers. They pulled up in front of the building. Sean stepped out of one of them and approached our car.

"Are you two all right?" he asked when Makayla rolled down her window, letting in a blast of cold air.

"We're safe enough, even though we're both shaking like leaves in the wind." She glanced in my direction. "Her leg's hurt, though."

Sean hurried around to the passenger side and yanked open my door. He inspected my flesh, speckled with a multitude of splinters and starting to turn a bluish purple. "That looks painful."

I shrugged. "It'll be fine. I kind of deserve it for not being more careful."

He hugged me tight and then held my gaze. His rugged face and kind blue eyes were a balm. "I'm glad you weren't seriously hurt," he said. I knew he was angry, but he was also too relieved to chastise us. In a flash, his demeanor changed and his gaze slid toward the decrepit apartment building. "Is he inside?"

At my nod, he said, "We'll take it from here. We need your statements, but I think you need to get your leg checked out, Lila. Makayla, are you okay to drive? Can you take her to the ER?"

"Yessir, Officer," Makayla said with forced bravado.

"All right then, we'll get your statements first thing in the morning. Just take care of that injury."

Reluctantly, I let go of his strong arm and climbed back in the car. As we drove away, I watched the policemen gathering at the entrance to Justyn's building. I hoped this would truly mark the end of the nightmare he'd created.

Having had all the splinters picked from my leg and my lacerations cleansed and bandaged, I was finally alone in my house, overcome with exhaustion and relief. I made myself a cup of chamomile tea and took it with me into the bath, which I had filled with honeysuckle-scented bubbles. Having wrapped my knee in waterproof bandages, I soaked in the aromatic froth, musing over the day's events. Issues had been resolved. Trey had decided to go to college. And Justyn's violence had been stopped once and for all. He was off the streets and in custody.

I hoped for Makayla's sake that she'd merely knocked him unconscious. Makayla didn't have a mean bone in her body and would feel terrible if he died, despite the fact that he was a murderer. I wished we had stayed to see Sean and his men carting Justyn off, so that I'd know for certain that she hadn't killed him.

An unwelcome thought penetrated my relief. What if he'd regained consciousness while Makayla and I were waiting in the car? What if he'd come to and run away through a rear exit? What if . . . ?

I dunked my head underwater to drown out those thoughts. Justyn was apprehended. It was over.

A few minutes later, I was wearing my soft flannel Hello Kitty pajamas that Trey had given me last Christmas. Feeling cozy and warm and ready to tuck into bed with a book, I walked around the house to make sure I'd locked the doors and windows.

After inspecting the window above the kitchen sink, I poured myself a glass of water and drank thirstily, draining the glass. As I brought it down, my breath caught in my throat. Staring at me through the glass was a face; a dark, shadowy face with angry eyes.

Justyn had come for me!

Chapter 16

But it wasn't Justyn.

He'd been haunting my dreams since Melissa's murder, so naturally I assumed that the twisted, hateful face on the other side of the glass belonged to him, but it didn't.

It was hardly any comfort that I wasn't staring at a killer, because the intruder looked furious and desperate enough to commit his own act of unspeakable violence.

"Jasper!" I shouted, refusing to let the co-op leader see how much he'd scared me. "What the hell are you doing here?"

I have no idea whether he heard me or not, but his eyes flashed with a cold light and then he disappeared from view. My courage wavered and I limped into the living room and grabbed the fireplace poker. With my free hand, I dialed 911 and reported my emergency as quickly as possible.

The operator asked me to stay on the line, so I dropped the phone into the pocket of my robe and turned off the lamp. The darkness instantly became heavy, weighed down by my fear. Every noise seemed amplified. My shallow exhalations, the whisper of my slippers on the floorboards, and the rustle of the hem of my pajama bottoms as I moved were far too loud.

I nearly screamed when I saw a long shadow fall across my front porch. And when I heard the rattle of the doorknob, I had to bite down on my fist to keep the terror in check. My door was locked, but if Jasper was determined to get into the house, he only had to smash the pane, reach in through the hole in the glass, and unlock the dead bolt.

Dozens of scenarios crowded my head. I could stand here, the iron poker raised over my shoulder, and wait for Jasper to walk into the room. Swinging with all my might, it was possible that I'd knock him out. Then again, I might not. If I injured Jasper without rendering him unconscious, the pain could serve as a catalyst, fueling his rage to the point where he would lash out, attacking me until his fury was spent.

Hide! a part of me silently shrieked, but I instantly rebelled against that notion. I wasn't about to crawl under the bed and cower. This was *my* house.

There was a scratching noise against the wood of my front door, and I pictured Jasper picking the lock. The image made me livid. How dare this drug-dealing pseudo-hippie try to break in? I refused to become another crime statistic. In fact, I planned to turn the tables on this creep.

As quietly as possible, I hurried through the living room and into the kitchen. After grabbing a coat from the hook on the back of the door, I pulled out the *Eat, Sleep, Read* key chain from a drawer and headed outside.

My injured leg throbbed in protest as I crossed the lawn, tiptoed through my dormant garden, and slid a key into the padlock affixed to the shed. I'm not sure why I kept the tiny building locked, but I'd bought a new set of tools after moving into my house, as well as a leaf blower and a self-propelling lawn mower, and had decided to err on the side of caution. Now I was glad that I did.

Because this was a bona fide potting shed, there was a pass-through window cut out of the rear wall. It was made of the same sturdy hardwood as the shed and slid open and closed like a barn door. Below the window, there was a small table and a ledge to hold seed trays and clay pots. I removed the padlock from the window's wooden panel, grabbed a hoe, and, leaving the front door open a crack, snuck around to the back of the shed.

Hesitating for a moment, I considered the holes in my impromptu plan, but then I sucked in a deep, steadying breath and pushed the hoe through the opening in the window, knocking a stack of pots and a pair of gardening shears to the floor of the shed. The sound reverberated in the still night and I tensed. Would it be enough to lure Jasper away from the front of the house?

Pulling the hoe outside again, I slid the wooden panel closed, locked it from the outside, and waited.

There was no doubt that Jasper could move with stealth. He'd walked the woods of Red Fox Mountain for years and had told Trey that he knew exactly how to plant his feet to deaden the sound of his footfalls. He claimed to have been taught this technique by a member of the Cherokee Tribe, and if he'd been telling the truth, I might not be aware he'd entered the shed until it was too late.

"I know you and Trey are in here," his voice suddenly hissed.

Jasper was close—so close that I had no problem imagining him as a lion on the hunt as he stalked over the grass and shriveled flower stalks. Luckily for me, I heard a crunch as his shoes came in contact with some of the pottery shards and knew he'd entered the shed.

I rushed around the building, slammed the door, and clicked the padlock into place a heartbeat before Jasper slammed into the door.

"Trey, let me out!" he roared. "You're making a big mistake. You and your sweet mama are going to pay. You ruined me."

Blood was rushing through my veins with such force that his words barely registered. Leaning on the hoe, I panted for a moment, stunned that I'd succeeded in trapping Jasper. On the other side of the door, he continued to shout threats and expletives until my anger flared red-hot.

"How dare you?" I hollered back at him. "How dare you abuse my son's trust and then show up at my home in the middle of the night? How dare you sell harmful drugs to kids? They might not know better, but *you* should. So help me, Jasper, if you come out of that shed I will bash your brains in with this garden hoe."

Jasper's incensed pounding ceased.

"Do you realize what you've put your sister through?" I continued mercilessly. "How scared she is? If it weren't for Trey, she would have fallen apart by now. You broke her heart, Jasper. What do you think will happen to her now?"

My words were met with silence. It lasted for a long time. A breeze rustled through the bare branches of the oak tree in the far corner of my yard, and I gazed up at the ink black sky, finding comfort in the presence of the high stars.

"Where is she?" Jasper finally asked in a soft, defeated voice.

"With Trey and my mother. She'd like to go to college but doesn't have the money. Her big brother ran away with all of it. She's got nothing but the clothes on her back." I was being cruel, but I couldn't help it. Jasper deserved to suffer for betraying and endangering so many others.

A thud came from inside the shed, and when

Jasper spoke next, his voice was lower to the ground and I could only assume that he'd sunk to his knees, literally floored by guilt and regret. "I hid my ATM card in one of the birdhouses at the clearing," he said. "You know the place. Iris brought you there after Marlette was killed. The password is Iris's birth date. Please . . . tell her . . ." he trailed off.

A shrill siren cut through the night's hush. The cops had entered the neighborhood and would be pulling into my driveway in a matter of seconds.

"I'll tell her where to find the bank card," I assured Jasper.

The sirens grew louder. Rotating white and blue lights suddenly illuminated the side of my house, throwing multicolored beams into the shrubbery and trees.

"Lila!" Sean called out.

"Back here," I yelled in reply, my voice sounding hoarse and tired.

A car door slammed, the beam of a flashlight wobbled over the grass, and I could hear him running toward me.

"Wait," Jasper pleaded. "Tell Iris that I'm sorry. I grew greedy and forgot my purpose. Tell her that I never wanted to hurt her. Or anyone else. That I was happiest when things were simple. I screwed it all up and I'd do anything to make it right. Will you help my sister?"

"I will," I promised, and then Sean was there.

Dropping the hoe, I wrapped my arms around his neck and breathed in his familiar scent. His hands encircled my waist and he kissed my forehead and my cheek before finding my lips. He kissed me deeply, urgently, and I knew in that moment how worried he'd been.

"I can't leave you alone for ten minutes," he growled when he finally released me.

I handed Sean the shed key. "Jasper's inside. I don't know what his intentions were, but I think the fight's gone out of him."

Pointing at my garden hoe, Sean asked, "Did you assault him?"

"No. I was just holding on to this in case he got out." I dropped the tool onto the ground and looked up as a second policeman jogged toward us. "I'm cold and my leg hurts, so I think I'll head inside. Besides, I don't want to watch you guys take Jasper away. This place is my only haven." I made a gesture meant to encompass the house, the yard, and the shed. "I'd like to wake up in the morning still feeling that way."

Sean nodded and then, leaning close to me, whispered, "Officer McKeon will be booking Jasper. I'm staying here tonight."

When I looked surprised, he barked out a laugh. "Oh, Lila. You're hurt and we're both too damned exhausted for more than a hug and kiss good night followed by eight hours of spooning." His eyes were shining with mirth. "Listen, lady, you've closed two open cases in one day. You're making the Dunston Police Department look inept, so I'm sleeping over to make sure that you've gone off duty for the rest of the night. Got it?"

Smiling, I said, "Got it. And I'm hoping that the sudden decrease in the crime rate means that you and I will be spending more time together."

He pointed at my leg. "Just don't be in any rush for that to mend, because when all my paperwork has been filed, I'm going to spend my time sweeping you off your feet."

I liked the sound of that.

I met up with Makayla at the police station the next morning. Sean had driven me there so I could give my statement, and Makayla appeared to do the same. I waited for her in the lobby while she finished, and then she offered to give me a ride home.

"I don't know how I'll manage to get through my day," Makayla said as she started the engine. "I hardly slept a wink last night. Couldn't get that nasty, evil man out of my mind. I was relieved that my bash on his noggin only gave him a slight concussion. The last thing I'd want to do is kill somebody, even if he's a lowlife, scumbag murderer." She looked at me. "How'd you sleep?"

"Surprisingly well. Knowing that both Justyn

and Jasper were in police custody helped." I couldn't keep from smiling, "Besides, having Sean sleep over made me feel safe. I conked out as soon as my head hit the pillow."

She raised her eyebrows. "Just like that? You and Romeo didn't knock boots first? I'd think you'd be clinging to that man like a kudzu vine."

I shook my head, amused by the image. "I crawled into bed and was gone." My cheeks got hot. "Though it was really tempting to spend the whole morning in bed. Too bad neither Sean nor I could play hooky today. At least we got to snuggle for a bit." Wanting to keep the memory of those brief moments to myself, I changed the subject. "Did Sean tell you what made Justyn track Melissa and Tilly down?"

She nodded. "Something about him being desperate to get ahold of his mother's medical records. Why he couldn't have gone through proper channels is beyond me. I know filling out paperwork is a drag, but Lordy, he didn't have to go postal over a little bureaucracy."

"Well, it's a bit more complicated than that. Apparently, he'd recently been diagnosed with juvenile diabetes and had to give himself daily injections, something he hated. He blamed his birth mother for his condition and wanted to confront her," I began.

Makayla made a sympathetic noise. "That's a tough illness to have."

"It wasn't just the diabetes that was tough." I sighed. "This is going to sound like I'm defending him, which I'm not, but he had a hard and love-less childhood in Dunston and then grew up to enjoy a hard and loveless adulthood in the same town. He wanted someone to pay for that. In any case, Social Services wouldn't give him his mother's identity, but the clerk he spoke with inadvertently revealed the caseworker's name. That was Melissa Plume. That started him on his quest for vengeance."

"But why hurt Melissa?" Makayla shook her head, perplexed. "What did he have against her? She wasn't the one who gave him up when he was a baby."

I shrugged. "I don't think he intended to kill her. He just wanted information from her. He wanted to scare her into telling him about his mother, Tilly. And he confused me for her at first and that's why he left me the raven's feather and came after me in the hallway of the town hall. Unfortunately, when he finally did manage to get Melissa alone, something in him snapped. Perhaps her answers frustrated him and he attacked in a rage. Perhaps he blamed her for placing him in all those unhappy foster homes, since she was his caseworker. I guess he was already pretty unstable."

"What was with the feathers?"

"He wanted to let Melissa know that he was

following her—that he knew about her life, both public and private. She has a blog and, like her business card, the graphic design includes a quill. Because her last name is Plume. Get it?"

Makayla nodded.

"That's also how Justyn knew she'd be in Inspiration Valley," I explained. "She posted on her blog that she planned to attend our conference."

"I'll never look at a crow the same way again," Makayla mumbled. "And we all know he went after Tilly next."

I nodded sadly. "With no formal education and no family support, Justyn could only land thankless, low-paying jobs. He worked as a housepainter, as a roofer, and for a landscape company mowing lawns. And what he saw during those years as he changed from a boy to a man was what a real family looked like. A loving family." I thought of Trey and felt a lump in my throat. "He saw mothers singing lullabies and dads throwing baseballs in the front yard. He saw parents and children gathering around the supper table to enjoy a home-cooked meal. He saw pictures taped to refrigerators and Christmas trees surrounded by presents. He saw all that he'd never had, and it turned him into a monster."

Makayla had tears in her eyes. "He wanted someone to pay."

A loud sigh escaped my lips. "When he finally found Tilly, only to discover that she'd had other children after leaving him on the proverbial doorstep, he must have seen red. Especially since you only had to watch her with those kids to know that she clearly doted on them."

"It sure would have put salt in the wound to see what a loving mom she was to them. The same woman who gave him up so he could be passed from one foster home to another—who never tried to reconnect with him. Meanwhile, she's baking cookies and knitting scarves for her other kids." Makayla frowned. "I've got to admit that that boy had a bad time of it. Still, lots of people face rejection from their own mothers and don't go around murdering them."

"Tilly was no longer the drug-addicted teen-ager who gave birth to Justyn. She'd cleaned up, made a new life for herself, and wanted to forget all about her dark past. That's why she lied to me about knowing Melissa, so the old Tilly could remain buried." I shifted in my seat. "You know, even though she was messed up then, I think she thought she was doing the right thing by leaving him at a church so he could be taken care of. The teddy bear Justyn placed beside Tilly's body was the same one she'd left in the laundry basket with him before walking away forever. Her only gift to her son."

Makayla pursed her lips in disapproval. "Drugs will twist people's lives into all kinds of knots. Everything would have been completely different if Tilly hadn't gotten hooked on drugs when she was young." She glanced my way. "It's a good thing Jasper's little 'shroom operation at the co-op was closed down. Who knows how many more kids' futures would have been derailed by it."

I heartily agreed, pushing aside images of what might have happened if Trey had gotten pulled into those "meditation sessions." We were quiet for a while, each with our own thoughts, watching the road flit past.

"I wonder how my assistant managed the Sunday morning at the coffee shop," Makayla mused, breaking the silence. "Lila, we make a mighty sharp sleuthing team, if you ask me." She reached over and touched my hand. "But let's hang up our superhero capes and focus on being Bella Barista and Awesome Agent. Books, coffee, and a good-looking man are all the excitement we should be seeking from here on out."

On Monday morning, I showed up at Novel Idea scandalously late, hobbling up the stairs at ten. My knee was still giving me a lot of pain and I was moving slowly, despite getting some rest on Sunday. Vicky followed me into my office carrying a hot caramel latte and a stack of phone messages for me to sort through. "Officer Griffiths is quite the gentleman," she said, handing me the Espresso Yourself take-out cup. "He called and explained everything that happened this weekend and why you'd be tardy today. There was no need to worry, seeing as Ms. Burlington-Duke informed me that she wouldn't be in until eleven, but I would have covered for you in any case."

Thanking her for the coffee and the understanding, I examined a few phone messages. Most were from members of the media. I balled them up and tossed them in the garbage. "I plan to read an entire manuscript by lunchtime," I said to Vicky. "It was rewarding to help the police, but I belong here." I booted up my computer and was pleased to find T. J. West's manuscript waiting in my email inbox. I opened the file and hit the print button. Pointing at the document pages that quickly began to pile up in my printer tray, I said, "*This* is what fulfills me. And I've been distracted from my work for too long."

Vicky, who'd probably never been diverted from a task her entire life, nodded in approval. "I'll see to it that no one disturbs you. We have a staff meeting at one, and Bentley was very clear that no one was to eat lunch before that time."

A little perplexed by my boss's order, I grinned at Vicky and promised not to sneak to Catcher in the Rye for a sandwich or have a large pepperoni pizza delivered on the sly. Then I settled down at my desk, read through a dozen emails, and picked up T. J. West's manuscript. Seven chapters later I sighed with contentment. Not only did I love the book, but West's charming characters and bucolic setting had also allowed me to put aside all thoughts of Justyn or Jasper. I sipped my latte, read, and welcomed the feeling that I had made it through a dark and ugly time and could look forward to a calm, peaceful winter.

West's book concluded with a festive Thanksgiving scene, and I realized that I'd soon be celebrating the same holiday in my new home. While pulling up West's contact information on my computer, I imagined the people I hoped to see at my table. Trey, my mother, Sean, Makayla, and Iris, too. Just picturing their faces as I entered the dining room carrying a behemoth turkey made my heart flood with warmth. I dialed West's number to offer him representation and knew that I had much to be thankful for.

"Lila!" Zach burst into my office seconds after I'd finished talking to an ecstatic T. J. West aka Thomas Jefferson Wipple.

"Do you have a low-key setting, Zach?" I teased. "You're always so revved up."

Zach looked confused by the question. "Why wouldn't I be? I have the coolest job ever, I'm single, I'm good-looking, and women find me irresistible!"

"Must be that incredible modesty that draws them to you." I laughed. "Are you here to make sure I'm not late for the meeting?"

He flopped into the chair on the other side of my desk. "Guess again! Actually, don't guess. We don't have time for that. I wanted to tell you that not one, not two, but *three* studios are bidding on the rights to the first book in Calliope's new series. I fielded the calls this morning. I hope that's okay, seeing as she's your client."

My mouth hung open. I'd only been a literary agent for a couple of months and I'd never dreamed that someone I represented might have their work turned into a movie or television show.

"I'm glad you did. After all, aren't you Mr. Hollywood?"

Zach puffed out his chest importantly. "I sure am. We'll split the commission on any sales to film studios. Lady, you might be trading in that scooter for a sweeter ride. I could see you tearing down the road in a convertible Vette. A yellow one."

I shook my head. "That's your style, Mr. Hollywood. I love my scooter and I'll borrow my mother's truck when I want to go on a long-distance drive."

My comment piqued Zach's interest. "And who will you be visiting? Someone *special?*" He wriggled his eyebrows suggestively.

"Yes," I said, gathering a pen and notebook in preparation for the staff meeting. "My son. Come January, he'll be a college freshman."

Zach leapt out of his seat and waited for me to

leave the room before following. "Hey! Trey could write a book about his experiences on Red Fox Mountain. I could totally sell it to a TV studio. Impressionable kid corrupted by drug-dealing hippie, et cetera, et cetera. If I had a screenplay of those events, I'd be fighting off producers with a stick. Especially since the leader escaped."

I halted just outside the conference room. "Not a chance, Zach. Trey needs to look ahead. Maybe Jasper would like to pen an autobiography. You could stop by the jail and ask him. Franklin could be his agent and you could sell the film rights. It's a win-win."

Completely missing the note of sarcasm in my voice, Zach's face lit up with enthusiasm. "You are *so* brilliant." And with that, he bounded down the corridor and into Franklin's office. Without knocking, of course.

In the conference room, everyone was already seated around the table, except Zach, who darted in behind me and plunked himself into a chair. As soon as they noticed me, the chatter in the room stopped, and as if by mutual arrangement, Franklin, Flora, and Jude jumped up and threw their arms around me.

Bentley peered over her diamond-studded glasses and smiled. "Lila, I appreciate that you're here today, considering."

"We are so glad you're okay," Flora exclaimed,

enfolding me in an embrace. "We heard all about what happened over the weekend."

"Yes, we understand you're quite the hero," Franklin said. "Tracking down the murderer of Melissa Plume and Tilly Smythe."

Jude pulled out a chair. "Have a seat, milady. I believe you sustained an injury during your adventure."

"Thanks." Grateful to get the weight off my leg, I sat down. "But how did you find out?"

"I heard a news report on the radio when I drove in this morning," Zach replied, "but we got the important details from our own Miss Vicky."

"I thought they should know," Vicky said, sitting perpendicular to Bentley, ramrod straight with her hands clasped on the table. "I hope you don't mind."

I shook my head. "No, not at all."

As Franklin returned to his chair, he asked, "Lila, do you know what prompted that young man to murder those two women? I can't imagine."

As succinctly as possible, I summarized the connections between Tilly, Melissa, and Justyn.

"Well," Vicky said, "his actions are quite a commentary on the societal issues of drugs and unwed mothers and the foster care system."

"Some young people make mistakes that can end up having a dramatic impact on others. They don't mean to be hurtful; they're just immature and foolish." Flora lowered herself to her seat. "I can't help but think that Justyn Kershaw might not have turned into such a rotten apple if he hadn't had such a rough start to his life. Such a sad and lonely childhood."

"He was a boy who grew into a man who made bad choices," Jude noted. "One can choose to have their past dictate their future or leave it behind to set a new course for their life. Justyn used his past as an excuse to do wrong."

"He's not the only bad guy Lila helped bring down." Zach clicked his pen several times. "She got that dope-dealing hippie tossed into the slammer, too. Our Lila's a force to be reckoned with."

Bentley cleared her throat. "We are all grateful that Lila's involvement contributed to making our small part of the world safer, but perhaps we could get the meeting started?"

We shuffled our chairs to get comfortable and directed our attention to Bentley, who removed her glasses and began. "I called this meeting because I wanted to commend you all on a very favorable few weeks. First on the agenda, I would like to applaud Vicky, who, although she has only been with us a short time, has been running this office with extreme efficiency and flawless professionalism. I can't imagine how we managed without her."

Vicky's cheeks turned a dark shade of pink,

and she blinked behind her glasses as we all clapped our agreement. "Thank you," she said. "I'm only doing my job, and this is a lovely place to work." She cast me a sidelong glance. "There's never a dull moment."

Bentley held up her hand. "And we cannot underestimate the success of our first book festival. Not only did our agency benefit from the exposure; I believe we signed three new authors as a direct result of the event. To show my appreciation for your hard—"

A knock on the open door interrupted Bentley. Big Ed walked in carrying a tray containing a mound of sandwiches. "Where should I put this, Ms. Burlington-Duke?" he asked, glancing around the room, obviously eager to divest himself of his burden. He must have struggled to bring it up the stairs.

Bentley waved her arm in the direction of the credenza against the wall. "Put it there, thank you."

I was so busy watching Ed that I had failed to notice Nell enter the room. She was right behind him, encumbered by a large cake box on which was stacked packages of plates, napkins, and cutlery. Ed put the tray down and turned to remove the items from the top of the cake box. Shoulder to shoulder they arranged the lunch buffet and unveiled the cake, a beautifully decorated confection in the shape of a large open book. When they were satisfied with the presentation, their eyes met. It was more than a look of congratulations at a job well done. I could almost see a spark travel between them, and in that moment I knew for certain that Big Ed had finally found the courage to ask Nell out.

"Will there be anything else?" Ed asked when he pulled his gaze away from Nell.

"No, thank you," Bentley said. "It looks wonderful. Now," she continued once Big Ed and Nell had departed, "as I was saying, to show my appreciation for all your hard work, I am treating you to lunch today."

"Woo hoo!" Zach blurted out. "I'm starving." He pushed himself out of his seat.

"Before we dig into the food let's get through the agenda." Bentley directed a steely look at Zach that caused him to sit back down. She continued by confirming recent signings and sales. Each of us shared our client news, and Vicky explained her new system of tracking statistics for the agency.

"That about covers all the business items," Bentley concluded. "Any other concerns or announcements?" She regarded us. We all shook our heads. "Jude and Lila, don't forget about finding a ghostwriter for Marlette Robbins's sequel. I know you've been busy, but the publisher is getting impatient, so I'd like you to get on that right away."

Jude glanced in my direction and nodded. "I think we can find some time to put our heads together," he said, winking at me.

"Definitely," I concurred. This project excited me, and I was eager to focus my attention on book-related tasks, having had my fill of crime fighting.

"I have one final announcement to make before we indulge in our repast," said Bentley, perching her glasses on her nose and peering at a sheet of paper. "I am thrilled to announce that the construction of the Marlette Robbins Center for the Arts is on schedule and it will open in the spring with a huge celebratory event featuring books and food." She looked up with a smile. "Two things none of us can live without. Famous chefs will prepare items from their cookbooks in front of an audience, and any big-name authors who feature food in their works will be invited. That's where we come in. Would anyone be willing to volunteer in coordinating this extraordinary event with the Arts Center staff?"

I pictured myself standing beside Rachael Ray, helping her prepare Moroccan spiced lamb with a pistachio and mint couscous, and before I realized what I was doing, I had raised my hand.

"Lila? You have time for this?" At my nod, Bentley quipped, "As long as you've given up your unpaid position with the Dunston Police Department, you've got the job."

The rest of the agents burst out laughing and made their way over to the platter of sandwiches. I held back and watched, savoring this moment. These were my coworkers, my friends. I had my dream job, my son was on a good path, and our world was safe once again. Life was good.

I helped myself to a Moriarty panini, smiling a little as I took a bite of tender roast beef and potent horseradish. This was as close as I wanted to come to a shady character ever again.

Center Point Large Print
600 Brooks Road / PO Box 1
Thorndike ME 04986-0001 USA

(207) 568-3717

US & Canada:
1 800 929-9108
www.centerpointlargeprint.com